DEVOTED ENOUGH

OTHER BOOKS
BY KELLY ELLIOTT

Love in Montana (Meet Me in Montana Spin Off)

*Fearless Enough**
Cherished Enough
Brave Enough
Daring Enough
Loved Enough -
Forever Enough
Enchanted Enough
Perfect Enough
Devoted Enough
*Available on audiobook

Boston Love Series

*Searching for Harmony**
*Fighting for Love**
Falling for Her
Longing for You
*Available on audiobook

Holidaze in Salem

A Bit of Hocus Pocus
A Bit of Holly Jolly
A Bit of Wee Luck
A Bit of Razzle Dazzle

The Seaside Chronicles

Returning Home
Part of Me
Lost to You

Someone to Love

**Series available on audiobook*

Stand Alones

*The Journey Home**

*Who We Were**

*The Playbook**

*Made for You**

*Available on audiobook

Boggy Creek Valley Series

*The Butterfly Effect**

*Playing with Words**

*She's the One**

*Surrender to Me**

*Hearts in Motion**

*Looking for You**

Surprise Novella TBD

**Available on audiobook*

Meet Me in Montana Series

Never Enough

Always Enough

Good Enough

Strong Enough

*Series available on audiobook

Southern Bride Series

Love at First Sight

Delicate Promises

Divided Interests

Lucky in Love

Feels Like Home

Take Me Away

Fool for You

Fated Hearts

*Series vailable on audiobook

Cowboys and Angels Series

Lost Love

Love Profound

Tempting Love

Love Again

Blind Love

This Love

Reckless Love

*Series available on audiobook

Austin Singles Series

Seduce Me

Entice Me

Adore Me

*Series available on audiobook

Wanted Series

*Wanted**

*Saved**

*Faithful**

Believe

*Cherished**

*A Forever Love**

The Wanted Short Stories

All They Wanted

*Available on audiobook

Love Wanted in Texas Series

Spin-off series to the WANTED Series

Without You

Saving You

Holding You
Finding You
Chasing You
Loving You
Entire series available on audiobook
*Please note *Loving You* combines the last book of the Broken and Love Wanted in Texas series.

Broken Series

*Broken**
*Broken Dreams**
*Broken Promises**
Broken Love
*Available on audiobook

The Journey of Love Series

Unconditional Love
Undeniable Love
Unforgettable Love
*Entire series available on audiobook

With Me Series

Stay With Me
Only With Me
*Series available on audiobook

Speed Series

Ignite
Adrenaline
*Series available on audiobook

COLLABORATIONS

Predestined Hearts (co-written with Kristin Mayer)*

*Play Me (*co-written with Kristin Mayer)*

*Dangerous Temptations (*co-written with Kristin Mayer*

*Available on audiobook

SWEET ROMANCE/CLOSED DOOR

Kelly Elliott writing as Ellie Grace

Saved by Love

Amnesia

Cover Design by: Hang Le
Interior Design and Formatting by: Elaine York, Allusion Publishing, www.allusionpublishing.com
Developmental Editor: Kelli Collins
Copy Editor: Elaine York, Allusion Publishing, www.allusionpublishing.com
Proofing Editor: Julie Deaton
Proofing Editor: Elaine York, Allusion Publishing, www.allusionpublishing.com

For more information on Kelly and her books, please visit her website www.kellyelliottauthor.com.

DEVOTED ENOUGH

KELLY
ELLIOTT

Joshua Ty
Hunter
Mason
Nathan
Christopher
Rose
Marie
Morgan
Elizabeth
Lily Hope
Blayze
Lucas
Tanner &
Timberlynn
Shaw
Ty Jr &
Kaylee Shaw
Brock &
Lincoln Shaw
Beck Shaw
Bradly
Michael
Stella Shaw &
Ty Sr Shaw
Avery Grace
Dirk &
Merit Littlewood
Shaw Ranch

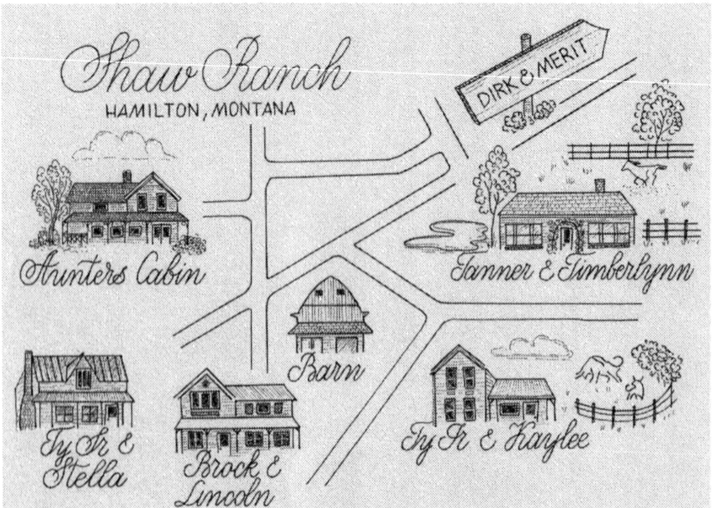
Shaw Ranch
HAMILTON, MONTANA
DIRK & MERIT
Hunters Cabin
Tanner & Timberlynn
Barn
Ty Sr &
Stella
Brock &
Lincoln
Ty Jr & Kaylee

Prologue

Nathan

Sophomore Year of High School

"Why do I have to bring it to her? Can't Lily, or what about her mom? Can either of them come and get it?" I asked my mother as she stood in front of me, arms folded over her chest.

"Because your father is out of town, your sister has plans, and I have a meeting I need to attend tonight. Grace is in Missoula caring for her sick mother."

"Mom, you know how much Haven gets under my skin."

"Nathan Shaw, that young girl has had a crush on you since middle school, and that shouldn't make her get under your skin."

"It's not just that, Mom."

"I'm not asking you to simply take something to her, Nathan."

"But–"

She held up her hand. "But nothing. I also want you to give this casserole to Haven. I'm sure her father hasn't made her anything decent to eat since Grace has been gone."

My mother's voice was filled with dislike for David Larson. Haven wasn't very fond of her father either, at least based on the few times she has spoken about him. "Do you not like him?"

She huffed. "Never mind how I feel about him. I promised Grace I'd make sure Haven was okay."

I sighed. There wasn't anything I wouldn't do for my mother, but Haven Larson? Going to her house and seeing her wasn't something I really wanted to do. It wasn't that I didn't like her; I did like her, but if my friends found out, they would tease me. Not that I couldn't handle it, but it would most likely get people teasing Haven, and I didn't want that. Haven got a lot of shit in school for not having money. The girls teased her for her clothes and the fact that she walked dogs as a job. I thought they were all jealous of her. She had the most beautiful grayish-blue eyes, brown curly hair, and the cutest dimples that appeared when she smiled. From the gossip making the rounds at school, her father wasn't especially nice to Haven or her mother, Grace. No one was sure why, though.

"Fine, I'll drop off the casserole and her backpack. But it was her fault for leaving it here after her lessons."

My mother gave Haven horseback riding lessons for free since she was good friends with Grace. If you ask me, Haven spent way too much time here at our place and not enough time at her own home.

Kissing me on the cheek, she opened the door to the truck. "Be careful driving, Nate."

"I will, Mom. You be careful driving to your meeting too."

She leaned in and kissed me once again. "Thank you, sweetheart."

With a wink, I replied, "Anything for you, Mom."

She rolled her eyes. "The apple didn't fall far from the tree."

It took me about forty minutes to get from the ranch to Haven's place. Her parents didn't live on the best side of town, but it wasn't the worst either. They had a simple, two-story house that I had only ever seen from the outside.

I pulled up and parked in front of the house. Haven's father's truck was parked in the driveway. Grabbing the backpack, I got out of the truck and made my way to the passenger side to get the casserole. As I walked up to the door, I heard a loud scream come from inside the house, and my heart felt like it was about to nearly jump out of my chest.

"That's Haven," I said to myself as I quickly went to the door and was about to ring the doorbell when I heard the faint sound of more screaming for someone to leave her alone. I reached for the door, and it was open. My heart hammered in my chest, and I had no idea what I was walking into. When I heard a crash come from upstairs, I dropped the backpack, put the casserole on a side table near the door, and then dashed up the steps. Haven's voice guided me to where I needed to go.

"Please don't do this. Please!"

I ran up the steps. The room where her voice was coming from was down the hall.

"You know what will happen if you don't keep your damn mouth shut."

For a moment, my footsteps faltered. That was Haven's father's voice.

"Please…don't do this! Please, stop!"

I pushed the door open to see David forcing Haven's hands above her head as he moved over her. For a moment, I was frozen in place. Was I seeing what I thought I was seeing?

When she let out a small cry, I ran, grabbed him by the shirt, and yanked him off of her. Then I pulled back my fist and punched him. He stumbled back and fell to the floor.

"Nate!" Haven cried out as she scrambled to the other side of her bed.

"What in the hell were you doing to her?"

David wiped the side of his mouth and stood. "You need to turn around and get the hell out of my house."

I balled my fists together, prepared to continue this fight, and shook my head. "How could you do that to your daughter?"

"Nate, please. Please don't make him mad."

I looked at Haven, and that was when I saw her bruised cheek. "Did he hit you?"

Her eyes darted away, and I had never in my life felt such anger. Turning back to David, all I felt was burning rage, and all I saw was red as I lunged for him, knocking him back onto the floor. Then I just started hitting him in the face over and over until I felt Haven pulling at me.

"Stop! Nate! You're going to kill him, stop!"

I let her pull me away as I stood and looked at the man lying on the floor, covered in blood. "Doesn't feel so good getting hit on, does it, asshole? Next time fight someone who can fight back."

David looked up at me and smirked as he went to wipe the blood from his lips. "What are you going to do, kid?"

"I've already called the police."

Haven gasped next to me. "What?"

Looking at her, I felt the anger rise up again. She looked terrified. So I whispered to her, "I haven't, Haven, but I will."

"No! Please, Nate."

I shook my head in disbelief. "How could you let him get away with this, Haven? If he'll do that to his own daughter, what will prevent him from doing the same—or worse—to someone else? It's settled, we're calling the police."

David stood, spit out some blood, and bolted out of the room like his ass was on fire. I followed him. "If you think I'm going to let you leave this house, you are crazy."

David quickly beelined it for his bedroom, went to the closet, and grabbed a duffle bag.

"What do you think you're doing?"

"If you think I'm going to jail for this, you've got another thing coming, kid."

I went to walk over to him again, but felt Haven take my hand and pull me. "Nate, please. Let him go. Please."

I turned to look at her. "But, Haven, he…"

The look in her eyes caused my voice to trail off.

She swallowed hard and whispered, "Please. I can't have anyone find out. Please."

David walked by us and down the steps.

"Haven, he was hurting you. He looked like he was about to..." I closed my eyes and drew in a deep breath. "His own daughter. We can't let him get away with that."

She frantically wiped her tears away. "I can't…I can't do this. Please, I'm begging you."

"Stay here," I said as I quickly went downstairs. The front door slammed, and I ran out to catch David before he took off. Grabbing him, I pushed him against the truck.

"I swear to God, if you ever come back to Hamilton, get anywhere near Haven, or so much as attempt to contact her, I won't be calling the cops. I'll be digging your fucking grave. And I won't be alone…every male member of my family will happily help bury your sick ass."

He smirked and pushed me away. "Ain't nothing here for me anymore anyway."

Slipping into the truck, he shut the door, started the engine, and rolled his window down. "Don't worry, boy, she's still intact if you want a go at her."

I reached in and grabbed him again, hitting him this time with my left fist. The blow wasn't as hard, but it caused him to step on the gas and drive away, knowing I wouldn't stop with just one hit the longer he stayed there.

I wasn't sure how long I stood there, watching his truck, before I looked around. No one had been outside when I punched him, but I wasn't sure if anyone might have seen or heard anything from their house.

Remembering Haven, I ran back into the house and up the steps to find her in bed. Her legs were pulled up to her chest, her chin on her knees as she rocked back and forth. I slowly moved closer and sat down on the bed.

"Are you okay?"

Tears streamed down her face, and she nodded. I pushed a brown curl behind her ear. "Haven, why won't you let me call the police?"

She lifted her head and shook it. "It would destroy my mother, and I only have a handful of friends as it is, I don't want to lose them. I can't, Nathan. I can't go through with that. I just…can't."

Reaching for me, she grabbed onto my arms. "Promise me, Nate, promise me right now that you won't tell a soul. Not even your parents."

I closed my eyes. "Haven, I think we need to tell someone. What if he hurts others too."

She closed her eyes. "He got fired from his job today, and that was why he was so angry and wanted someone to take it out on."

Taking her hands in mine, I swallowed the lump in my throat and asked the one thing I wasn't sure I wanted to know. "Has he ever done…that before?"

Haven looked down at the bed. "He's hit me before."

"It didn't look like he was trying to hit you when I walked in."

More tears slid down her face as she closed her eyes. "He's made me watch him do…that to himself and he's touched me once. He said he would kill me and Mother if I ever said anything to anyone."

"Touched you how?"

She shook her head. "Please, Nate. Please. I can't tell you."

"Did he rape you? Have intercourse with you?" I needed to hear it from her mouth because I didn't believe a damn thing that he told before he drove away.

With a shake of her head, a sob slipped free. "But I think he would have had you not been here."

I wanted to destroy something. No, I wanted to get in the truck and go hunt that motherfucker down and kill him, just like I threatened to do before he left.

But I had to be strong in this moment for Haven, had to be the calm in her storm. "Hey, it's okay. It's okay now."

Haven buried her face in her hands and cried. I put my arm around her as she dropped her head to my shoulder, and it felt like she sobbed for hours. In truth, it had only been about thirty minutes.

"What if he comes back?" she softly asked.

"He won't."

"How do you know?" she asked, lifting her head and staring up at me with those eyes of hers. They looked blue today, most likely because she was wearing a blue top.

"Because I told him if he ever sets foot in Hamilton or tries to contact you, I'll be digging his grave."

She didn't say anything, only stared at me.

"I'm so sorry, Haven. I'm so…so fucking sorry."

"It's over, and I won't ever have to see him again."

Wiping her face, she moved away from me, and I took that as a sign to stand up. She did the same.

"Promise me, Nate, right now, that you won't tell a soul."

I closed my eyes and dropped my head back. "Haven, every ounce of me says I need to tell my parents. The police need to know."

"I'm already the laughingstock at school, Nate. This will only make everything worse."

"But you have friends who will help you through this."

She let out a bitter laugh. "Do you think the small handful of friends I have will help? It doesn't matter that he never forced me to…" Her body shivered. "Rumors will start, and I can't do that. My mother just got this job at a dentist's office, and I can't ruin that for her. Please. I'm begging you, Nate."

I rubbed at the instant pain in my neck. Everything inside of me screamed this was wrong. But when I looked at Haven, tears in her eyes and a broken look, I found myself saying, "I promise you, I won't ever tell anyone."

A look of relief crossed her tear-stained face, and she closed her eyes. "Thank you, Nate. Thank you for everything."

She threw herself into my body, and I wrapped my arms around her and held her. The last thing I would ever want to do is hurt Haven Larson. And if keeping her secret meant she would be spared from any more hurt, then that was what I would do.

◆ ◆ ◆

Senior Year of High School

Haven Marie Larson.

She was going to be the death of me one of these days.

"Hey, Nate, what's with the frown?" Lizzy Hathaway asked as she flashed me a bright smile. Her blue eyes lit up with that familiar glint of desire.

"No reason," I said as I focused back on Haven riding the horse around the arena.

"Haven is so weird."

Turning to look at Lizzy, I fought to keep the anger out of my voice when I asked, "Why do you say that?"

Motioning out to Haven, who was attempting to get the horse she was on to settle down, Lizzy sneered, "She is obsessed with animals. I mean, she walks people's dogs. That's her job. Dog walking. She spends more time with them than she does humans."

"What is your job?"

Lizzy laughed. "I'm in high school, Nate. I don't work."

"That's not a reason. I'm in high school, and I work."

"On your family ranch. That doesn't count." She waved her hand in the air again. "That's like chores."

I wanted to laugh. It was hardly like chores. It was hard work.

"What are you doing here, Lizzy?" I asked as I focused back on Haven in the arena with my father next to her.

"My mother is here to talk to your mom about training a horse we bought. I want to do barrel racing."

I nearly laughed. "Do you even know how to ride?"

She scoffed. "Of course, I know how to ride."

Raising a brow, she folded her arms over her chest. "I can ride a horse, Nate. If you want to go to a private spot, I can show you how good I can ride."

"I'll pass."

She huffed before turning on her heels and marching away from me. Turning my focus back on Haven and my father, I watched as she expertly handled the horse. It had taken me months to stop having nightmares about Haven and her father. I had almost broken down a few times and told my parents. Two years later, the urge to hurt someone was still there, but not as strong. And her good-for-nothing father had kept his word. He hadn't stepped foot in Hamilton. Not even for the divorce. I had a feeling Haven had told her mother what had happened because for the last two years she's been glued to Haven's side, and had only recently started letting her come to the ranch alone.

I was so enthralled in my thoughts and watching her that I didn't hear my mother walk up and stand beside me.

"She's the only one who can ride that mare."

All I did was nod.

"I just had to turn away business."

Looking at my mother, I asked, "Lizzy's mom?"

"Yes. The woman bought a horse and expected us to train it to barrel ride with their daughter, who had never even sat on a horse before. And they needed her to be ready by early next year so she could ride in the rodeo."

I laughed. "Sounds like Lizzy."

My mother sighed. "I want you to help Haven with Lady when she is done with your father."

I looked at my mother and asked, "Why do I have to help her? She's more than capable of caring for the horse when she's finished."

It wasn't like I didn't want to be around Haven; I did. Too much, probably. She was all I could think about, and I knew she liked me. Or at least she did a few years back. Now, she hardly looked at me when I saw her in school. My reputation didn't help, even though it was more talk than reality.

Raising a single brow, my mother stared at me. I took a step back and nodded my head. "Of course, I'll help her."

A brilliant smile spread across her face. My mother was beautiful. Her brown hair was pulled back low, and her blue eyes sparkled as if she knew something I didn't.

"Thank you, Nathan. I know you normally avoid Haven, but since your father and I need to leave as soon as her lesson ends, I don't want her feeling alone."

I sighed. "I don't ignore her. I just avoid her."

Her hands went to her hips. "Nathan, what in the world do you have against that girl? So she had a crush on you; surely she's gotten over it."

Casting a glance out, I saw Haven biting down hard on her lower lip as she tried to get Lady to walk in a circle around Dad and his gelding, Prancer. Her control of the mare was impressive since the damn thing was scared of everything, including the other horse and rider.

"I don't have anything against her, Mom. She just…I don't know."

She laughed and then gave me a side hug. "Oh, Nathan, sweetheart. One of these days you'll look at that girl out there, and you won't want to avoid her."

"Is that because she's going to move out of Montana, and I'll never have to see her again?"

Her smile grew bigger. "No, you're going to feel something in here." Placing her hand on my chest, she slowly shook her head. "And that is going to change everything."

My heart felt like it about dropped to the ground.

"If you're talking about love, Mom, I am not going to fall in love. Ever. I like girls too much to settle down with just one, and it would be wrong to lead Haven on."

She pointed to me. "I'm going to pretend I never heard that. Go head into the barn; they're finishing up."

Doing as I was told, I headed to the barn and did a few quick chores as Haven cooled down Lady. Next, I filled a bucket with warm water for Haven to wash down the mare. A few minutes later, I could hear the horse's hooves. I watched as Haven tied her horse up and removed the saddle. I walked over and took it from her.

"I'll get that for you."

Haven smiled. "Thanks, Nate."

I pointed to the bucket. "Brought this out for you."

She thanked me once again and quickly got to washing down the horse. I took her saddle and brought it back to the tack room. Not many people had their own saddles, but Haven did simply because she was here so much and loved helping my father break new horses in. It was my mother who suggested she just leave her saddle here. She had bought it used but took care of it like it was gold.

When I returned to the paddock, Haven was rubbing a dry towel around on Lady. She then took a handful of hay and put it out for her to eat.

"Was she very sweaty?" I asked, walking up and leaning against a pole as I watched Haven put the wick-smart blanket on Lady.

"Not really. It was a nice, cool day, and we didn't work that hard. Your dad said to put her out to pasture since the sun is out, and it's warming up."

I glanced down and watched as Lady took a long drink. I smiled. "She really does trust you, doesn't she?"

Haven gave the mare another pat before going to get a bit more hay for her. All the animals seemed to trust Haven. It was clear she threw all of her love into taking care of them, and it broke my heart because I had a feeling I knew the reason why.

"I can put her out if you need to leave."

Without looking at me, Haven replied, "That's okay. I don't mind, and I don't have anywhere I need to be right away."

"How is the dog walking going?" I asked as I watched her lift each leg and inspect Lady's shoes.

Haven's face glowed with a wide grin, and I couldn't help but smile back. What was it about this girl's smile that made me feel…happy? It was unlike any feeling I had ever had; only her smile brought it out.

"It's going great. I've got five now and devised a great way of walking them all simultaneously. It's a belt I came up with and you attach their leashes right to it."

My brows shot up. "You're not afraid of them dragging you?"

She laughed, and I tried to ignore how it felt like a bolt of energy raced through my body.

"They're all well-behaved dogs. I'd like to learn to do some training someday."

"What happens when you leave for college?"

She stopped running her hand down Lady's neck and looked at me. "I'm not going to college."

"You're not? How does your mother feel about that?"

She shrugged. "Can't go to college if you don't have any money."

"Scholarship?"

Haven shook her head. "I can't leave my mom."

I wanted to ask her why but kept my mouth shut.

"Besides, I have a plan, and if I stick to it, I'll be fine without going."

"What does your mom think about your plan?"

"She's okay with it. She also knows that I've gotten a few scholarships, but even with that, I can't afford to go."

I kicked a nonexistent rock on the ground. "I'm sorry, Haven."

She shrugged. "It's okay. I've got enough money saved up to hopefully be able to buy my own house someday. I plan on learning how to train the dogs as well. I've been reading about it for the last year."

"Reading about dogs?"

Nodding, she untied Lady and started walking her toward the south pasture gate. "Yeah. And our vet knows a girl who trains, and she offered to teach me. If that follows through, I won't have to pay for the classes. More money to save up."

Following her, I marveled at how different she was from most other girls in my senior class. Was it because of what her father had done to her? We hadn't ever spoken about it again except once when she asked if I had kept her promise.

Haven stopped at the gate before opening it. Once it was open, Lady walked into the pasture. "Will you remove her blanket in a bit?"

"Sure."

We watched as Lady trotted out to the middle of the pasture where a small group of horses were grazing. She saddled up to Thunder, my horse, and she let out a whinny.

Haven laughed. "Spicy girl."

"Thunder doesn't seem to mind," I said with a soft laugh.

We turned and walked back to the barn, neither saying anything. Once inside, Haven started toward the small office. I assumed she was getting her things to leave.

I walked to a stall to check on another horse.

"Hey, girl," I softly said as I opened the door and walked in. Reaching into my pocket, I pulled out a small peppermint stick and handed it to her. She bit off a piece and started bobbing her head.

Moving my hand lightly over her neck, I chuckled. "Like that, don't you?"

I heard Haven let out a small yelp. I quickly entered the room and saw her standing on a ladder, reaching for something in the rafter.

"What in the hell are you doing, Haven?"

"There's a kitten stuck up here, and I'm trying to get it."

The ladder wobbled.

"Didn't anyone ever tell you not to stand on the top of a ladder?" I said as I held onto the bottom rungs.

"I couldn't reach her; I needed to get higher."

"Get down, Haven."

"Not until I get the kitten. She's afraid."

Rolling my eyes, I looked up. "Just get down, and I'll get her."

"I can get her; I just need another inch or two," she said, lifting up on her toes and stretching.

"Fuck, Haven! You're going to fall."

She wobbled, and I thought for sure she was coming down. Suddenly, a white and orange kitten appeared, and Haven was heading back down the ladder.

"Hold it still for me."

"What in the hell do you think I've been doing?" I shot back, moving out of the way when she descended. She got off the ladder and held the kitten up to her face.

"You bad little girl. You scared us."

"No, you scared us. Climbing up on that ladder like that. You could have gotten hurt."

Suddenly, Molly, the barn cat, came walking into the room. She took one look at her baby and meowed. Haven set it down, and Molly picked it up and carried it off.

"She must have been moving her litter," Haven said with a smile. When she looked back at me, her smile faded. "Why are you scowling at me?"

"Do you have any idea how bad that could have turned out? You could have fallen and broken your neck."

She winked, and it felt like someone sucker-punched me. I forgot for a moment how to breathe. "But I didn't."

"But you could have!" I shouted.

Tilting her head, Haven asked, "Nathan Shaw, were you worried about me?"

"No. Yes. I mean, anyone would have been. Why do you have to do such…stupid things?"

Her head drew back, and it felt like the air had been pulled from my lungs momentarily. A look of hurt passed over Haven's face. I cursed myself because I had made a promise never to hurt her.

"I'm sorry, Haven, I didn't mean to say that."

Clearing her throat, she whispered, "I need to leave now."

She started to walk but tripped and stumbled. I reached out and caught her, but I also lost my footing. As I held onto her, we both started to fall backward. Luckily, the bed that my cousins had in here for late nights working caught us. Haven lay over me, both of us in shock. Then we burst into laughter.

Her blue-gray eyes seemed to lighten as she laughed. A loose strand of hair fell in front of her face from her ponytail. Before I could stop myself, I pushed it behind her ear. The feel of my fingers brushing over her skin instantly made my body come alive.

Haven's smile faded slightly as we lay there, neither of us moving.

"Haven," I whispered as my eyes drifted to her perfectly pouty lips. When her tongue dashed out to wet them, I lost all sense. Cupping her face in my hands, I drew her down to me and kissed her. It was slow and almost awkward at first until she opened her mouth. The kiss turned deeper, and before I knew it, I rolled us over. Haven spread her legs open, and I settled between them, pushing my hard length into her, causing us both to moan. Her fingers sliced through my hair as if she was clinging onto me, afraid I would stop kissing her.

"Fucking hell," I gasped as I ripped my mouth from hers and started to kiss along her jaw and down her neck. My hand slipped under her shirt, and when I cupped her perfect breast in my hand, she arched her back. I wasn't sure when I did it, but I had taken her shirt off and pulled her bra down, exposing a tight nipple to the cool air. My mouth covered it, and when I gently bit down and then soothed it by licking, Haven moaned my name. I liked hearing her say it as she lay there on the verge of falling apart.

"More, Nate. Please, I need more."

Still kissing and sucking her nipple, I undid her jeans and slipped my hand in.

"Oh, God," she whimpered when I slipped my fingers inside of her. She was soaking wet.

"Do you like that?" I asked as I playfully bit her earlobe while whispering to her.

"Yes."

Knowing that I was about to make Haven come did something to me. I felt confused and I wasn't sure why, but I wanted to hear her cry out my name as she came.

Her hands were all over me. In my hair, gripping my shoulders, running up and down my back. When she slipped her hands under my shirt, my entire body shivered. When she reached for my jeans, I froze.

"No, don't stop! Please!"

"Don't," I quickly said.

"I want to touch you, Nate. I want to make you feel good too. Please, don't stop."

And just like that, reality came crashing down around me like waves in a storm when her words reminded me of that day I found her and her father.

I couldn't do this. Not to Haven. I had no intentions of settling down with anyone, and to do this would lead Haven on. That was the last thing I wanted to do. I pulled my hand out and sat back, trying not to look at her chest rise and fall with each deep breath. Haven stared up at me, confused.

"This was…this was a mistake. I can't do this."

"What?" she asked, a shocked expression on her beautiful face.

I scrambled off the bed, reached for her shirt, and held it out.

Haven lifted on her elbows. "You're stopping?"

Rubbing the back of my neck, I said, "It was a mistake, Haven."

She blinked at me a few times, and I could see she was fighting back tears. "Why? I thought you wanted…um…it felt like you wanted…"

I shook my head. "It was a stupid mistake."

Haven snatched her shirt from my hand and quickly put it on. She stood and appeared to be dizzy for a moment. When I reached out to steady her, she jerked away.

"Haven."

She cut me off and said, "You don't have to say it was a mistake again, Nate. I got it. If touching me repulses you, why in the world did you kiss me?"

"What?"

She pushed past me and headed out of the barn.

"Haven, will you wait a second."

Once she got to her car and went to open the door, I put my hand on it. "Wait."

"For what? You made it clear you made a mistake—a stupid one. I'd like to leave before I'm humiliated even more."

"I didn't mean to do that…I got carried away, and it just happens with guys."

She spun around and stared at me; her mouth dropped open. "Oh my God. You, of all people, to say that to me. Wow. Thanks for making me feel even better. I'm glad to know that any woman can make you hard, and want to fuck her with your fingers. Oh, except for the girl who is tainted."

Her harsh words felt like a slap, and I stepped back. She slowly shook her head. "I would have given myself to you, Nathan, willingly without regret. I will never make that *mistake* again."

I closed my eyes. I couldn't stand to see the hurt on her face. The sound of her car door opening caused me to look at her again.

Stop her. Tell her how you feel about her. Tell her it has nothing to do with what happened.

Opening my mouth to say something, I quickly shut it. When Haven slammed her door closed, I jumped.

I stood frozen in the same spot as I watched her back out and drive down the driveway. Once her car was out of sight, I stumbled back and reached for something to steady myself. I wasn't sure what in the hell I was feeling, but there was one thing I knew for sure. I could never…ever again…kiss or touch Haven Larson.

Chapter One

Nathan

Present Day

Lightning lit up the darkening skies while thunder rumbled through the valley. The storm that was predicted to move in later this afternoon was making an early appearance, and I wasn't the least bit disappointed about that. I loved storms, especially fall storms. Something about the thunder echoing off the mountains made my heart feel happy.

"Looks like this one is going to be a big one!" my cousin Josh called out over the increasing wind.

I nodded and shut the gate, ensuring it was locked securely.

"I hope we don't get any lightning strikes in the valley. Everything is still dry from the summer," I said as I jumped into the ranch truck and shut the door right before the heavens opened and rain poured down.

"I've got a good plan in effect if anything does happen," Josh said from the truck's driver's side. He quit his job as a firefighter not long ago and started working full time on the ranch. I wasn't sure why he gave up his dream job of firefighting, but I knew our grandfather's sudden and unexpected death had something to do with it. One thing he did do, at the request of our oldest cousin, Blayze, was come up with a plan in case of fire. A few years back, a wildfire had burned a few hundred acres of the Shaw Ranch, and Blayze never wanted to see that again. Fires were something you couldn't control, but you could have a plan of action to keep the damage to a minimum, and that was precisely what Josh had been working on. The first thing he did was start working on clearing the entire fence line of the ranch. It's not a small feat, but we got it done. Our cousin, Beck, who a few years ago had been a recent addition to the family, was in charge of the clearing. The guy was a Shaw, for sure. He was out there with the workers clearing and hauling brush. He was our Uncle Beck's son, but he never got the chance to meet him since he died before Beck was even born. Originally from Texas, after Beck's mother died, he found the name and information for his father's family. One trip to Hamilton and Beck fell in love, not just with Montana, but with Avery Littleton, our cousin, not by blood. The rest, they say, is history.

"We need to swing by my folks' place. Mom and Dad aren't back from Las Vegas, and I need to make sure Lady is stable."

"Have you called Lily?" Josh asked.

Lily was my sister and was married to Maverick, who worked as a horse trainer for my mother and father. He was more of a horse whisperer, working on the more troubled horses. They lived in the small house on the back of my parents' spot on the ranch. I knew they would ensure everything was in order, but I wanted to swing by and check myself.

"I did, no answer. She and Mav might be rounding in the horses; I'm not sure. I tried to text Maverick also and no reply from him either. Lady is afraid of thunder if left out to pasture. It doesn't seem to bother her when she is stabled for some reason."

"That horse is one of the strangest horses I've ever known." Josh laughed. "Does Haven still come and ride her?"

I nodded even though he wasn't looking at me. The rain was coming down so hard it was hard to see even with the wipers going at top speed.

"Yeah, at least once a week, according to my mother and Lily."

We drove silently for a moment before Josh said, "I think they're getting close to getting the loan sorted. Haven and Sophia aren't happy with the contractor, though." He glanced out the window up at the sky as if he could see anything. "If we keep getting rain like this, they won't break ground anytime soon."

"I'm surprised they're not waiting until after winter to start on it."

"They've still got some time to get things done, and according to the girls, they want to be open by late spring or early summer."

"Makes sense," I replied.

Josh's girlfriend, Sophia, was partners with Haven. Originally, she was going to work as Haven's assistant, where she would do administrative tasks, which she does now, but after hearing Haven's plans to open a dog park, she was on board and offered to be her partner. Haven jumped at the chance to have Sophia on board, and both women were a force to be reckoned with. Currently, Haven runs a dog walking service where she picks up dogs in a van and brings them to locations where she can let them all off-leash and walk. She does that twice a day, five days a week. And when she isn't doing that, she volunteers either at the animal shelter or helping out with displaced animals. She had also placed a few horses with my mother and father in hopes that they, Lily, or Maverick, could help them so they could be adopted.

Josh looked out the windshield again. "It's crazy how fast this rain is coming down."

"I have a feeling we're going to have a crazy winter."

"Yeah, I do as well. We could use the snow, though, after the little bit of rain we got last spring and this past summer. Plus, last winter was pretty mild."

I nodded once again. Before we pulled down the drive that would lead to my parents' part of the ranch, Lily called.

"Hey, sorry for the delay. We're good here. Haven was able to get Lady into her stall."

My heart dropped. "Haven? She's there?"

"Yeah, she was here before the storm moved in and offered to help us. It's crazy cause once Lady knew Haven was here, she wouldn't have anything to do with me or Maverick."

I smiled. "Sounds about right. So, you guys are all good? You don't need me and Josh to help with anything, right?"

"We're good. I'm trying to convince Haven to stay until the storm clears up some, but she's insisting she needs to head on out."

I frowned. "Sounds like her. Stubborn as a mule."

Josh laughed, clearly knowing I was talking about Haven.

"We're heading back to the main barn to ensure everything is battened down. If you need anything, give me a call."

"Sounds good. Thanks, Nate. I love you."

"Love you too, sis."

I hit End and looked out the passenger window. I couldn't see shit with the rain coming down in sheets, but my mind was swirling with thoughts of Haven. What in the hell was she thinking being out in this storm? They said it was going to be bad, with even some flooding expected with how fast it was coming down.

"What are you huffing about over there?" Josh asked as he pulled up to the main barn and parked next to our cousin Hunter's truck.

Hunter and Blayze were brothers, and Uncle Brock's only two sons. Their sister, Morgan, didn't live on the ranch and instead lived with her husband, Ryan, on their ranch where they raised and trained horses. To say the entire family ran the ranch was an understatement. All the grandkids lived on the ranch except for Morgan and Rose. Josh and I technically didn't live on the ranch, but we purchased land that butted up to the ranch when we received our trust fund from our grandparents. Every acre was then incorporated into the original ranch. Just like everyone else, Josh and I had our allotted acres of the ranch.

"I'm not huffing."

Josh laughed. "Dude, you were sighing big time."

A loud crack of thunder hit, and we jumped.

"Shit," we both said at the same time.

"Let's make a run for it!" Josh said before he opened the truck door and stepped into the storm. I couldn't even see him running because the rain was falling so hard.

So I did what any self-respecting male would do, I drew in a deep breath and ran for cover.

◆ ◆ ◆

Once it was clear the storm was not letting up, I decided to head home. Blayze assured me that I wasn't needed, and after spending much of yesterday in the saddle of my horse checking the fence line and hauling hay up to the loft, I was ready for a hot bath. My body ached. There were ranch hands who were responsible for the hay hauling, but I volunteered to help out. It was a good workout and kept me in shape, and I never minded a hard day's work.

The road to my property was already flooding, so I left by the main gate. When I went to turn left onto the road, I noticed a car pulled over and someone bending down to look at their tire. I couldn't tell if it was a man or a woman. I turned to the right and pulled up behind them. Grabbing an umbrella—not that it would do much good—I jumped out of my truck. I knew who it was the second they stood and turned to me.

"Haven."

Rushing over to her, I held the umbrella above her. Not that I'd somehow make her drier, I mean, she was soaked.

"What's wrong?" I called out over the rain and wind. It was so windy Haven had to grab onto the car to keep from being blown around.

"My tire is flat, and when I checked the spare, it was flat too."

Frowning, I looked at the car and back to her. "We have to stop meeting this way!"

Haven rolled her eyes. The day before Halloween, I found her on the side of the road with a flat tire. I had offered to help her then, albeit with a lot less rain pouring down, and we ended up arguing. I walked away with a black eye from her elbow. She hadn't done it on purpose, or so she said, but I'm still questioning that.

"Why are you standing out here in the rain?" I shouted.

"I was trying to decide after I looked at the flat if returning to Lily's was worth the risk."

I shook my head. "You'll ruin your rim. Besides, the ranch roads are starting to flood. It's like a tsunami out here, and the temperature is dropping quickly."

She nodded. "I can't get a hold of my mom."

"Just leave the car and come back to my house with me."

Her eyes widened, and I knew she was about to say no. Then I saw that her lips almost looked blue.

"Damn it, Haven, you're freezing. Just come back to my place, get warm, and wait until the rain settles down, and then you can deal with the car."

She looked at her car and then back at me. Worrying her lower lip, she looked like she was about to shake her head, but I held up my hand.

"Walking back to the ranch will take you hours, and have I mentioned that you're turning blue? Just get your things, and let me take you to my place."

With a sigh, she nodded. "Let me grab my stuff."

Following her with the umbrella to the passenger side, she grabbed her purse and a large bag. Clutching them both to her chest, we quickly made it over to my truck. After helping her in, I ran around the other side of the truck. I threw the umbrella in the back seat and jumped in the front.

"I have never in my life seen so much rain come down so fast!" Haven said as she pushed wet hair from her face. Even soaked and looking like a drowned rat, she was beautiful.

I shook my head to get rid of those thoughts. Haven was off limits. "Yeah, it's coming down in sheets." I reached over and turned the heater on and her seat warmer.

"Thank you for stopping. I can't believe I didn't have an umbrella in my car. I just cleaned it out a few weeks ago, and I took it out and forgot to put it back in."

"I'm just glad I took that exit off the ranch, or who knows how long you'd be sitting there. It's a long walk to any of the houses on the ranch, especially from where you were broken down."

She laughed until it faded away. "The road is flooding, Nate. I've never seen these roads flood before."

I could hear the fear in her voice. "My place isn't that much farther up the road."

We drove past the gate that led to Josh's place. Just a bit more until we got to my place. Haven was right; the ditches were flooded, and water was moving onto the road.

"Do you think my car will be okay?" she asked.

"I'll call a tow truck as soon as we get to my place."

Her arms involuntarily wrapped around her body as she started to shiver. I reached over and turned the heater up to max.

"Better?"

She shivered. "I'll be better soon."

My driveway came into sight, and I silently sent up a prayer. If she didn't get warm soon, she would catch a chill. Even though Grams says that's all made up. "You can't catch a cold from being wet." She would always say.

I pulled in, hit the opener for the gate, and drove down the drive. When my house came into view, Haven said, "A log cabin? You built a log cabin?"

I smiled. I knew I was beyond blessed with having my own land, my own custom home, and all before I turned twenty-two. The one thing I never did was take any of it for granted. My smile faded as I realized Sophia, Josh's girlfriend and Haven's business partner, had never told Haven what my house looked like. Not that I expected her to, but a part of me was disappointed Haven hadn't snooped and asked. She used to always be in my business.

That was before the barn incident, though.

Pushing those thoughts away as well, I replied, "Yeah, I've always liked them."

She peered through the windshield and squinted. "It's hard to tell with all this rain, but it almost looks historic."

There went my smile again. "That is exactly what I was going for. I'd show you the front, but I assume you want to get dry and warm as soon as possible."

She rubbed her hands together before blowing into them. "You would assume correctly."

I pulled into the garage, turned off the truck, and shut the garage door. Haven was getting her items and quickly caught up to me at the door to the house. I unlocked the door and turned off the alarm.

Flipping my lights on, I heard Haven from behind me.

"Wow! And we're only in the mudroom."

Laughing, I reached into a cabinet and got a towel for Haven.

"I'm getting your wood floors soaking wet."

I walked into the laundry and grabbed a robe.

"You can change out of your clothes in here and put them in the dryer. I'll show you to the guest bedroom, and if you want to take a hot shower, I can give you something of mine to wear."

She looked at me and narrowed her eyes. "Why are you being so nice to me?"

I blinked a few times. "Do you honestly think I would leave you on the side of the road in a storm, Haven?"

She shrugged, and I didn't want to admit how much that hurt.

"What are you wanting in return?"

This time, my mouth dropped open. "I don't want anything."

She sighed. "I'm sorry to be a pain in the ass."

"You're not. But get out of those clothes before you catch a cold."

She saluted. "Yes, sir. Right away, sir!"

Rolling my eyes, I exited the laundry and shut the door.

"This laundry room is like a dream! Mine isn't even a quarter of this size in my apartment."

I walked into the living room and turned on the lights. They all flickered right before a loud crack of thunder.

Haven let out a small scream and I couldn't help but chuckle. That's what she gets for assuming I wanted something in return for helping her.

"That was close," I said as I moved into the kitchen to turn a few more lights on. As the storm approached closer, it was getting darker outside. Given how dark it was, it was hard to believe it was nearly three in the afternoon.

"Um, I put my clothes in the dryer."

Turning to see Haven in nothing but my robe, I cleared my throat. "Right. I'll show you to the guest bedroom, and after you get warmed up and changed into something, I'll give you a tour. If you want one."

When I glanced back to see if Haven was following me, I noticed she was looking everywhere as she followed me through the living room and to a set of stairs.

"Down here is the guest suite. It has a full-size bathroom and a walk-out to the patio. I doubt you'll want to go out there, though," I said when I reached the bottom of the steps. "To the right is the guest room."

"And to the left?" she asked.

"The family room and bar area. I know it's a strange set up with the kitchen and main living room up stairs, but I wanted the view for up there and a patio for down here."

We walked into the guest bedroom, and she took a deep breath. "Nate, this is stunning."

"I'd like to take the credit, but I have to give it to Rose. Our in-house designer. She did all of the interior."

"She is amazing," Haven said as she entered the room. "Is that reclaimed wood on the wall behind the headboard?"

It was strange to be having a normal conversation with Haven. Whenever we found ourselves together, we threw out jabs at one another. This was a welcome change, and I couldn't help but wonder if maybe we could be friends and move past…well, the past.

"It is. Much of the wood on the walls and the ceiling beams are reclaimed. It was important for me to re-use as much as I could. All the wood outside the house is from an old 1800's cabin."

She slowly shook her head. "It's stunning."

"Thank you. It's smaller than Josh's house, with just three bedrooms, but it works for me."

I showed her to the bathroom, and she grabbed onto my arm. "It's like a spa in here. Look at that bathtub."

With a chuckle, I said, "You can take a bath if you want. I'll run up to my room, which is right above here, and grab you something to wear. I'll leave it on the bed and meet you in the family room. In how long do you think?"

She eyed the bathtub like she longed to get into it. "I'll take a quick shower just to warm up."

I nodded. "Fresh towels are in here." I pointed to a cabinet. "And there should be some fresh soap and shampoo if you need it in the cabinet by the tub."

"Thanks. I won't take very long."

"Take your time. I don't think we'll be leaving anytime soon. I'll call about your car as well."

I left her alone in the bathroom and shut the door. I closed my eyes and drew in a few deep breaths. Knowing she was naked under that robe was driving me insane. Who was I kidding? There is no way I could be friends with Haven. Not when the only thing I wanted to do when I was near her was kiss her.

With a shake of my head, I headed to my room to get her something to wear.

Chapter Two

Haven

I stood in the middle of the massive bathroom and did a three-sixty.

"Holy crap," I whispered as I took in all the rich woods and soothing colors. From what I could tell, all the cabinets in the entire house were a dark shaker style. The bathtub was a huge soaker tub that sat in front of a large picture window. I was dying to know what the view looked like from that window.

The shower was also oversized and all glass. I removed Nate's robe and laid it over the small bench in the room. I stepped inside the shower and laughed.

"What in the heck are all the knobs for?"

I pressed myself against the stone tile wall and turned one of them on. The rain shower came on. I adjusted it to hot and then started playing with the other ones. Water came from everywhere, so I quickly turned them off and kept the rain shower on. I hadn't grabbed any soap or shampoo. All I really needed to do was rinse off with some hot water to get warm.

Closing my eyes, I dropped my head back and let the water run over my face and down my body. It felt so dang good.

A light knock on the bathroom door pulled me out of my trance.

"Yeah?" I called out.

"I put some clothes on the bed for you. It was the best I could find until yours are dry."

"That's perfect. Thank you, Nate."

I paused to see if he said anything else. As I stared at the door, I frowned. Why was he being so nice to me? He was usually very standoffish and avoided me like the plague. Seeing me looking like a drowned rat probably made him feel sorry for me. And why did I have to have another flat when he came across me? It was just my luck, at least when it came to Nathan Shaw.

After getting good and plenty warm, I shut off the water and dried off. Using the towel Nate had given me earlier, I wrapped that around my head. I opened the bathroom door slightly to ensure Nate wasn't still in the bedroom. He wasn't, and he had shut the door when he left. A small part of me was disappointed.

"Stop that, Haven. He made it perfectly clear ages ago that you aren't his type."

I stepped out and looked around the guest room once again. It wasn't anything over the top, with a simple queen-size bed with an iron bed frame sitting against the feature wall. Three large windows were at the top, most likely allowing light into the room. A small sofa sat to one side, and on the other side was a giant picture window, with a smaller window to the left and a glass door to the right. Above the picture window was another smaller window. The view from the room must be crazy nice. I peeked out to see a table and two chairs out back, but with the rain and the darkening sky, I couldn't see anything else.

In the corner was a small antique writing desk with an oil lamp sitting on it. I smiled as I walked over to it. I ran my finger along the glass and smiled as I thought about the oil lamp my grandmother used to have on her writing desk. This lamp was a beautiful piece, and I couldn't help but wonder if it was a family heirloom. Just like that, however, I was reminded that my father broke my grandmother's lamp one night when he was angry with my mother.

I sighed and turned away from the desk. What must that be like to have things like this passed down through families. I chewed on my lower lip. I wouldn't know. The only thing I had ever gotten was a small inheritance from my grandmother that I was going to use for the dog park. Unfortunately, my mother fell on hard times, and I had to use the money to get her mortgage payments caught up. My father came from a poor family who made their living either farming or mining. My father had left home when he was fourteen because his father was abusive. The apple hadn't fallen far. I closed my eyes and forced myself not to go down that road. It had taken me years to learn to drown out what that man had done to me.

Turning, I saw the clothes Nate had put out for me: a Montana State T-shirt, black sweatpants, and an oversized sweatshirt with the Shaw Ranch logo. I picked up the sweatshirt and brought it up to my nose, taking in a deep breath as the smell of Nate filled my senses.

"Stop it, Haven," I said, dropping it back to the bed. I was glad he brought the sweatshirt since I also put my bra in the dryer. After slipping on the T-shirt and the sweats, which I had to tie super tight to keep them from falling off, I put the sweatshirt on. He had even put a pair of wool socks out for me. I put them on and headed back into the bathroom. I towel-dried my hair and then glanced around for a blow dryer. I found one in a cabinet and was able to dry my hair. My curls would be out of control since I had no product or hair straightener in it, but it would have to do. I had long ago stopped trying to impress

Nate Shaw. He wasn't interested in me, and I would do good to remember that.

I opened the guest bedroom door and walked down the hall. To my right was a door leading outside. I walked past it and into the family room and abruptly stopped. Two things had my mouth hanging open.

One was the insanely beautiful room with rustic wood planks adorning the walls and the large beams on the ceiling.

Two, Nate stood in black sweatpants and a blue T-shirt, and his feet were bare of shoes or socks.

He's barefoot. In sweats. Looking hot as hell.

"Oh, God," I whispered under my breath. *Why am I being punished this way? Why?*

I walked farther into the room and stopped again when I saw Nate walk over to the wood pile.

"Holy. Shit."

Nate looked up from where he was building a fire in the fireplace that I hadn't even noticed. The back side of the room had floor-to-ceiling windows with sliding doors that led out back. A large sectional sofa faced the fire in the middle of the room. Above the fire was a large TV screen. When I turned to my left, I slowly shook my head. A rustic bar made from more large timbers of wood and a stunning black granite counter stood. Behind it were more cabinets, a lighter color than the rest of the cabinets in the house. They held different types of liquor. There was a sink, and as I walked closer, I asked, "Is that draft beer?"

Nate laughed. "Yeah. A request from my cousins when we were designing this area."

Turning, I looked at a room made of three sides of glass that held wine inside of it. The wall with all of the wine had a black rod system that held all of the wine. It looked like it was made of reclaimed wood.

I looked at Nate. "This room should be in a magazine."

He winked. "It was. Rose has a friend who works for an architecture firm in Boise, and he designed this whole room, and it was featured in some architecture magazine. They were here for days staging it and taking pictures."

"I've never seen anything like it. Do you like wine?"

Nate shrugged. "I can drink it, but it's not my go-to. That is." He pointed to the draft beer, and I laughed. This easy conversation between us wasn't normal, but I liked it. The intimacy of it. Maybe a little more than I should.

"Speaking of, would you like something to drink?"

"That would be nice."

"I could make a hot toddy, or a simple glass of whiskey should do the trick."

Smiling, I said, "Whiskey sounds good. I've never had it before."

Nate paused and glanced over his shoulder. "What?"

"Nope," I said as I popped my P while sliding onto the bar stool. There were two.

He laughed softly, and I ignored the slight tremor that went through my body at the sound.

He isn't interested in you like that, Haven.

When he turned around and handed me the whiskey, I was again struck by how handsome Nate Shaw was. His brown hair looked like he had run his hand through it multiple times, and those eyes of his. Were they gray or silver? Maybe the lightest of blue. I just couldn't tell. All I knew was I had never seen eyes that color before.

"Thank you," I said as I took the whiskey glass and brought it to my nose. It was sweet and fragrant and had what I could only describe as a grassy or hay-like scent. I took a drink and started to cough.

"Holy shit!" I hit my chest. "That hit the back of my throat, and it burns!"

Nate laughed. "I'm not a fan of whiskey at all."

"Why did you give it to me then?" I asked.

"You wanted something to warm you up."

"A spiked pumpkin latte would have been better."

Nate looked around and held up his hands. "I'm all out of pumpkin spice. Sorry."

"Can I have a beer instead?"

He winked, and my heart felt like it somersaulted in my chest. I remembered the last time he winked at me like that. Senior year of high school in his parents' barn where we almost…almost slept together until he stopped it. I knew why he stopped. He knew what my father had almost done to me and had stopped him when I was sixteen. Had he not shown up, he would have for sure raped me. I knew in the back of his mind I was—I am—damaged goods, and no man wanted that. I couldn't honestly blame him, but sometimes, the way he looked at me…was confusing.

I pushed the memory away. It did little good to think about it. Besides, I had heard that Nate had a revolving door of women coming and going.

"Bottle or draft?"

"I'll give the draft a try."

Nate pulled out two glass mugs from a little refrigerator and filled them with the frothy beer. He handed one to me, and we held up the mugs and clinked.

"Here is to a good draft beer."

I chuckled and took a sip. Turning in my seat, I looked over the room once again. "Nate, this is beautiful. I can't even imagine your view with these windows."

"It looks out toward the ranch, and I must say, it's a killer view. So, I, um, heard through the grapevine that you were hoping to buy a house."

Turning back to face him, I tried to hide the sadness on my face. "I was thinking about it, but I've soaked all my savings into this dog park, including the money I had saved up for a down payment on the house. I had an inheritance from my grandmother that was going to help with getting the dog park going, but life happened. It's okay, though; my apartment is fine."

"By the way, how is it you don't have any dogs of your own, Haven? As much as you love them."

"I can't have one while I'm in an apartment. I mean, I guess I could. I would just feel so bad keeping it locked up in a small, one-bedroom apartment. I get my fair share of love from dogs, though, with my job."

"How many can you fit on that bus?"

Why was he being so nice to me? He never seemed the least bit interested in what I did. He hadn't said anything negative or cracked a bad joke or anything. I was honestly surprised he had even stopped to help me. No, wait, was that fair of me? No, it wasn't, and I instantly felt guilty for thinking it.

"Why are you staring at me like that?" Nate asked with a raised brow.

I shrugged one shoulder, took a sip of the beer, and then said, "I'm just confused about why you're being so nice to me, even asking about my job."

A look of hurt crossed his face, but it was gone as quickly as it had come. "What do you mean?"

I let out a humorless laugh. "You're not cracking any jokes about my job or poking fun at me. That's not like you."

"You act as if I'm mean to you constantly."

"You are, Nate. You normally do whatever you can to avoid me."

He rubbed the back of his neck, obviously uncomfortable with my directness. "I'm not trying to be mean to you, Haven."

"To answer your question," I said, looking down at the beer. "We can fit sixteen on the bus."

"Sixteen! And you're taking them out there on your own?"

"Owen helps sometimes."

A look passed over Nate's face, but I couldn't read it.

"Sophia said you guys went out, like on a date or, umm, just to hang out. Was that before he started working with you?"

I nearly spit out the beer in my mouth. "No! We've gone out to dinner a few times, and he's asked me out on a date, but I told him it was best to keep the relationship strictly friends. He agreed since we work together."

"What does he do for you, I mean, the dogs?"

"Owen drives the bus and helps in the beginning sometimes with the poop bags."

"Poop bags?" Nate asked with raised brows.

"Yeah, they all go potty before our hike."

All he did was nod.

"Ted comes sometimes as well."

Nate's jaw clenched, and he turned away to clear his throat.

"What's wrong?" I asked, curious why he had reacted that way to Ted's name.

I waited for him to say more but changed the subject when he didn't.

"So, care to take me on a tour?"

He smiled. "Sure. You've seen down here. There is a half bath right out here."

I left my beer and followed him through the family room to peek into a nicely decorated half bath. There was a rustic cabinet that held a copper bowl sink. The room was painted a light shade of green with only a few decorations. It was simple, and I liked it.

"You said Rose did all of the decorating?" I asked as I followed him up the steps to the main floor.

"She did a lot of it. My mother and Lily had a hand in it as well."

We walked back up the steps, and Nate walked into a room. "Another guest bedroom. This one is smaller and doesn't have as nice of a bath as the one downstairs."

The room was simple, with finished-out walls and no wood. The feel of the room was a bit more modern, with light taupe walls and carpet on the floor. It was the first room I had seen carpet in. The bathroom was also contemporary, with more of a streamlined look to the cabinets. There was nothing rustic about this bathroom at all. There was also a pretty decent-sized shower and no bathtub.

"This has a very modern feel to it."

"This would be Rose. She wanted to do something completely different for those guests who might want a different feel than the rest of the house. I have to say, it is my least favorite room."

I smiled and followed him out of the bedroom and through the hallway to the front doorway. The hallway was like a passage from one side of the house to other, with the family room open below. A beautiful wrought-iron railing ran along the one side of the hallway until we reached the other side of the house where the kitchen was. We walked into the kitchen, and I got a better look at everything. Dark rustic cabinets with beautiful black finishes made the room feel like I had stepped into the past. Large rock columns flanked the sides of the sizeable six-burner stove. A built-in microwave with a coffee station was to the right of the stove. The backsplash behind the stove was a large slate of stone framed with a large wooden beam. It was beautiful.

"Wow, the kitchen is beautiful."

Nate smiled. "Thanks."

The island held the sink and was surrounded by a stunning slab of granite. It was off-white with brilliant golds and browns. In front of the island, a wooden table seated four. The rock column under the table matched the other two near the stove. Tall wooden chairs with leather seats sat around the eat-in table.

Another large rock column separated the kitchen from the formal dining area. In a small nook, a beautiful wood table sat. The legs were large, stump-looking pieces of wood. It was unlike anything I had ever seen before. The windows faced the front of the house, but I still couldn't see anything with the rain and darkness outside.

"This table is stunning," I said as I walked around it.

Nate smiled as he looked at the table. "My father and I made it. I bought the chairs for it, but we made the table. It's one of my favorite things in the house."

I looked at him and grinned. "I can see why. I bet it's heavy."

"You have no idea." He turned and pointed to the living room. "And the living room, of course. I like how open this all is. The sliding doors can open all the way, leading to a balcony. That looks down into the backyard. The covered patio outside of the family room is under that balcony."

"Beautiful," I replied, looking at the tan sofa covered in decorative pillows. Two oversized leather chairs sat on either side, facing a large rock fireplace. The rustic wood mantel matched the same wood used for the dining room table legs. There wasn't a TV in this room, which I thought was odd. Didn't guys love giant TVs?

"What if you want to watch football and you're cooking?" I asked.

Nate looked confused, and when he scrunched up his face, he looked adorable. "What?"

I pointed to the fireplace and around the living room. "No TV."

He laughed. "This is more of a formal living room. I watch TV downstairs or in my room."

"Oh," I said, sounding a little too breathy after his mention of his bedroom.

He turned and walked down the hall.

"Here is another half bath," he said, opening the door to a simple bathroom. It contained a pedestal sink and toilet. The color was the same as the half bath downstairs. "The laundry room, and if you go up these steps, it's my bedroom."

He started up the steps, and for half a second, I almost didn't follow him. Did I want to see his bedroom? A place where he has most likely brought countless women. Ultimately, my curiosity about his private space won out, and I quickly caught up with him.

"This space is over the three-car garage and a bit more private than the rest of the house. I honestly couldn't decide if I wanted this to be my bedroom or the guest bedroom you used earlier."

I suddenly remembered my car. "Speaking of garages, what about my car? I almost forgot to ask."

"Already called Hank and he was going to pick it up for you. I asked him to bring it here; I figured you would want that."

"Yes, thank you for that."

He smiled and walked into a large bedroom. The walls were covered in what looked like the same reclaimed wood on the outside of the house, at least what I could make of it in the pouring rain. On one wall there was a giant rustic wrought-iron bed with a cedar trunk at the base of it.

"That trunk is beautiful."

"Thanks," he said as he walked over and opened it. Inside were covers and sheets. "Found it at an estate sale a few years back and grabbed it. Figured I would use it someday, and turns out it is the perfect fit for this room."

I nodded. On the wall opposite the bed was a large-screen TV with a fireplace under it. An oversized leather chair with an ottoman sat to the side, and I couldn't help but picture how nice it would be to curl up in that chair and get lost in a book with a roaring fire.

When I turned to look at the rest of the room, Nate stood with his fists clenched and his jaw tight. Was he uncomfortable having me in his room? Hopefully he didn't think I thought something would happen. Pulling my gaze off him, I returned my gaze to the bed. A strange ache filled my chest as I again wondered how many women he had brought back here and slept with in that very bed.

There was a large dresser against one wall, and the fourth wall was nothing but floor-to-ceiling windows with a French door that led out to what I was guessing was another balcony.

"This room is like out of a magazine, Nate."

"I like it," he said as he moved toward a door. Opening it, we walked into a huge walk-in closet with hardly anything. One side had some clothes hung up, but the other side was empty. I wasn't even sure I had enough clothes to fill a quarter of the space in this closet. Walking through, we entered the bathroom.

"Oh, wow," I softly said, turning around to take it all in. Against one wall were two tall cabinets that were floor to ceiling. In the middle of those sat a long counter with two sinks that seemed to hover between the two larger cabinets. The wood was the same color as the kitchen, but they didn't have the same rustic finish. They were mounted off the floor and gave a very spa-like feeling.

Directly across from the sinks sat a large soak-in tub. Next to it was another sizeable walk-in shower encased in glass. The shower tile matched what was behind the sinks: small square tiles in different shades of gray and white. And the best part? The floor of the shower was large river rocks.

"Wow. I have no words to describe this bathroom other than…wow."

"Thanks," he replied with a soft laugh.

We stood awkwardly before Nate cleared his throat and asked, "Should we head back to the family room? Beer is probably getting warm."

“Yeah, we probably should.” I nodded as I quickly exited the bathroom and bedroom and headed back down the steps. I knew that Nate was wealthy, or that his family was. But I hadn’t realized just how wealthy.

I walked into the laundry and checked my clothes. They were almost dry, thank goodness. When I turned around, Nate was standing there. He didn’t seem as tense as he was when we were upstairs, and I was glad. I wasn’t sure what in the heck was wrong with him.

“They’re almost dry,” I said, barely saying it loud enough for anyone to hear.

He gave a single nod, smiled, and walked away.

I closed my eyes and prayed Hank would get here soon. I just needed my car, a new tire, and a quick escape from Nate Shaw’s house.

Chapter Three

Nathan

Haven couldn't have gotten out of my bedroom fast enough, and I thanked the stars above for that. Having her in my room, near my bed, nearly drove me mad. I had to clench my fists to keep myself from reaching out and touching her. She looked hot as hell in my clothes, even with them hanging off her small-framed body.

I followed Haven back downstairs. She slipped into the laundry room to check on her clothes. I told myself to keep walking but instead, stopped and watched her like an idiot. She turned, and our eyes met. Haven swallowed hard before finally saying almost on a whisper, "They're almost dry."

The best I could do was smile before I turned and walked toward the kitchen. My stomach growled, and I glanced at the clock. It was five.

"Um, if I can change my tire some place out of the rain, I can get out of your hair."

I opened the refrigerator to look for something to eat and poked my head around it to look at her. "How did you learn how to change a tire?"

She laughed. "I had to learn to do all kinds of things after my father left. My grandfather used to tell me I needed to learn those types of things so I wasn't stranded on the side of the road."

She paused, then smiled as if thinking of something funny.

"I guess it didn't work because that was how you found me not once, but twice."

"Yeah, but honestly, there was no way you or I could have changed that flat tire. Not in that storm. Plus, not only was your regular tire flat, but even your spare was flat. I'm not sure that there is a manual or YouTube video to help with that trifecta."

Haven nodded and then looked at the food I had taken out. "What are you doing?"

I had taken out eggs, an onion, bell peppers, and an avocado. "I was going to make us something to eat. I'm starving. You?"

As if just realizing it, her hand went to her stomach, and she chuckled. "My stomach just growled. Omelet?"

"If that sounds good to you."

"You cook?"

I looked at her with a disbelieving expression.

"What makes you think I can't cook? 'Cause I'm a guy?"

"No," she replied, her arms folding over her chest. "You just seem like the go out to dinner or order takeout kind of guy. Not I'll whip you up an omelet."

I grinned. I knew the following words I was about to say would piss her off. "I've been complimented plenty of times for my cooking skills."

Haven snarled her lip. "By who? Your grandmother?"

I laughed. There it was. Damn, she was easy to provoke. "By other women...and my grandmother."

"Oh, you mean the ones you sleep with? How nice of you to stick around long enough to cook them breakfast."

Was that a hint of jealousy I heard in her voice? "It's usually in the middle of the night. I'm not a hang around and wait for morning kind of guy."

Haven rolled her eyes and then looked around, obviously wanting to change the subject. "Bread?"

"That large cabinet in the corner is the pantry."

She walked over, opened the door, and stepped into the large walk-in pantry. Two seconds later, she was walking out with the loaf of bread. Turning to face me, she asked, "Do you want me to help cut up anything?"

I pointed to the onion. "I hate cutting them up, so if you want to, I won't argue."

She looked like she was about to object, and when I raised a brow, she straightened her shoulders and said, "Knife, please."

I handed her a knife and watched as she started peeling and cutting the onion. Her blinking was so rapid that I had to wonder how she could even see to cut.

"Getting to you?"

"Nope, not at all," Haven said.

Standing next to her, I started to cut up the bell peppers. Haven was trying to discreetly wipe her eyes and keep from sniffling. I couldn't help it, a small chuckle slipped free.

"You sound like it's getting to you."

She sniffled again. "I don't know what you mean."

Poking my head around her, I laughed as I saw tears streaming down her face. Haven quickly wiped them away and nudged me with her elbow. "Go away and let me cut this!"

"That is exactly why I hate cutting onions. My mother told me once to cut them by the running water."

Reaching for the faucet, Haven turned on the water, and I laughed again. This time louder. I could hear her sighing before she resumed cutting.

Once Haven finished the onion, I handed her a container to put it in and left some out for the omelet. Haven took it and put it in the refrigerator.

"Do you mind if we have some cantaloupe as well?"

I looked up from where I was whisking the eggs. "Have at it."

Haven took it out and placed it on the counter. "Where are your plates?"

I pointed to the cabinet next to the stove using the spatula. "Plates and bowls in here. This drawer is all the silverware."

"Thanks. Did you want cantaloupe as well?"

"That sounds good," I replied, moving around the veggies as they cooked. "There should be some orange juice in the fridge if you want some."

"Should I go get the beer we left downstairs?"

Turning to look at her, I screwed up my face. "You want a beer with eggs?"

Haven laughed, and I tried to ignore how I felt hearing that laugh. That laugh had haunted me for way too many years.

"No, I mean, should I go dump it out?"

I waved her off. "Nah, it's okay. I'll get it later."

Haven made the toast while I finished up the omelets. Sliding them onto each of our plates, I asked, "Sit in here at the bar or the dinner table?"

She glanced over her shoulder. "Do you mind if we eat at the table?"

"Not at all."

I took our plates and walked them to the dining room table. Haven set the bowl of cantaloupe and plate of toast down onto the tabletop.

"Do you want any jelly or jam or anything?" I asked before sitting down.

"No, this is all wonderful, thank you."

She took a bite and moaned. I couldn't help but laugh. "It's just eggs, Haven."

"I know, but I didn't realize how hungry I was. I spent much of today with Lady and Clover."

"Clover?"

Haven finished chewing. "Your mom helped me find Clover a few months ago. She was a rescue horse. They were going to just send her off to some horse farm in Idaho, but your dad worked out a deal so I could take her. I didn't have to buy her, which was good for my pocketbook since every dime I have is going to the dog park. Then your parents offered to board her and they're not charging me near enough, so I try and help out around the barn when I have some free time."

"I didn't know you were boarding a horse with them."

She shrugged. "You wouldn't unless you asked about Clover."

Rubbing the back of my neck, I said, "I guess that tells me I don't go see my folks nearly enough."

Haven chuckled. "To be fair, they have a lot of horses. Especially once word got out about how good Lily and Maverick are with troubled horses. Clover adores Maverick. He's really helped her come out of her shell."

I smiled. "I did know that Maggie got a new pony."

Maggie was my sister Lily and Maverick's four-year-old.

"She did, and she is so cute on it!"

We ate the rest of our meal in comfortable silence. When it was time to clean up, Haven jumped up to help.

"I'll wash, you dry?" she asked.

"I can just put everything in the dishwasher."

She looked down at the dishwasher and then up to me. "Are you sure?"

I laughed. "Do you hand wash your dishes?"

"It's just me, so I don't normally have much to clean. I guess I'm just used to it."

"How about I rinse, and you load?" I asked with a smile.

She nodded. "That works for me."

Another crack of thunder hit, and we both jumped.

"That is some storm out there. I knew it would be raining a lot, but I didn't think this much was supposed to come down. I bet we have a crazy winter."

I nodded. "I was just telling Josh they're saying we will have more than normal snow this winter."

"Oh, joy," Haven said, loading the last dish into the dishwasher. "We really need the snowpack, though, for next summer."

Grabbing a dishcloth, I quickly cleaned up the stove and counters, turning to see Haven watching me.

"What?"

She slowly shook her head. "I don't know; it's strange to be in your house and watch you cook and clean up."

Smiling, I said, "I don't mean to brag, but eggs are not my specialty."

A slow smile appeared on her pretty face. "Oh, really? What is?"

"Spaghetti and meatballs."

Her eyes went wide. "*That* is your specialty? Spaghetti and meatballs? I was thinking you were going to say something fancy like chicken cordon bleu or something."

"I don't even know what in the hell that is. If you want fancy cooking, Josh is your guy. He likes to cook. One time, he made this whole made-from-scratch dinner for Sophia. Even made her favorite dessert."

Haven's face softened. "That was sweet of him."

I nodded and tried not to look at how adorable she looked in my clothes. Haven must have seen me looking at her because she said, "My clothes are probably dry by now."

"Yeah, um, you remember where the laundry room is?"

She smiled and nodded. "I'll just grab them and run back downstairs and change."

"Sounds good."

"Did you want me to put more wood in the fire downstairs?"

Looking at her, confused, I asked, "The fire?"

"Yeah," she said with a tilt of her head. "You started a fire downstairs in the family room."

Shit, I had forgotten all about it.

"I'll take care of it."

With a nod, she turned on her heels and went to the laundry room, then down to the guest bedroom.

I tried to gain my equilibrium. Having Haven in my home, in my clothes, in my bedroom, and eating at my dining room table was not in my cards for today. I needed to remember why Haven Larson was off limits. Her father had hurt her in ways that I still couldn't wrap my head around, and I was the last guy who needed to be messing around with her emotions. She deserved someone far better than me.

Before I could head back downstairs, the doorbell rang. I knew instantly it was Hank. I quickly went to the door and motioned for him to come in.

"Holy crap," he said as he left his umbrella on the porch and walked in. "It is coming down in sheets."

"How are the roads?"

"Some are flooding, some are fine. I tell you what, though, if the temperature keeps dropping, we may get flurries."

I glanced past him to look out the window on the door. It was a downpour out there.

"Haven's car?"

"It's in your driveway." He looked past me.

"She's changing back into her dry clothes."

Hank nodded, then leaned in close. “I didn’t have her size tire, so I couldn’t bring it. Nate, all of her tires need to be replaced. They hardly have any tread on them. I know Haven’s mother can’t help her, but she needs new tires.”

“That bad, huh?”

He nodded.

Frowning, I said, “I was going to see if you could take it in and plug it.”

Shrugging, he said, “I can, but it won’t last much longer. I don’t even give it from here to her place in town.”

I reached up and stroked the stubble that was growing on my chin. “She needs to be able to drive it once this weather settles down.”

“I can take it back to the garage and see what I can do.”

“Damn, I’m sorry I had you bring it here. I thought you could just bring a spare tire with you.”

“I would have if I had it. I’d be worried about her driving in this rain on the other three tires, though.”

Nodding, I said, “Take the spare with you. It might be in better shape. I’ll pay for it all, and if she needs new tires, just bill me for that.”

Hank rubbed his neck. “Haven won’t like that.”

“How do you know Haven won’t like that?” I asked in irritation.

He looked up at me with a surprised look. “She’s so independent and likes to take care of everything herself.”

How in the hell did Hank Walker know that about Haven?

“Hey, Hank!” Haven called out as she walked down the hall to both of us. “Is my car here?”

“It is, but you aren’t going anywhere until you get the tire fixed.”

“Can it be plugged, do you think?”

He shrugged like he had done only seconds ago with me. “Maybe, but the tread is pretty bad, Haven. You’ll be lucky if it lasts until you get home.”

She chewed on her lower lip. “How much is it for a new tire?”

“I can get you a quote when I return to the shop.”

“I can pay for it.”

Haven’s head snapped to the left as she looked at me. “Thank you, Nate, but not necessary.” She focused back on Hank. “Just do what you need to do to get it fixed. I need my car to get home.”

“I can give you a ride home,” Hank said with a smile. “Once I fix the tire, I’ll put it back on your car and bring it to you.”

I was sure my mouth was hanging open as I watched Hank blush and fiddle with his baseball cap while waiting for Haven to agree.

Finding my voice, I said, “I’ll give Haven a ride home. Probably best that you just take her car with you then, Hank. I’m sorry to make you come this way for nothing.”

“No problem at all.” He turned to Haven. “What would you like for me to do, Haven?”

“If you wouldn’t mind towing the car to the shop. I, um, well…if you think it needs a new tire, go ahead and put one on. That would be great, and if you could be mindful of the cost.”

Hank looked at me, then back to Haven. “Truth be told, Haven, all the tires need replacing.”

With a lift of her chin just a bit higher, she smiled. “Okay, just give me the best deal you can.”

He tipped his head. “Will do, Haven. I’ll let you know when I’ll bring the car back to you.”

Haven smiled and walked to the door, opening it for Hank. He stepped outside, grabbed his umbrella, and headed outside.

The car was still on the flatbed of his truck, so at least that was good.

Shutting the door, Haven paused for a minute. She looked like she was in deep thought.

"Haven?"

Jumping, she turned and looked at me. "Would you mind giving me a ride home now, please? Since you sent Hank away."

She walked past me, slightly bumping into my arm.

I followed after her. "I didn't send Hank away. I figured it would be easier to take you home while he took your car back to the shop."

Spinning around, she pointed her finger at me. "What gives you the right to try and pay for my tire?"

Taken aback, I stared at her. "What?"

Flipping her hand toward the door. "That whole knight in shining armor bullshit. I don't need you to pay for my tire, Nate."

"No one has ever claimed I was a knight in shining armor, Haven. I was just trying to help you out."

"Well, I don't need your help, Nate. I can take care of myself."

I folded my arms over my chest. "You certainly did a few hours ago when you were standing on the side of the road with a flat tire, which I might add is the second time I've found you that way in the last month! Why in the hell are you driving around on bald tires, Haven? It's dangerous."

Her fists balled up. "Not all of us can afford to drive around in brand-new trucks and live in beautiful houses. Some of us are paycheck to paycheck kind of people, Nate. Every ounce of money I have goes into my business and the upcoming dog park. Excuse me if I let my tires go, but it is not your concern."

I dropped my arms to my sides. "You're right."

She opened her mouth to say something, then quickly shut it and swallowed. "I'm right?"

Nodding, I held up my hands. "It is none of my business."

"That's right. It's not. And I'm not irresponsible."

"I never said you were."

She huffed. "You certainly implied it. And you embarrassed me in front of Hank by offering to pay."

"How in the hell did I embarrass you, Haven? The guy told me you couldn't afford new tires, not the other way around."

I headed toward the steps to the family room and waited to see if she followed. It took her half a second, but she was definitely following me.

"I'll just call Ted. He can come and pick me up."

"Great," I replied. "If you need my address for *Ted*, let me know."

"You really are a jerk."

Stopping, I turned to face her. "Why is that, Haven?"

"You're just…you're being too nice. You want something."

I let out a bark of laughter. "You think you have me all figured out. Because I offered to bring you to my house so you could get warm and dry and fed you dinner because I was secretly hoping to just push you over the kitchen island and fuck you as payment for my good deeds."

Her cheeks turned bright red.

The fire had gone down and I closed up the glass doors. I turned to see Haven had already dumped out the beer and had washed both glasses. They were sitting on a hand towel drying.

After ensuring everything was okay and I had given Haven enough time to call this Ted guy, I headed to the main floor. Haven was standing in the kitchen, leaning against the counter, her arms folded over her chest. I walked toward her and stopped.

"Is he on his way?"

Her lips pressed into a tight line, and she looked out the window into the darkness. I waited patiently for her to say something.

“He, um, he doesn’t think it’s a good idea to get out in this weather with some of the roads flooding.”

I nodded. What kind of pussy ass guy leaves the girl he is dating stranded at another man’s house?

“Do you want me to drive you home, Haven?”

Her gaze lifted, and I was gutted to see the emptiness in her beautiful eyes. Haven was always so full of energy, and to see her looking defeated, for lack of better words, left me remembering the last time I saw that look in her eyes. A strange ache squeezed my chest.

“If you don’t mind, I’d like to head home.”

I nodded. “I’ll just go change.”

Turning, I made my way to my bedroom and tried to tell myself there was no good reason to insist she stay the night. If she wanted to leave, then so be it. It was honestly for the best. Having her in my home was almost too much to take. My heart also knew that the sooner she left, the better.

Chapter Four

Haven

I watched as Nate turned and headed to his bedroom to change. Turning away from him, I paced the kitchen while wringing my hands. I hadn't expected Ted to drop everything and drive to the Shaw Ranch to pick me up. We'd only been on a few dates, and he was a great guy, but we weren't exclusive—he was probably with a woman.

Closing my eyes, I mumbled, "Stupid, Haven. Stupid. Stupid. Stupid."

While Nate was changing, I quickly made my way back to the guest room to clean it up. I brought the clothes Nate had given me to wear and put them in the laundry room. As I made my way out, I didn't see that he was right there and I bumped into Nate. He grabbed me by my arms to steady me.

"Whoa, you okay?"

The feel of his hands on my body made me tremble, and I quickly took a step back. "Yes, sorry about that."

I quickly looked him over. He was wearing jeans, cowboy boots, and a long-sleeve navy shirt. I groaned internally. Why did he have to be so good-looking? It made it that much harder to dislike him.

Nathan stepped back and motioned for me to walk ahead of him.

"I put the clothes you let me wear in your hamper."

He only smiled and nodded as he reached for his truck keys. "You ready to head out?"

Another loud crack of thunder shook the house. When was this storm going to move on? I felt a moment of guilt, knowing I was risking our safety by making him drive in this weather.

"Let me grab my stuff."

We made our way out into the garage, and Nate held the door open as I climbed up into the truck. He shut it and walked around to the driver's side. He got in, started the truck, and opened the garage doors.

Looking behind me, I watched as the rain poured off the house. Even Nate's driveway looked like it was flooding.

He pulled out and started down the drive, trying to avoid the massive rivers of water. When he got to the main road, I stared at the water running down the ditches and washing across the lower parts of the road. No wonder Ted didn't want to come out in this.

Nate went to pull out when I said, "Wait!"

He turned and looked at me. "Did you forget something?"

"Yes," I replied as I met his gaze. "My damn common sense. Nate, we shouldn't be driving in this storm. Look at the water. If something ever happened, I would never forgive myself. It's not like I live down the street; I'm in Hamilton. This is stupid."

He stared at me as if waging some internal battle. Sitting back, he asked, "What do you want to do?"

I twisted my hands together in my lap.

"I can take you to Josh and Sophia's if you feel more comfortable there."

Turning to look at him, I felt myself frown. Was it my imagination, or was he trying to push me away once again?

Before I could say anything, he said, "I don't mind you staying at my place, but if you want to leave, I understand."

Swallowing the lump in my throat, I asked, "Would it be terrible if I just stayed the night? You won't even know I'm there, I swear."

"Now you want to stay here? Before, you couldn't get out of my house fast enough."

Sighing, I said, "My common sense took hold. Look at it, Nate. It's raining cats and dogs."

He leaned forward, looked out his front window, and nodded. "Yeah, it is. It hasn't let up over the last few hours either."

"Well, now that I can see how bad it is, I don't think it's a good idea to drive in it."

Nate sighed. "Okay, then I'll turn back."

Nate pulled out into the street, reversed the truck, and then headed back down his driveway. I was positive he thought I was a nut case.

"You probably think I'm crazy."

"I don't think that at all," he said, pulling his truck back into the garage. He shut the garage door and exited his truck while I did the same. We walked back into the house, and I stood there like a complete idiot in the hallway while he walked on. He turned and stared at me.

"Haven?"

I could feel the tears building up in my eyes, and I blinked rapidly to keep them at bay. The last thing I wanted to do was cry in front of Nate Shaw.

Nate started to make his way back to me. "Hey, what's wrong?" he asked, bending down to look in my eyes. When I said nothing, his hands came up to cup my face. "Haven, you don't have to stay here if you don't want to. I can take you to Josh and Sophia's house if you want."

I shook my head. How did he not see the way he affected me? How his touch made my entire body shake with desire.

What was it about me that repulsed him? I closed my eyes and said, "I think I'm just tired and cold. I just…"

"You just what?"

It felt like everything was weighing down on me. Everyone always comments about how happy and positive I am, even when inside I'm drowning. I took on this project of building a dog park and was soaking every ounce of money into it, and I didn't even have the necessary funds to put tires on my old car. I barely had enough to keep myself afloat. And to top it off, the icing on the proverbial cake, I was in love with a man who didn't want anything to do with me.

I lifted my head, and the moment I saw those eyes, I lost control and cried. Not just the tears that slowly slide down your face, where the hero reaches up and wipes them away. No, I had to burst out in sobs—the kind that shakes your body and makes your nose run instantly.

"Shit," Nate said as he pulled me to him. I buried my face in his neck and just rapid-fired all of my problems. Everything was muffled, and I was glad for that because, truth be told, I didn't want Nate to hear all of my issues. He was the last person I wanted to tell my woes to, but at the same time, it was nice to say it out loud.

Suddenly, I was lifted off the floor and carried over to the sofa. Nate sat down with me on his lap as I buried my face into his neck. Now that the dam was broken, I couldn't stop it. All the feelings, every single one that I'd kept buried deep down inside over the years, the ones about my father, my mother working two jobs to keep up with the house, and me trying to help her and secure a future for myself…it was all coming up to the surface. I could feel his hand move up and down my back as he softly told me everything would be okay.

"Shh, it's okay, Haven. Don't cry. Please don't cry."

The more he told me not to cry…the more I cried. I wasn't even sure when the last time I had cried was. That was a lie. It was the night Nate rejected me. And here I was, in his arms, crying like a damn baby.

"Tell me what's going on, sweetheart. Why are you so upset?"

I wanted to grab onto his use of the word sweetheart and analyze it, read more into it than was probably there, but I knew it was useless. Nate had made it clear time and time again that he had no feelings for me. Yet, he held me while I cried, which had to mean something, didn't it?

No. No. No.

I wasn't going to read into anything. Nate leaned back on the sofa, taking me with him. The tears just kept coming. I finally relaxed against him, and the last thing I remember before crying myself to sleep was Nate's soft voice.

"It's okay. I'm here, and I won't let you go."

◆ ◆ ◆

I blinked my eyes open only to shut them because of the sunlight pouring into the room.

Sunlight?

Sitting up quickly, the room spun slightly. I had to close my eyes to get my equilibrium back. I slowly opened one eye, then the other. It took me a hot second to realize where I was.

Nate's guest room. The same room he had brought me into to shower and change. Turning to my left, I sighed when I noticed that the side of the bed was still pretty much made up.

Swinging my feet over, I stretched my arms up and let out a long breath. I must have slept like the dead. I looked at my Fitbit to see what time it was and nearly choked on the air I sucked in. It was almost nine in the morning. Catching sight of my phone on the side table, plugged in and charged, I grabbed it. There was a text from Sophia.

Sophia: Good morning! Nate texted me last night to let me know you had fallen asleep and that your car was at the shop. I hope it's okay, but I figured you were still sleeping when I hadn't heard from you earlier this morning. I took it upon myself to text the morning and afternoon groups this morning to cancel today due to the weather. With all the rain and flooding, I didn't think you would be taking the pups out, or that some of the roads would even be passable.

Me: Morning, Sophia. I'm so sorry, and I must have been more tired than I thought. I just woke up, and that's perfectly fine. I wouldn't have been able to get there in time. Did you happen to let Owen know?

Sophia: Yes, I let him know.

Me: I owe you, Sophia.

Sophia: That's what partners are for! I've got your back.

I let out a long breath and set the phone back on the table before heading into the bathroom. I couldn't help but smile when I saw a brand-new toothbrush with toothpaste on the counter. After washing my face and brushing my teeth, I looked at my hair, which was a mess. In the end, I left it alone. I usually wore my hair up in a ponytail, but today, it fell around my shoulders in wild curls.

"I'll just pretend it looks good," I mused as I stared at myself in the mirror. I had zero makeup on, my hair was a rat's nest, and I was about to see the man I had been in love with for as long as I could remember.

Closing my eyes, I drew in a deep breath and slowly let it out. "You have to move on, Haven. You have to let go of this stupid fantasy."

When I opened my eyes and saw my reflection in the mirror, I wasn't sure if I wanted to cry or laugh. I had spent the night in Nate Shaw's house. Had most likely fallen asleep in his arms, and Lord knows what he thinks of me after that crying fit. What I wanted to do was crawl under a rock and hide. For as many times as I had wanted to see Nate, this was one rare moment I didn't.

But I was stronger than this. So instead of hiding out in the room, I turned on my heels and started up to the main floor for the kitchen.

As I walked up the steps, I could smell bacon. My stomach growled, and I placed my hand over it, taking a deep breath through my nose. I hadn't realized I was so hungry.

I swayed slightly when I saw Nate standing at his stove, wearing nothing but sweats, no shirt, no shoes, just sweats. I squeezed my eyes shut.

You're moving on, Haven. Moving. On. But damn, did he make it really difficult to move on when he was shirtless and wearing sweatpants.

Opening my eyes, I cleared my throat and said, "Good morning."

Nate jumped and then glanced over his shoulder at me. His eyes went wide and his mouth fell open some. I looked away from his intense gaze and said, "So, ummm, obviously my hair has a mind of its own. Do you know where my ponytail holder is?"

When he didn't say anything, I looked at him. He was staring at me with a look I had never seen before.

"Your hair," he softly said.

Feeling embarrassed, I reached up and touched it. "I know, it's a mess. Hence the ponytail thingy that I need."

He shook his head. "It's beautiful, Haven. I forgot you had such curly hair."

His words rattled the inside of my chest, and it took me a few seconds to find my voice.

"Um, yeah, I wear it up a lot. Makes it easier when I'm dealing with the dogs."

Nate cleared his throat and slightly shook his head before he turned back to the bacon. "I think you should wear it down more."

My eyes went wide at his admission. "Did you just give me a compliment, Nate?"

He glanced back at me. "Don't make it seem like I've never complimented you before."

My arms crossed my chest as I let out a humorless laugh. "You haven't. Ever. Not once."

A look of...regret...crossed over his face. Impossible. I clearly had misread it.

"I find that hard to believe."

Deciding to let this conversation go, I asked, "Did you need me to help with anything?"

"If you wouldn't mind watching the bacon for me. I worked out this morning and started the bacon when I got out of the shower, but I need to change."

My eyes went over his body. He was built, but not overly built, like some guys at the gym with muscles that are way too big. Nate's shoulders were broad, and his chest was bare of hair, which made my fingers twitch to touch his skin. Then you had his lower midsection, which had the perfect set of abs, indented in all the ways that abs should be. His sweats hung low on his hips—Lord, give me strength—and the pain in my lower lip alerted me that I was biting down on it.

"You okay, Haven?" Nate asked.

My eyes jerked back up to his, and I nodded. "Yep. Fine. I'll, um, I'll take care of the bacon."

He nodded and walked off, leaving me to grab onto the counter and take a few deep breaths. It was suddenly sweltering in that kitchen.

Once I pulled myself together and reminded myself, *again*, that I was moving on from Nate, I walked over to the bacon and flipped it. I made my way to the pantry and took a quick look. We had eggs last night, so I was hoping to make something different. When I spied pancake mix, I smiled. I also found a can of pumpkin puree, pumpkin spice, and vanilla. Nate's pantry was stocked with everything one would need to cook. He may not do fancy, but he clearly liked to cook.

A thought suddenly occurred to me. What if he was dating someone, and I didn't know? Wouldn't Sophia have said something? No, why would she? Lily…would she have mentioned it?

I shook my head. No one would mention it because no one knew how I felt about Nate. Okay, just because he had food in his pantry didn't mean it was because he was dating someone. And besides, who cared? Not me. I was moving on.

Lining up what I needed to make the pancakes, I looked around the kitchen. "Where would the mixing bowls be?"

"That cabinet right there. What are you doing?"

Nate had walked into the kitchen and up to a cabinet. When he opened the door, I saw the bowls. I reached in and took out a medium mixing bowl.

"I'm making us pumpkin spice pancakes."

He raised a brow.

"You do like pumpkin, don't you?"

"Of course I do."

Smiling, I said, "Great. My mother used to make this for me on the first day of fall every year."

Nate laughed. "You're a bit late. Fall was back in September."

"It's November, Nate, and the Official Fall Rules state that pumpkin spice can be eaten any time of the year."

"I'll take your word for it. So, umm, what do you need me to do?"

"You take care of the bacon, and I'll handle the pancakes."

I mixed up the ingredients and poured some batter onto the griddle. The smell of spices and pumpkin filled my senses. "I love this time of year."

Nate took out two plates and set two glasses of orange juice down on the kitchen table. He then got out syrup and butter.

"Do you decorate for fall?" Nate asked.

"I normally do, but this year, I've been so busy getting things going for this dog park that I haven't had time to do it. I will decorate for Christmas, though. It's my favorite holiday."

Nate pulled out his phone and read a text he had gotten while I put the large plate of pancakes down on the table.

"Ready to dig in!"

He glanced up and smiled. "Those look and smell good."

I felt my cheeks heat slightly. "Hope you like them."

Nate took a fork and grabbed three pancakes while I took two. He put a bit of butter on it and some syrup. I hadn't even realized I had been holding my breath until he took a bite and moaned in delight.

"That's good, Haven. Dare I say better than my mother's."

Smiling, I took a bite of mine. They were good, and it took all I had not to devour them. I was starving.

We ate in silence for the first few minutes. Nate broke it when he looked up at me and asked, "Haven, can I ask you something and you don't have to answer it if you don't want to? But I was just wondering why you were so upset last night? You cried so hard that you cried yourself to sleep."

I wiped the corners of my mouth with the napkin and sighed. "I was hoping you would forget about all that."

He shook his head. "Not a chance when a woman is in my house—and in my arms—crying."

Shrugging, I said, "I guess the dam broke. It's been a stressful few months, and with my car getting a flat tire and a few weeks ago it needed a new battery…well…things are just *stressful*."

"Is there anything I can do?" he asked.

My gaze lifted and met his. He seemed so damn genuine and it broke my heart knowing how much I really liked him, but that he would never be mine.

With a soft smile, I shook my head. "Thank you, but it will all work out. I think I was just tired."

Nate nodded as he leaned back in his chair. When he said nothing, I cleared my throat and stood to clear the table.

Reaching for his plate, Nate said, "Leave it. I'll clean up."

"I don't mind helping you clean up."

The doorbell rang and interrupted our moment, and then Nate stood. "That's Hank. He's brought your car for you."

"What?" I asked in surprise. "He brought it here?"

Nate started toward the front door. "I figured you'd need it, and when the weather had cleared up, I called him to see if he could drop it off."

"Oh," I said as I followed him to the door.

"Morning, Hank," Nate said, reaching out to shake the other man's hand.

"Good morning, Nate and Haven. I've unloaded your car, and it's ready for you."

Glancing past Hank, I saw my car sitting in the driveway. "Did you have to put a new tire on?"

Hank nodded. "I had to. There was no way I could plug that tire again."

"Again?" Nate asked. "Oh, was that the same one from last month?"

I nodded and focused on Hank. "Thank you, Hank. Can I drop by the shop later today to pay you?"

He smiled. "Of course you can, Haven. There's no rush. I'm just glad I found the right tire at another store for you this morning."

Nate turned and looked at me. I could tell he wanted to say something, but he pressed his mouth into a tight line.

"Right. Well, thank you again, Hank. How are the roads?"

"Minor flooding on some roads, but you won't have any issues getting home. The sun is out and drying things up as we speak. I'm just glad we didn't get ice or snow."

I wrapped my arms around my body. "The temperature has dropped, that's for sure."

Hank looked up. "Winter is right around the corner, so it's no surprise we are getting this crazy weather."

When he looked at Nate and me, he smiled. "I'll be heading off. Let me know when you want to get the other tires replaced."

"Thanks, Hank!" I called after him as he headed down the porch steps and to his tow truck.

After he got in and pulled off, Nate shut the front door and started for the kitchen again.

I followed and helped him clean up, even though he had told me not to. We worked in silence, and I couldn't help but notice something had shifted with us over the last day. What it was, though, I couldn't say.

"Thank you for picking me up and letting me stay here."

Nate tossed the dish towel over his shoulder and flashed me that drop-dead gorgeous smile of his.

"No problem at all. I'm glad you got your tire fixed. Are you taking any dogs out today?"

"No, it's too wet. Sophia told me she had sent out a text to let the dog owners know."

Slipping his hands into his jeans pockets, Nate looked around the kitchen. "Thanks for helping me clean up, and for the delicious pancakes."

"Sure," I said with a smile. "I should get going."

"Do you have everything?" Nate asked as he followed me into the living room.

"Yep." I picked up my small bag and purse. "Thanks again."

He walked me to the front door and out to my car. Right as I was about to get in, Nate spoke.

"Haven, um, wait a second. There's something I needed to say; I mean, I wanted to talk to you about." He cleared his throat. "I wanted to talk to you about something."

Pausing, I looked into his silver-blue eyes and tried to ignore how my heart sped up. His eyes were dancing with something I had only ever seen once before from him, and it was a long time ago.

He tore his gaze away from mine and kicked at something on the ground. "Last night…something–"

The sound of a vehicle pulling up the driveway caused us both to turn and see who it was.

"Ted?" I said in complete shock.

Ted pulled up behind my car and got out, a smile on his face. "You have your car!"

I looked at Nate, my car, then back to Ted. "Yes, Hank brought it over just a little bit ago."

Ted walked up and leaned down to kiss me on the cheek. "I was worried and saw you were still at this location, so I thought I would come to see if you still needed a ride home."

"Are you tracking her?" Nate asked, a tone of bitterness in his voice.

Ted looked at Nate and held out his hand. "Ted Reynolds."

At first, I didn't think Nate was going to shake Ted's hand, but his good manners won out. He reached out and pumped once before dropping his hand.

"Nate Shaw."

Ted smiled as he said, "Nice to meet you, Nate."

Confused, I looked at Ted. "How did you know I was still here?"

He held up his phone. "Find my friends app on your phone."

"I shared my location with you last night; I didn't think it would still track me."

"It did. It looks like you don't need me after all."

Rocking back and forth on his feet, Ted looked between me and Nate before he settled his gaze on me. "I'll follow you back to your place unless you need to go walk the dogs."

"No," I said with a shake of my head. "Today's appointments were canceled."

"Great! I don't have any clients today, so we can spend the day together." Facing Nate, Ted said, "Thank you for coming to my girl's rescue last night."

My head drew back some, and I stared at Ted. *My girl?* What in the world was up with that? We'd gone out on a few dates, and I was suddenly his girl when I knew he dated other women.

Nate forced a smile, and I could see a tic in his jaw. "Sure thing."

If I hadn't known better, I would have thought Nate was jealous.

Impossible.

"Ready to leave?" Ted asked as he reached for my hand. I quickly pulled it back. I wasn't sure why, but it seemed like the right thing to do at that moment.

With a forced smile, I said, "Why don't you head out, and I'll meet you at my apartment."

Ted's smile faltered slightly, but he quickly recovered. "Sounds like a plan. It was nice to meet you, Nate."

With a single head bob, Nate replied, "You too."

Once Ted was back in his truck and turning around to head down the long drive, I asked, "How did he get through your gate?"

"It was open for Hank."

Nodding, I faced Nate. I smiled and asked, "What were you going to say before Ted showed up?"

Nate's eyes suddenly changed. They looked void of emotion, unlike only minutes before when he looked at me, and they seemed to sparkle.

His hands returned to his pockets, and he stepped away from me. "Nothing. It doesn't matter anymore."

"Are you sure? You seemed serious about something that happened last night."

He shook his head. "It's nothing."

I chewed nervously on my lower lip. "You're sure?"

His face lifted, and his gaze met mine. For a second, I thought he would step closer and kiss me. Instead, he took another step back.

"See you around, Haven."

I nearly put my hand to my chest when I felt a sharp pain, almost like a knife was pushed into my chest. It was just like at the barn. He was pushing me away for some reason.

I opened my car door once again. Before I slipped inside, I looked back at Nate. "Thank you again."

He held up a hand and simply said, "Yep."

Slipping into the car, I turned it on and backed up into the driveway pullout to turn around. I started to pull out and looked in my rearview mirror, only to find Nate watching me as I drove away.

Once on the road, I put my hand to my mouth and let out a soft, humorless laugh. I would probably never find out what Nate was going to say to me. And knowing that made my eyes fill with tears.

Chapter Five

Nathan

It was the middle of November, and after yesterday's storm, everyone was reminded of what was right around the corner.

Winter.

After the morning meeting with Blayze, Hunter, Josh, Beck, and Brock, it was decided that we needed to start our winter checklist. That meant ensuring we had plenty of hay, the winter pastures were ready to go, and none of the fences required repair. Our water troughs were functioning, and the generators were fired up and tested.

I loved the ranch in the winter. It was a much slower pace and less hectic. Once winter set in, however, there was still work to do. The cows still needed to be fed, water needed to be broken up if frozen, and the usual daily chores that came with ranch life still needed to be completed. Anyone who worked on a ranch would say they enjoyed winter because it allowed them to rest before the calving season. The fact that it hadn't even snowed yet was a bit disheartening. We needed the snowpack in the mountains. The massive amount of rain we got was good, but we needed snow.

"You coming with us hunting this weekend?" Josh asked as he shut the barn doors that housed our winter hay. It would need to have some more hay brought in, which Josh and I would take care of this week.

"Who is us?" I asked.

"Me, Blayze, Hunter, Maverick, and Beck."

"Elk?" I asked.

"I think Beck, Hunter, and Blayze are going for deer. Maverick and I are going for elk."

"Um, I'll let you know."

We started back toward the main barn in one of the ranch trucks. I could feel Josh turning and looking at me every so often.

"Want to talk about it?"

I looked at him. "Talk about what?"

"Haven being at your house two nights ago and you not acting like yourself since."

I laughed gruffly. "What do you mean not acting like myself?"

"Dude, half the time you are so lost in thought you don't hear anything anyone says. Hunter asked you three times this morning if you could check the winter pastures and you never even looked at him. You were staring off at something on the floor."

I rubbed at the back of my neck. "Sorry, I didn't realize I was tuning you guys out."

"Did something happen between you and Haven?"

"What?" I asked, snapping my head to look at my cousin. "No. Nothing happened. Besides breaking down into tears and crying so hard, she cried herself to sleep."

Josh stopped the truck, put it in Park, and then turned his body to look at me. "What in the hell did you do?"

"Me?" I asked. "I didn't do anything. She just broke down. I think she's stressed about money. Her car needs four new tires—well, three now—and she mentioned all her savings was going into this new dog park."

"Sophia said all the numbers for everything are starting to come in. They have some donors, me included, but they still have to put up some serious cash."

"Do they need more donors?" I asked.

"I don't think they know of anyone else to ask."

I nodded and stared out the front window. "Could I donate? Anonymously, like I don't want anything in return."

Josh raised his brows. "You want to donate to Haven's dog park? And you want to do it anonymously? Why?"

"She went off the rails when I suggested I could pay for her tires. I thought for a second she was going to punch me in the nuts. It was pretty clear to me Haven doesn't like to take help from anyone. Plus, things with her and me are...complicated."

"Or, maybe she thought you were offering her a handout."

I huffed. "A handout? I was trying to be nice and offer to help her. Unlike that douchebag she is dating. He wouldn't even come and pick her up. He did, however, show up the next morning and declared he had been tracking her."

That caused Josh to shoot his brows up once more. "Are you kidding me? How is he tracking her? I'm surprised Haven would allow that. I think they've only been out on a few dates, according to Sophia."

"Something about she shared her location with him, probably when she was stranded on the side of the road, and she never turned it off or something. She didn't seem very pleased. The guy is a dick, and he interrupted us right when I was about to..."

"About to what?" Josh asked.

Inwardly cursing at myself, I looked out the passenger window. "Nothing."

"Oh, no. You don't get to say something like that then let it go. What were you about to do?"

I sighed, dropped my head against the seat's headrest, and said, "Tell her something has changed between us. I felt it, and a part of me wanted to explore that, but it was probably for the best that he came when he did."

When Josh didn't say anything, I lifted my head and looked at him. He was staring at me, his mouth gaped open.

"You were going to tell Haven you're attracted to her."

I let out a bitter-sounding laugh. "I think I'm beyond attracted. When she was crying in my arms, and I could hardly understand a fucking thing she was saying, the only thing I could think about was hurting someone. Or taking away her worry or making her smile again. I was gutted listening to her cry in my arms. When she finally fell asleep and I carried her to the guest room, it took everything I had not to climb into that bed and hold her while she slept. I didn't, of course, but I was up all fucking night thinking about how much I wanted to be with her. I stupidly thought that maybe if I told her, I don't know, we might try it. Dating."

"Holy shit. As in, exclusively date her?"

I shrugged. "I was just caught up in the moment. The last thing Haven needs is a guy like me in her life."

"A guy like you? What does that mean?"

Looking at him like he had lost his mind, I said, "I'm not exactly known for being with one woman. The last thing I would ever want to do is hurt her. Trust me, she's been hurt enough for a lifetime."

"How do you know that?"

I looked away from Josh. "I can't tell you."

"You can't or won't?"

"Can't. It's not my story to tell, and I made Haven a promise. A long time ago."

Josh ran his hand through his hair. "So you're afraid of hurting Haven, so that's why you avoid her because you do have feelings for her and you think you'll hurt her."

I nodded.

"But then something shifted, and you were willing to give it a try, but Ted showed up and stopped you from telling her how you were feeling?"

"You got it. He kissed her on the cheek, and they were going back to her place and…"

"And?"

Looking at my cousin like he'd lost his damn mind, I said, "She's dating him, Josh. I can't tell her that suddenly I've developed these feelings for her and expect her to tell Ted the douche to leave. Besides, I'm not even sure I should tell her."

"Have they been sudden, the feelings for Haven?"

I stared at my cousin for what felt like forever before answering him. "No. That night in my parents' barn, all those years ago, it took every ounce of energy I had to stop what we were doing. I wanted nothing more than to be with Haven in every way possible, but I can't."

Josh's brows shot up. "Why the hell not?"

"I told you, she's been hurt before."

"I heard that, but, Nate, why do you think you'll hurt her?"

With a shrug, I replied, "I've spent so many years flirting with women and having meaningless sex. I'm unsure I would know how to be in a serious relationship. What if I tell Haven how I feel, we date, and things don't go well? You and I both know she's liked me for as long as I can remember. I don't want to be another man in her life who hurts her. I won't be another man who hurts her. Just seeing her cry last night, and it had nothing to do with me, about destroyed me."

"Wow. Did I just hear right? You're scared of dating Haven?"

Rolling my eyes, I sighed. "Don't tease me right now, Josh."

He held up his hands as if in defeat. "I'm not teasing you, Nate. I think this is big. It takes a lot to admit you have feelings for Haven, but to say you're scared of hurting her takes guts. It's about time, though."

"I don't know. Knowing I was about to tell her and seeing that guy show up made me realize that I almost set myself up for failure. What if I had told her, and she said she didn't feel the same way?"

He smiled softly. "And what if she said she did?"

With a shake of my head, I said, "It's complicated, Josh."

"Then explain it to me, Nate."

I sighed. "That night in the barn, when things were getting heavy, I was ready to go all the way until I remembered what happened to her. And I couldn't do that to her, and I didn't know how to tell her that. To tell her that if we did this, I wasn't sure I would be able to commit myself to her. Hell, I was only eighteen, and what if I slept with her and that just scratched an itch for me, but meant more to her? I didn't want to see that hurt in her eyes. So I freaked and told her it was a mistake. That what we were doing had been a mistake. You didn't see the look of hurt on her face. She looked like she hated me in that moment, and I have a feeling she thinks I stopped for another reason altogether."

"Why didn't you just tell her the truth?"

"I tried, but she left without giving me a chance to explain."

"She doesn't hate you now, Nate. You don't see the way she looks at you."

Frowning, I asked, "What do you mean?"

"When Haven doesn't think anyone is watching her, she stares at you like she is longing for something. I'm going to guess that something is you."

"She stayed with me the other night and never once made it seem like she wanted anything from me."

"Did you make any moves on her? You even said she fell asleep in your arms, and you put her in the guest bedroom."

"I wasn't about to put her in my room! I would never presume she would want to sleep in my bed."

Josh grinned. "And that would make Granddad pretty damn proud of you. You did what any gentleman would do, but look at it from Haven's point of view. If she is still attracted to you, she might have seen that as another example of how you're not interested in her. You also go out of your way to crack jokes and poke fun at her."

"Because it was easier to have her dislike me than to look at me with those sad eyes of hers."

Josh shook his head. "You might as well pay me that thousand dollars we bet. You should see yourself right now. You've got it bad, Nate."

I sighed and said, "Fuck you, Josh."

He laughed, took the truck out of Park, and headed toward the main barn as I stared out the window and wondered what in the hell I should do now. I had finally been ready to admit my feelings for Haven, and now I wasn't sure what I should do.

◆ ◆ ◆

A week had passed since Haven had stayed the night at my house. In that time I had done nothing but dream of her when I was asleep, and thought of her when I was awake. Every time I thought about her crying, I wanted to punch a hole in the wall. A small part of me wondered if some of her pain was still from what her father did to her, and that made me feel sick. I had almost asked her if she ever went to a therapist for what happened to her. Someone to talk to about it. It couldn't be good to hold that all up inside of you. Countless nights I closed my eyes and pictured her as a scared little girl whose father hurt her.

"Fucking asshole," I said as I pulled into Hank's garage and parked my truck. I had tossed and turned all night, thinking of what I could do to help ease some of Haven's stress. It was why I was now standing at the door.

"Are you going to just stand there or come in, Nate?" Hank asked, causing me to turn and see him at the open bay of one of the garages.

"Hey, Hank," I replied, reaching out to shake his hand.

"What's on your mind?" he asked, a smirk appearing at the corners of his mouth.

"Why do I get the feeling you know why I'm here?"

He laughed. "It didn't take a rocket scientist to see how you reacted when I offered to give Haven a ride home, or how you look at her."

"It's not what you think, we're just friends. Besides, she is dating someone."

He shrugged. "If you say so. I'm guessing you're trying to figure out how to get her new tires without her knowing it was you."

I pointed to him. "Yes. She's stubborn and nearly flew off the handle when I even suggested buying one tire."

Hank laughed. "I was there, I remember."

Looking around his garage, I asked, "Any suggestions?"

"Short of stealing her car and bringing it here, I have nothing."

I rubbed at the back of my neck. "Shit."

"Listen, I've known Haven and her family for a long time. They've always struggled financially, and after that low-life daddy of hers left, her momma has worked as hard as she can to provide. I know firsthand that neither she, nor her daughter, will take a handout."

"It's not a handout. She can pay me back if she wants."

"You tell her that?"

I shoved my hands into my jeans pockets. "No. I haven't talked to her since she left my house that day."

A text came through on Hank's phone, and he chuckled. "Today might be your lucky day, Nate Shaw. Haven is on her way to drop off her car."

"Why?"

"Another flat. She wants me to see if I can plug it."

"Where in the hell is this girl driving where she is getting so many flat tires?"

Hank let out a humorless chuckle. "They're so bald I'm not surprised. I can't plug another one, Nate. The tires need to be replaced."

"Do you have them in stock?"

He nodded. "Made sure after that day I had them. I had a feeling I'd be getting a visit from you."

Turning to look at him, he just laughed. Wisdom definitely came with age, I guess.

"Can I pay for them now before she gets here?"

He motioned for me to follow him to his office. After paying for them, I quickly headed out.

"Nate, what do I tell her when she magically has three more new tires?"

I thought for a moment. "Tell her someone was paying it forward, and she was the lucky recipient."

He narrowed an eye at me. "And if she asks me who that person was?"

With a smile, it was my turn to shrug as I said, "Tell her it was Santa Claus."

As I walked out of the office area of Hank's garage, I heard him laugh. Maybe even a 'ho ho ho' came out of his mouth. I climbed up into my truck and pulled out. I let out a sigh of relief that I hadn't run into Haven on my way out.

The next stop was my lawyer's office. I needed to find out how to donate anonymously to the new dog park coming to town. If I couldn't have Haven the way I wanted, I would make damn sure she wasn't stressed about money.

Chapter Six

HAVEN

I stared down at my car and the new tires that replaced the ones that literally had zero tread on them. "Hank? Why does my car have all new tires on it?"

He looked at the car, nodded, and said, "It does seem to have new tires on it."

My hands went to my waist. "Hank?"

He held up his hands. "It wasn't me, Haven. Someone was, um…paying it forward. They said to take care of the next customer, and you happened to be that customer. Pure luck."

Narrowing my eyes at him, I said, "Did this someone have a name?"

Hank grinned. "Santa Claus was the name I believe he gave."

I tilted my head and regarded him. "Is that so?"

"Yep, that is the way of it."

Sighing, my hands dropped to my sides. "Was it Ted?"

Hank choked. "Ted?"

"Ted Reynolds?"

Hank laughed. "The farrier?"

"Yes."

"Why would it be him?"

I could tell from his surprised response that it hadn't been Ted who had done the good deed.

When I didn't answer, he said, "Are you dating him?"

"Well, I mean, we've gone out a few times."

Hank whistled and said, "Nate know?"

My heart felt like it dropped to my stomach. "Nate did this?"

"What makes you think that?"

I narrowed my eyes and pointed to Hank. "Hank, you never were a good liar. Was Nate Shaw playing Santa Claus today?"

He closed his eyes as he scrubbed his hand down his face. "Well, damn it. Please don't tell him I told you."

I blinked a few times, looked at my car, then back to Hank. "Nate bought my tires?"

He nodded. "He said if you wanted to pay him back, you could, but I think he wanted to do this for you, Haven."

My mouth opened, and I quickly shut it. I didn't even know what to say, but I shouldn't be surprised. My mind drifted to the other night when he held me while I cried. He was so tender, and when he whispered he would be there for me, it had been the cause of more tears because I knew he would never be there for me the way I wanted.

"Nate did this," I said again as I faced my car. "Why would he do that?"

"I'm guessing it's because he cares for you and didn't want to see you driving around with unsafe tires."

Snapping my head to look at Hank, I asked, "He cares for me?"

"Haven, you didn't notice how he got jealous when I offered to give you a ride home last week?"

"He did?" I asked, feeling a little spark of hope in my chest.

"Yes, ma'am. He was not about to let me take you home."

My mind drifted back to Nate wanting to tell me something but stopped when Ted showed up. Damn it all. What was he going to say?

"Thank you for telling me, Hank."

"Now, you're not going to go off and yell at him for doing something nice for you, are you?"

Smiling, I shook my head. "Me? Yell at Santa Claus? I don't want coal in my Christmas stocking, Hank."

Hank winked. "Haven, you also might want to think twice about Ted Reynolds."

Curious, I turned and faced him before slipping into my car. "Why's that?"

Hank looked down at the ground nervously before his eyes met mine. "He isn't known for being a one-woman kind of guy, if you catch my drift."

The news of Ted should have made me feel sad. Instead, it did nothing. Absolutely nothing.

"Thanks, Hank. And thank you for working me in today."

He waved as I slipped into the car. I started it, pulled out of the drive, and headed to my meeting with Sophia and our lawyer with a little bit of stress lifted off my shoulders…and it was thanks to Nate Shaw. Of all people. He'd saved me more than once, so why I was surprised baffled me.

◆ ◆ ◆

I was sure Sophia and I looked like idiots sitting at the meeting table with our mouths hanging open.

Sophia spoke first. "Who was it?"

Pete Mitchell lifted his shoulders. "They wanted to remain anonymous. The check came from another lawyer's office only minutes before the two of you showed up. It is made out to the LLC you both set up."

My finger went to the check and pulled it closer to me. The check was for three-hundred-thousand dollars. "Is this legit?" I asked, even though I heard him say it was from another law office.

Pete shook his head. "It's a donation to your business. You could use it for whatever you want. The dog park, pay off your bus or current debts, whatever you'd like. There was no stipulation with it."

Turning to Sophia, I slowly shook my head. "Who has three-hundred-thousand dollars to just…"

My voice trailed off.

"What is it?" Sophia asked.

Tears started to build in my eyes as I thought about earlier when I picked up my car. "He put new tires on my car."

Pete and Sophia looked at one another and then back to me.

"Who put new tires on your car?" Sophia asked.

Pete handed me a tissue as I fought to keep my tears at bay. I cleared my throat once I knew I could speak without bursting into tears. "Nate. This check is from Nate Shaw."

"Nate?" Sophia asked in a surprised voice.

Pete looked at the check and then at me. "It's possible. The Shaw family does a lot for the community. This amount of money could have certainly come from them."

"Do you know who the law firm is that represents the Shaws?" I asked Pete.

He tugged on his tie as he looked at the check, then back to me. He hesitated as his eyes bounced from the check, to me, and landed on Sophia.

"It's this law firm listed on the check, isn't it?"

Nodding, Pete replied, "It is, yes."

Sophia drew in a sharp breath. "Do you really think it was Nate?"

I nodded. "I know it was."

"Why would he want to remain anonymous, though?"

Pete spoke then. "It could be for several different reasons."

With a shake of my head, I said, "I know why he did it."

"Why?" Pete and Sophia asked at the same time.

A part of me wondered if Nate did it because of what my father had done to me all those years ago. Was it guilt that made him do it? Knowing what a low life of a father I had, or was it simply because he wanted to do this for…me?

Looking at Sophia, I said, "The why doesn't matter right now."

"I know Nate, he won't take this check back or he'll deny it was him who sent it."

"What do you think we should do with it?"

She glanced at the check and then thought for a moment. "I think you pay off the bus loan and business credit card."

Pete nodded his head in agreement.

"That is still leaving you—us—with a good amount of money left. I think we put it aside for anything that might pop up. Having some money in the bank is always good, right?" Sophia asked Pete.

"I agree with what Sophia is suggesting. You don't have a lot of debt, which is good. But this donation can help even more with that. And like Sophia suggested, you should put it in the bank and hang onto it. With the donations that have come on board and the money the two of you are bringing, you don't have to have any more of a down payment to get the business loan. You're set there."

I nodded. "Okay. Yes, I think we should do what you suggested, Sophia."

She smiled, as did Pete.

"If it was Nate Shaw who gave you this money, he either really loves dogs or…"

My head snapped up to look at Pete. "Or?"

"Or he has a heart of gold."

Sophia chuckled. "Or he has a strange way of showing someone he has feelings for them."

By the time our meeting was over and Sophia and I walked out to the parking lot, my mind had gone over every possible reason I could think of why Nate Shaw would drop a shit-ton of money into my lap. Or my business lap, if you will.

"Your mind is racing, Haven."

"Do you know that when I picked up my car, I thought Ted had paid for my tires? Ted? The guy who has never even held a door open for me. How could I have been so stupid?"

Sophia stopped at her car. "How did you find out it was Nate?"

"By mistake. Hank slipped and said it was Nate. I should have known. The night he picked me up in the storm, he had wanted to pay for the new tire, and I went off on him."

"Why?"

I shrugged. "Pride mostly. My mother was always so adamant about not taking handouts. That a man always wants something in return. When I heard Nate say he would pay for it, I got embarrassed and used anger to deal with it."

"Then I have to ask this, Haven, how are you taking it that he gave you three-hundred thousand?"

"He didn't give it to me; he gave it to our business. And where does a twenty-two-year-old get that kind of money? I mean, his house is beautiful, he has a brand-new Ford F250 truck, and he's dishing out three-hundred-thousand-dollar checks?"

Sophia looked around, wondering if she should say anything. Ultimately, she said, "I know the grandkids all received a trust from their grandparents. That's how Josh and Nate bought the land and built houses. Please don't let Nate know I told you.

I don't think it's a big secret, but I don't think they want me going around telling people. You're not people, though. I mean, you are, but you know what I mean."

"I know the Shaws are a wealthy family, but, Sophia, he gave us three-hundred-thousand dollars. Why?"

Sophia gave me a soft smile. "The same reason Josh donated or, I would assume it's the same reason."

My gaze met hers. "I want to think I know why, but it's Nate. We have a history."

Her brows rose. "What kind of history?"

I closed my eyes as that night in the barn returned to me. "Our senior year of high school, I worked with a horse at Nate's parents' barn. We were the only ones left in the barn, and I was trying to save this kitten, and let's just say I ended up on the bed in the office. Things happened, and I was so gloriously happy, Sophia. I can't even begin to tell you how long I had, or if I'm being honest, I have liked Nate. Things went pretty far, but not that far. He just stopped and said it was a mistake. He kept repeating how what we had done—what we'd almost done—was a mistake."

Sophia took my hand in hers. "He got scared, Haven. He's still scared."

With a shake of my head, I felt the tears starting to build. "No, I don't think that's it. He knows something about my past and I'm afraid…I'm afraid…"

"You're afraid of what?" Sophia asked.

"That my past is what is keeping him from moving on from friendship. I know he cares about me, that is evident with what he did about my car and the donation."

"I think he more than cares for you as a friend. You should see him when your name gets brought up. Something in him changes, and he lights up. And don't even get me started when I mentioned you had gone out with Ted. I thought Nate was going to tear his hair out."

My chest ached. "Why can't he admit he has feelings if he truly does have them?"

Sophia thought for a moment. "I wish I had that answer for you, sweetie. The only person who knows that answer is Nate."

I nodded. "What do I do now? Do I tell him I know the money and the tires, that it was all from him?"

Sophia shrugged. "I could ask Josh if you want me to. He would have a better insight into Nate. But, if you think whatever it is that was in the past is the reason he is friend zoning you, just ask him."

I closed my eyes and tried to push away the nausea that I felt any time I thought of my father. I wasn't sure if I would ever be able to talk about those years, especially to Nate. What if he looked at me differently because of my father and how horrible of a person he was to me and my mom.

Drawing in a deep breath, I asked, "If you tell Josh, will you please ask him not to say anything to Nate that I think it's him?"

"Of course. And you can trust Josh. He won't say anything."

I gave her a weak smile.

"I need to run. Please let me know if you need me to do anything for tomorrow's pick-ups."

"Yes, of course," I said with a nod. "Go enjoy your evening with Josh."

Sophia pulled me into a hug. "Call me if you need anything."

"I will. Have a good night."

"You too, Haven."

The drive back to my apartment was a blur. What was I going to do? Did I confront Nate and tell him I knew the money was from him? Do I not acknowledge it? I was confused. One second Nate Shaw was cold, the next hot as all get out. So the biggest mystery was what did he want from me?

Once I entered my apartment, I dropped my things on the floor and headed to my bedroom. Face-planting onto the bed, I let out a yell before rolling over and staring up at the ceiling. A part of me thought I should be angry at Nate for giving me so much money, but another part was so overcome with relief that I felt like I couldn't think straight. Why would a man give someone three-hundred-thousand dollars for the heck of it? Did he think I would shove it back in his face and tell him 'no, thank you'? No, he is banking on me not finding out it was from him.

Closing my eyes, I thought about how I had reacted to the tire. Of course, he would most likely think I would turn it down. He simply did it out of the kindness of his heart. That was a lot of money, though, for just the kindness of your heart.

My hands came up to my chest as I drew in a deep breath and slowly let it out. "Nate Shaw…what in the world are you doing and why?"

I reached for my pillow, brought it to my chest, and rolled onto my side. I was exhausted. The last thing I remembered before drifting off to sleep was silver eyes looking into mine, and Nate's soft words were an echo as I drifted off to sleep.

"Last night…something–"

"Something what, Nate?" I whispered into the pillow right before finally succumbing to sleep.

Chapter Seven

Haven

"I'm so glad you decided to come out tonight, Haven."

Rosie walked arm in arm with me as we headed toward the entrance of The Blue Moose bar. After a long week of meetings with lawyers, architects, and a few people who were making donations, I was ready to let loose and not think about anything. Or anyone. Everything was secure with the loan, but there was something off about the contractor, and I had informed the bank I was going to find someone else. The longer I delayed, the longer the project would be pushed out since winter was right around the corner.

"Lizzy!" Rosie called out as we walked through the entrance.

I grimaced when I caught sight of Rosie's older sister Lizzy. I hadn't seen her in years, and the first thing I thought of was the countless ways she flirted with Nate. Nearly half the school flirted with Nate and Josh. Lizzy was a year older than us and forever talked about how she would win Nate one day. I tolerated her then, and not much had changed since.

Lizzy looked stunning in a black silk jumpsuit and high-heeled shoes, which I was pretty sure were designer. Her blond hair was pulled up and swept back in a French twist. Her makeup was on the heavy side, but I remembered Lizzy was never caught without makeup on.

Watching the two sisters hug, I waited slightly behind them and glanced around the bar. It was a Saturday night, and since it was near Thanksgiving, there were hardly any tourists and mostly locals.

"Haven? Haven?"

My head jerked back to look at the two sisters. They were both looking at me with smiles.

"I'm sorry about that," I said as I took a few steps closer. "Lizzy, it's great seeing you."

She flashed me a wide grin. "I'm here to spread the news!"

Looking at Rosie in confusion, she shrugged. "I didn't even know she was back in town until this very minute. Mom is going to be pissed you didn't come to the house yet."

Lizzy laughed. "I was already home and shared my good news with them. Mom told me it was girls' night out tonight. That's why I'm here!"

Rosie watched her sister as she bounced on her toes. "Well, tell us!"

Holding out her hand, Lizzy showed off a massive diamond engagement ring. "I'm getting married!"

Rosie screamed, Lizzy screamed, and I jumped in shock.

"I had the same reaction," Josephine Carter said in my ear. Turning to see another one of my best friends from high school, I pulled her into a hug. She was also dressed to the nines in a beautiful dress that almost looked out of place in our local bar. She was rocking the look, though. Her dirty blonde hair was cut in a short bob, and her hazel eyes sparkled with pure happiness.

"Josephine! I had no idea you were in town."

She laughed. "I came to visit my parents for Thanksgiving and decided to stay the whole week! I ran into Lizzy at the airport in Missoula and caught a ride with her. We exchanged numbers, and she said everyone was coming out tonight, so I thought I would join. I'm exhausted from the flight in from New York City, though."

"I bet that's a long flight," I stated as Josephine and I followed Rosie and Lizzy to a large table toward the back. "Do you live in New York City now?"

Wrapping her arm in mine, she laughed. "Yes, and I love it! I can't believe we lost touch after high school. So much has happened in my life! I finished college in Boston and moved to New York after getting a job with a law firm."

"Wow, what are you doing there?"

"I'm a paralegal, and I love my job. Oh, Haven, living in a big city like New York has been so fun. My apartment is so tiny and costs a small fourtune, but it's worth it. One day I'll go back to school and become a lawyer; right now, I'm just enjoying life in the big city."

Smiling, I sat down in the chair next to the one Josephine had sat in, instantly realizing that I didn't have much in common with these people from high school, not that I ever did, though.

"What about you? Did you ever go to college? Are you still living here in Hamilton?"

"No," I said with a shake of my head. "Never could afford college. I grew my dog walking business and now take dogs out for hikes in a bus I bought. We go out twice daily with different groups of dogs, and I take them on different trails."

She smiled. "You always did love your dogs. I think that's amazing you've grown your little dog-walking business into something like that."

"That's not all!" Rosie said. "She is opening a dog park and has donors and everything. It's going to be incredible!"

Lizzy and Josephine both looked at me. "A dog park?" Lizzy asked, her nose wrinkled in disgust. "Why?"

I moved in my seat and silently wished I had stayed home now. I loved Rosie and Josephine, but Lizzy I could permanently do without her and her judgy ways.

"It's not just any dog park," Rosie went on. "It will be a membership-only dog park, and the best dog park in Hamilton. Hell, the state of Montana!"

I wanted to kiss Rosie. She had always been such a champion of mine, and I loved her for always coming to my defense.

Turning to Lizzy, I replied, "It made sense to me to open one. My dog-walking business has expanded, and I saw a need for a safe place for the dogs to go and play. Not everyone wants to let their dog go on a bus and hike a trail with a large group of dogs."

"Oh my God. You walk that many dogs?" Josephine asked, her hand over her heart. "How do you control them all?"

I gave a half-shoulder shrug. "They're all trained and listen well. They're also all off-leash when we're hiking."

"And it is so much fun!" Rosie added. "I've gone out with Haven a few times. The dogs are living their best lives."

Lizzy slowly shook her head. "I guess if being with animals all day is your thing. I couldn't imagine as that sounds literally gruesome."

I forced a smile. "Well, dogs are often more pleasant to be around than humans, if I do say so myself. So, what are you up to these days, Lizzy?"

She sat up straighter in the chair. "I own a boutique in the Bay Area."

"That's amazing," I said before giving the waitress my order. "Just a draft beer. Anything will be fine."

I thought about Nate and his draft beer at his bar in his family room and smiled.

Lizzy was still talking about her store, completely oblivious to the fact that I basically told her I preferred dogs over most humans, and my mind had been wandering and missed what all she said. I cleared my throat and pushed all thoughts of Nate away.

"It sounds like a great place!" I said when she was finally finished talking about how the color scheme of her store matched the house she lived in, which overlooked San Fransico Bay.

"It is. You girls should come and visit," Lizzy stated as she took out a small mirror and checked her lipstick, which looked perfect.

Yeah, I'll have to pass on that little adventure.

Lizzy and Josephine soon broke off into a conversation about city living and how they did not miss Montana one bit.

Rosie leaned in and said, "It's open mic night. You really should go up and sing."

Laughing, I turned to look at her. "I haven't done that in years."

"You have a great voice, Haven. You should."

"She should what?" Josephine asked. The waitress returned and gave everyone their drinks. Lizzy ordered some fancy cocktail while the rest of us had ordered beer.

"There is Candice!" Rosie cried out as she stood and waved her hands. "Over here, Candy!"

Candice Livingston approached our table with a wide grin on her face. She was dressed much like Rosie and me: jeans, a nice top, and cowboy boots. This was why Rosie and Candice were still my best friends.

Candice walked up to the table, looked at Lizzy and Josephine, and asked, "Did you just come from work or something?"

Josephine laughed. "Ha ha! I don't even think I own any cowboy boots anymore."

"I know I don't," Lizzy stated with a snide smirk on her face as she looked at her perfectly painted nails.

"Did you ever?" I asked.

All eyes turned to me, and I felt my cheeks heat. I hadn't meant for it to come out the way it did. But my reaction was instantaneous. Lizzy looked up in thought and then laughed.

"No. I don't think so!" Totally oblivious to my snide remark.

"Do you want a beer?" I asked Candice. "The waitress just came over, but I can go to the bar and get you one."

Candice placed her purse on the table and reached for my hand. "Let's go together."

I stood and we were soon making our way around the dance floor and to the bar. Once we were far enough from the table, Candice said, "I don't think I would have come if I'd known Lizzy would be here. Rosie didn't mention she was going to be in town."

Glancing back over my shoulder, I couldn't see our table anymore. "To be fair, Rosie didn't know she was in town. She's here to tell her family she's engaged."

Candice lifted her brows. "Is she? Wonder who the unlucky guy is."

Bumping her arm and laughing, I said, "Candy, don't be that way. It was a long time ago."

"Was it?" she asked, looking at me as we approached the bar.

I thought for a moment. "Yeah, five or six years ago."

Candice rolled her eyes. "Wild, seems just like yesterday. I still don't think I will ever be able to forgive her for sleeping with Matt."

Matt and Candice had been dating for three years in high school. During our junior year, Candice found them in an empty classroom. Matt was screwing Lizzy from behind as she was bent over the teacher's desk. Needless to say, she broke up with Matt and vowed to hate Lizzy for the rest of her life.

“She did you a favor. Matt was a jerk, and you wouldn’t have known it if she hadn’t arranged for you to find them.”

“I’ll take Bud Light, please,” Candice said to the bartender before focusing back on me. “I forgot she was the one who told me to meet her there.”

“Maybe she wanted you to see what a dick he was—all while seeing his dick in the process.”

Candice thought about it for a minute and then laughed. “Lizzy doing something good for another woman? Please.”

I tried not to laugh but failed. “That’s so true.”

After Candice got her beer, we turned to head back to the table when I heard my name. Goose bumps raced across my body when I realized I knew that voice. Turning, I saw Nate walking over to us, two guys following closely behind him. They looked familiar, but I couldn’t place them.

Smiling, I said, “Nate, fancy meeting you here.”

His bright smile made my heart trip over itself. “Some of the guys from the ranch wanted to go out tonight.”

Turning, he pointed to the first one. He was a bit older than us, maybe mid-thirties, with short, dark hair and beautiful blue eyes. “Haven, this is Clay, one of the ranch hands. And this guy, this is Bounty, another ranch hand.”

Bounty looked to be in his mid-twenties. His dark blonde hair and hazel eyes took both Candice and me in. Candice stepped forward and held out her hand to Bounty.

“Candice Livingston. It’s a pleasure to meet you, Bounty.” She turned to Clay. “And Clay.”

“Pleasure,” Clay said as he tipped his hat.

Bounty, on the other hand, took Candice’s hand and kissed the back of it. “Please tell me you’re available for a dance—with me—for the rest of the night?”

Blushing, Candice handed me her bottle of beer. “Let’s see what you’ve got, cowboy.”

And just like that, they made their way to the dance floor.

"That was quick," Nate and I both said simultaneously.

Laughing, I looked at him and was once again struck by how he could glance my way and my breath was instantly stolen from my lungs.

Clay slapped Nate's back. "Gonna go find the other guys."

Without taking his eyes off of me, Nate nodded. "Sounds good."

We stood there, neither of us saying anything, until I cleared my throat. "How have you been?"

"Good," he said, slipping his hands into his pockets. He seemed to do that when he was nervous or didn't know what to say.

"I got new tires on my car."

His brows lifted. "Really?"

I nodded. "Yep. According to Hank, someone wanted to pay it forward that day, and they paid for my tires. Can you believe that someone would be so generous?"

Nate gave a slight shrug as he looked everywhere but at me. "I can believe it. There are still some kind people out there. People who care about the welfare of others."

Chewing on my lower lip, I replied, "Yes, there are."

He looked over my head and out to the dance floor. "Crowded tonight, huh?"

I didn't bother to look behind me. I knew the dance floor was crowded. "Yeah, it sure is."

Nate looked down at me. "Would you like to dance?"

Surprised, I asked, "Me?"

He laughed. "Yes, you." Then his smile faded as he looked around the bar. "Unless you're here with someone."

"No!" I quickly said. "I'm just out with the girls."

He smiled again, and I had to force myself to stand upright and not let my wobbly knees get the better of me.

Nate took the beer from my hand, put it to his mouth, and drank it.

I watched as he put it on an empty table.

"Candice is going to be pissed you drank her beer," I said, letting him take my hand and lead me to the dance floor.

"Well, damn, and here I thought your lips had been the ones on it." And just like that, with my mouth wide open, the song changed from a pop song to a country one. It was Kelsea Ballerini's "Love Is a Cowboy." Nate raised his brows and gave me a crooked smile before drawing me to him. The smell of his woodsy cologne surrounded me as he touched my lower back and pressed me closer to him. I drew in a deep breath and slowly let it out as Nate moved us around the dance floor like we'd been dancing together for years. He was such a good dancer, and it was then that I realized that I hadn't seen him dance that much.

He spun me around and pulled me back, tucking my hand and his up against his chest. Everything Kelsea was singing I was feeling at that moment. Everyone else seemed to simply fade away, and when I looked up and saw him looking down at me, I couldn't pull my eyes from his. The song ended, and we stood momentarily staring at each other. When a faster song started, Nate winked, then pushed me out and spun me around as I let out a laugh. Pulling me back to him, he put his mouth against my ear and said, "Let's show these people the proper way to two-step."

Smiling, I nodded right before he took my hand and spun me in a few circles before he drew me back against him, and we danced as if we were in a couple's competition. I had never laughed and had so much fun dancing as I did with Nate to Shania Twain's "Boots Don't." When the song was finally over, I couldn't have wiped the smile off my face if I had tried.

"Why, Mr. Shaw, who knew you had that in you?"

He placed his hand on my lower back and guided us off the dance floor. "Back at you, Ms. Larson. When do you find time to dance?"

"When do you?"

"Touché."

I caught sight of Candice and Bounty still on the dance floor. I'd have to order her another beer once I returned to the table.

"Hey, Nate!" a cute little blonde said as she bounced on her toes right in front of us.

"Um, hey, Laurel."

"Want to dance?" she asked him without so much as giving me a second look. Of course, we weren't together, but I would never ask a guy to dance when he was so obviously with another woman.

"Not tonight."

The way he dismissed her caught me by surprise. He wasn't rude, exactly, but he seemed more annoyed than anything.

"Don't let me stop you two from dancing," I said when Laurel turned and walked away.

"You're not."

Okay…this is weird. Any other time I had seen Nate at The Blue Moose he avoided me at all costs.

"Well, um, that's my table," I said as I looked at where the girls were sitting. All of them were watching me and Nate with curious expressions. Rosie wore a smile while Lizzy frowned, and Josephine looked confused.

Join the club, Josephine. Join…the…club.

Before we got to the table, I turned and faced him. "Thank you for the dances, Nate. I had fun."

He smiled. "So did I. I guess…I'll, umm, see you around? Maybe we can have another dance in a bit."

I felt my teeth dig into my lower lip. How many times had I wished for Nate to ask me to dance, and here he was twice in one night?

Smiling, I replied, "I'd like that."

With a nod, he said, "Cool. I'll send another beer to your table for Candice."

I let out a chuckle. "Thanks. I'm sure she'll want it after all the dancing she's doing with your friend Bounty."

Nate looked over his shoulder to the dance floor before focusing on me again. He looked like he wanted to say something but changed his mind. He stepped away from me and rubbed the back of his neck. "I'll let you get back to your friends."

"Okay. Thanks again for the dance."

Nate turned and walked along the outside of the dance floor. He stopped at a table where a few other guys were sitting and sat down.

I drew in a slow, deep breath before I turned and walked back to the table. When I sat down, Rosie grabbed my hand and leaned in to ask, "How did that happen?"

"I'm not sure," I said as I reached for my drink. "He just asked if I wanted to dance."

Rosie looked over to the table and then back to me. "He's staring at you, Haven."

I rolled my eyes. "I'm sure he's not."

"What's going on with you and Nate?" Josephine asked. "I thought you two didn't get along."

"Did he ask you to dance?" Lizzy asked, sounding utterly shocked and a little pissed.

"Why do you sound so shocked?" Josephine asked. "Everyone knew Nate always liked Haven."

"What?" I asked as I looked around the table, this time I was the one in complete shock.

Lizzy rolled her eyes. "Oh, come on, Haven. Don't play that whole innocent thing on us. You liked him, and he liked you. I never could understand why you both acted like you didn't have feelings for each other."

I looked at Rosie, who simply shrugged.

"I don't know what makes you guys think he liked me. He could hardly stand to be around me."

Josephine and Lizzy both laughed.

"Do you know how often I tried to get Nate Shaw alone?" Lizzy said as she leaned across the table. "He turned me down every single time. No one ever turned me down."

Josephine asked, "Remember when Callie…oh, what was her last name…anyway, she tried to get Nate to make out with her at the party down by the wall?"

"The wall! Oh my gosh, I haven't thought about that place in forever!" Candice said as she sat down between Lizzy and Josephine.

The wall was just that—a wall that ran through one of the parks in Hamilton. Every Saturday night, people met there to party. The local police had shown up a time or two over the years, which had caused everyone to run and hide in the woods that the park backed up to.

"What was that girl's name who claimed she had snuck away with Nate and gave him a blow job?" Josephine asked Candice.

I moved about in my seat, not liking where the conversation was going. The last thing I wanted to hear about was Nate's conquests in high school.

Candice took a long drink of beer before setting it down as she seemed to try and catch her breath. "Callie Austin."

"Yes!" the rest of the women at the table said.

"It was Callie Austin who claimed she had hooked up with Nate," Candice said with a roll of her eyes.

Rosie laughed. "Everyone knows Nate never hooked up with anyone. He was a big flirt."

"Not true," Josephine stated as she wore a smug look.

"You?" I asked, not sure if I wanted to know the answer.

She jerked her head in my direction. "No! Girl, I knew how much you liked him. I would never do that to you."

I sat back in my seat and looked at Lizzy but quickly looked down at my beer.

"The summer before our senior year of high school, there was that field party in old man Johnson's field," Josephine started. "There was a girl from Missoula here visiting her cousin."

"Oh, right!" Rosie said as she pointed to Josephine. Turning to me, she said, "That was the night you and Nate got in that huge fight because he told you that you needed to go home because you were drinking."

My brows drew in as I tried to remember. "I don't remember that."

Candice laughed. "Because you had drank so much you could hardly walk. And Michael Mathews was hanging all over you."

"And Nate punched him," Rosie said. "Remember Josh had to pull Nate off of Michael because Nate kept hitting him."

"What?" I asked, leaning forward. "Why?"

Candice looked at me like I was insane. "He thought Michael was taking advantage of you because you were drunk. You guys got into it, and if I remember right, you said something…oh my gosh, what was it?" Candice looked around. "We were all so shocked."

"You said something like, just because you're repulsed with touching me doesn't mean another guy isn't," Rosie stated with a smile, as if she had just cracked the code to world peace.

"I said that?"

"Girl, you were so drunk. Do you even remember Josh Shaw driving you home?"

I slowly shook my head. "I don't remember that."

Josephine chuckled. "I'm not surprised; you were wasted. Anyway, that Callie girl kept coming on to Nathan, and after that, he was so worked up I just remember him taking her to his truck. According to her, they had sex in his back seat."

My stomach churned.

"Yeah, but you can ask anyone in our class; Nate never went that far with anyone," Candice said. When she looked at me, she frowned. "Haven, are you okay?"

I quickly nodded. "Yep. I'm fine."

Josephine's eyes went wide. "Oh, girl, I'm so sorry. You still like him."

"You do?" Lizzy asked, commenting for the first time.

Josephine took my hand in hers. "I'm so sorry I brought that up."

I forced a smile. "Honestly, it's okay. It's fine. I mean, it's not like I didn't know he was having sex with girls. Women, whatever. And a lot of them."

My four friends exchanged looks before Rosie said, "But he didn't. That's what we're saying. Nate was all talk in high school. Besides that Callie girl, he never hooked up with anyone. At least, not that I knew of."

Josephine, Candice, and Lizzy all nodded in agreement.

I wasn't sure if that made me feel better or worse. That small voice in the back of my head tried to remind me of why it was that Nate didn't want to touch me. Would he really be put off knowing that my father had abused me in the most horrible of ways? I wanted to think no, but his actions said otherwise. But the way he was looking at me earlier…oh, it was all so confusing.

The DJ got everyone's attention after the last song ended. "All right, folks, it's open mic tonight at The Blue Moose. Who is going to be the first person to come and sing?"

"Speaking of Nate," Rosie said. "He won't stop looking over here."

The rest of the table all looked to where Rosie's gaze was.

"Oh my gosh, you guys?" I said as I slid down in my seat.

"What is it about a guy in a baseball cap," Lizzy said as she fanned herself.

"Aren't you engaged, sis?" Rosie mused.

Lizzy stuck her tongue out at Rosie. "A girl can look."

"He's confused."

Everyone looked at Candice.

"Who?" I asked.

She slowly shook her head. "Oh my God. It all makes sense now. That night, he hooked up with that girl to try to forget about you, Haven!"

Rosie clapped. "Yes! Classic guy move. Sleep with one girl to try and forget about another. But the way he looks at you, be still my heart. The boy is currently melting over you."

"Nonsense," I quickly said as I waved Rosie's words away. "He doesn't look at me any differently than he does any other woman."

Candice snorted. "Please. The man cannot stop looking over here, Haven. You two like each other. Why aren't you doing anything about it? I could think of worse guys to hitch my wagon to."

"If that were me, girl, I'd be ditching my fiancé and be all over that tall, dark, and handsome man," Lizzy stated.

Rosie stood. "Come on. I've got the perfect song for you to sing. You sing it all the time."

"What? No!" I said as I pulled my arm free from Rosie's grasp.

"What song is it?" Josephine asked, clearly excited to find out.

"That Kelsea Ballerini one!"

"Yes! Yes!" Candice said as she stood up with Rosie. Both of them grabbed my arms and pulled me up.

"Guys, I'm not going to sing."

As they dragged me to the setup stage, everyone started to look as I actively tried to get away from my two best friends.

Rosie squeezed my arm. "You're making a scene."

"Me?"

"Hello, ladies," the DJ said when we stopped in front of him.

"Do you have the music for that Kelsea Ballerini reimagined song?"

He looked at us like we were crazy.

I sighed. "'Love Me Like You Mean It', the reimagined version."

He grinned. "I do have that one. Is that the one you're going to sing?"

When I went to turn and walk away, Rosie stopped me. "She has an amazing voice. And yes, that is the song she's singing."

"Cool. What's your name?"

"It's Haven Larson," Candice answered for me as she said it with a massive grin.

Staring at my two ex-best friends, I growled. "I hope you know that after this, you're both dead to me."

Rosie blew me a kiss while Candice said, "Break a leg!"

They scampered away, and I turned to the DJ. "I guess I'm singing."

He chuckled, then picked up the microphone. "Ladies and gentlemen, we have our first singer of the night. Ms? It is Ms., right?"

Laughing, I nodded.

"Look at that, guys, she's single."

A few whistles and some hollering went on for a few seconds before they calmed down.

"Ms. Haven Larson is going to be singing. Are you ready for it?"

The entire bar erupted into cheers, and I caught a glimpse of Rosie, Candice, Lizzy, and Josephine at the front of the stage. I should have stopped looking because leaning against a pillar with his arms folded over his broad chest was Nate. He was watching me, and when our eyes met, he smiled.

I looked down at my boots.

Why is he confusing me? He's being all nice and smiling and offering up dances and buying me tires and giving me money for my business. What in the upside down is happening?

I forced myself to look up and out into the crowd. Well, one thing was for sure, this was happening, so I might as well just go with the flow.

The microphone was on a stand, so at least I didn't have to move around. The music started, and I intended to look down at the girls, but instead, my eyes drifted directly at Nate and I started to sing.

When I got to the last sentence before the chorus, where she asked, "Do you have what it takes?" Nate's brows rose.

I looked away and moved my gaze around the crowd. It didn't take long before I loosened up and really got into the song. At the last chorus, I looked back to Nate.

When the song ended, the bar broke out into loud applause. I dared a peek at Nate, who had pushed off the pillar and was clapping. When our eyes met, he mouthed, "Wow, that was amazing."

Laughing, I got off the stage and was immediately hugged by all four girls.

"Jesus, Haven, why aren't you in Nashville singing?" Lizzy asked. "That was so good. You sounded just like her."

"That's sweet of you to say, Lizzy, but I don't think I'm that good." As I stole a glance back in Nate's direction, he'd started to walk toward me.

"You were terrific, baby!"

Shockingly, the sound of Ted's voice from behind caused me to turn around. He picked me up and spun me.

"Ted? Wait—what are you doing here?"

"Who is Ted?" Josephine asked.

Lizzy looked him over like a hungry wolf. "Yes, who is Ted?"

Ted smiled at my friends. "Um, this is my friend, Ted. Ted, these are my friends, Lizzy, Josephine, Candice, and Rosie."

"It's a pleasure to meet you, ladies."

I turned and saw Nate walking back to his table and my entire body deflated.

"Why don't you join us?" Lizzy said as she hooked her arm in Ted's.

"I don't mind if I do," Ted stated, walking with Lizzy back to the table.

"Where did Nate go?" Rosie asked. "I saw him walking over here."

I blew out a breath. "He probably saw Ted. That stupid jerk, Ted. I told him I didn't want to see him anymore. Why would he do that and make it seem like we were together still?"

When the DJ couldn't find anyone else who wanted to sing, he played another song.

"I love this Spicy Margarita song!" Candice said, clapping. She spun around and made a beeline to Bounty.

"I think she likes him," I said with a laugh. I scanned the table but couldn't find Nate. Where could he have gone?

"Let's go to the bathroom," Rosie said as she pulled me.

"I don't have to go to the bathroom."

Rosie tugged. "Yes, you do."

Laughing, I said, "What are you doing?"

Rosie looked past me, and I turned to see what she was looking at. It felt like someone threw ice-cold water onto me. My breath felt frozen in my lungs as a pain shot through my chest. You'd think I would be used to that feeling when it came to Nate Shaw. He was dancing with some girl, and it wasn't innocent dancing. The girl had her hands all over him. Granted, he wasn't touching her, but it still made my stomach roil.

"Haven, he probably saw you with Ted and…"

"And did exactly what he did with Callie?" I replied with a shake of my head.

Her face fell as she shouted, "I'm sorry they told you that story!"

I looked back out to the dance floor. Nate had his hands on the girl's hips as she moved her body like a yoga instructor. Was it my imagination, or did he push her away some? I would drive myself crazy if I kept watching them.

Turning away, I started back to the table.

"Haven!" Rosie called out.

Once I returned to the table, I said, "Guys, I think I'm going to call it a night."

"What?" Josephine said. "No, don't go. It's been so fun catching up. Sit down and have one more drink."

Unfortunately, the chair she offered gave me a direct view of the dance floor—and Nate and his little salsa partner.

I looked away when she lifted up to say something in Nate's ear.

The song changed, and Sia's "Gimme Love"' started. Nate looked like he was going to walk away, but the girl pulled him back and wrapped her arms around him. Nate reached up and untwined her arms from around his neck. He leaned down and was saying something in her ear.

Was he asking her to leave with him?

Rosie took my hand. "Haven, don't watch."

As if he could sense I was watching, he looked over to the table. Our eyes met, and I hated that the sting of tears burned my eyes. The girl reached up and placed her finger on his chin, drawing his attention back to her.

Looking down at my hands in my lap, I closed my eyes and cursed myself. I was being silly. It wasn't like Nate and I were together. So we had a couple of days where it felt like we might be able to be…friends.

Friends. Was that what Nate wanted? I had stupidly stood up there and sang that damn song with him watching me, and now I felt like an idiot. He had smiled, but maybe he had simply thought the song was good.

Oh, God. I didn't want to sit in a bar overthinking everything about Nate Shaw.

"I'm leaving," I said as I stood. Surprising Rosie, and even myself, with my sudden decision.

"No!" Rosie said as she stood too. "What about…"

We both turned and looked where Ted and Lizzy had been sitting.

"Where did they go?" I asked.

Candice said, "I just saw the two of them leaving."

"What?" Rosie and Josephine said together.

"Is she cheating on her fiancé?" Rosie asked.

Turning to face me, Josephine asked, "What about Ted and Haven?" As if Ted's departure broke my heart. Far from it.

I quickly said, "We're not together."

Turning to Rosie, I pulled her to me so only she could hear me. "I need to leave."

Rosie drew back and looked at me. I hated that Nate had once again nearly brought me to tears and that she could see it. I wasn't even sure why I was so upset. Nate hadn't ever promised me a single thing. So he was kind to me and seemed like he wanted a friendship. That was going to have to be good enough.

Rosie pulled me in for a hug. "Oh, Haven."

"I'll talk to you tomorrow, okay?"

She nodded. "Let me walk you out, at least."

I shook my head. "I'll get the bouncer to walk me to my car. Stay and have fun."

Rosie pulled me into a hug. "He's not worth the tears."

If she only knew what he had done for me in my past, and even recently. And how confused I was. "We're not together, either. He can dance or do whatever he wants. I'm just tired after a long day."

She smiled before she kissed my cheek. "Text me when you get home."

"I will."

Turning back to the table, I called out over the music. "Bye, girls!"

"Call me!" Candice said.

Josephine hugged me. "Maybe I'll see you again before I leave."

Without looking out at the dance floor again, I made my way around groups of people and to the exit.

"Hey, Jonny," I said to the bouncer. "Would you walk me to my car?"

He grinned. "Of course I will, Haven."

Jonny was two years older than me, and we had known each other in high school, but not that well.

Once I got to my car, I unlocked it and slipped into the driver's seat. I waved goodbye to Jonny. Once he was walking back toward the club, I dropped my head against the headrest.

"Why can I not get over you, Nate Shaw? And what is so wrong with me that you can't make the next move in my direction?"

Chapter Eight

Nathan

Once I returned to the table, I glanced over to where Haven and her friends sat. I had wanted to talk to her after she had sung that song, tell her how I was feeling, but that asshole Ted showed up, and the last thing I wanted to see was him hanging all over her. So I went back to the table and got suckered into dancing with one of my friend's cousins who was in town. I couldn't wait to get off the dance floor; her hands had been all over me.

Frowning, I searched but couldn't see Haven. Or Ted. They were gone.

"Shit," I said as I quickly made my way over to the table.

"Where is Haven?" I asked as I looked at Rosie, one of Haven's best friends. "I need to talk to her."

Rosie looked up at me and then to Candice, another of Haven's friends. "I do believe she went back to her apartment, right, Candice?"

Candice nodded. "With Ted."

Josephine Carter looked between Rosie and Candice and seemed confused, but only momentarily. She laughed and said,

"Oh, yes. She did leave with Ted. Didn't she say she was nervous because it was going to be their first time?"

Candice choked on her beer as Rosie pressed her mouth together into a tight line.

"Was I not supposed to say anything?" Josephine asked, looking like she had broken some girl code.

"What?" I asked, bouncing my gaze over the three of them. "First time for what?"

Rosie raised her brows. "Nate Shaw, if you have to ask that question, I wonder if your reputation precedes you."

I narrowed my eyes and asked, "Sex?"

"Don't say it like you don't know what it is." Candice laughed.

Without giving them another second of my time, I turned and made my way to the exit. As I walked away, Rosie said, "Better hurry if you intend to stop them!"

Once I got out of The Blue Moose, I made a dash to my truck, got in, and proceeded to break nearly every traffic law I could to get to Haven's apartment. I pulled into a visitor's parking lot and jogged up the steps to her apartment. The only reason I even knew were Haven lived was because I had overheard my mother and her mother talking about it when Haven moved in.

My breathing was fast and hard as I lifted my hand and pounded. It only took a few moments, and the door opened. Haven stood there, a confused look on her face.

"Nate? What are you doing here?"

I looked past her and didn't see the dick anywhere. Turning my attention back to Haven, almost breathless, I said, "Don't do this. I mean, at least not until we can talk."

Her brows pinched together. "What are you talking about? Don't do what?"

"Can I come in, Haven? I mean, after you tell him to leave. Please."

She looked unsure for a moment.

"I know he's here with you."

Her expression went from unsure to downright confused. "Who?"

"Ted."

After staring at me for a few moments, she shook her head. "Ted isn't here."

"You left the bar with him."

With a long sigh, Haven stepped back and motioned for me to come in.

"Take a look for yourself. There isn't anyone here but me. I left the bar alone. The bouncer even walked me to my car."

I walked into the apartment and quickly took it in. The walls were all painted white, and there were no pictures hanging on them. A sofa and a loveseat had fall and Thanksgiving pillows on them. Across from the couch was a blue cabinet with pictures of Haven's mother and one of Haven standing on an overlook with the Bitterroot River behind her and a pack of dogs around her. Above the cabinet was a TV mounted to the walls.

Haven had plants scattered throughout the open living concept. Her kitchen was on the small side, with a small table and four chairs in a bumped-out nook. Everywhere I looked, there were things for dogs…and cats.

"Your place is cute."

She glanced around before shrugging. "It's small but enough for me."

I nodded as I moved into the living room and saw what had to be the door to her bedroom. It was open and I couldn't see anyone in there from where I stood.

"Why did you think Ted was here?" Haven asked, moving into the kitchen and opening the refrigerator. She grabbed two bottles of water. Walking toward me, she handed me one. "I don't have any beer."

Thanking her, I took the bottle. “Thanks, and I don’t want any beer.”

Haven moved to the loveseat and sat. “So I’ll ask again… why did you think Ted was here?”

Following her lead, I sat down on the sofa. “The girls told me you left with him.”

Her brows shot up. “The girls?”

“Rosie, Candice, Josephine.”

A look passed over her face, but it was gone before I could read it. “Is that so?”

“You know, I didn’t get to tell you how great you sounded tonight.”

She leaned back and took a drink of the water before she said, “Shocked you remembered. You looked a bit busy dancing.”

I shook my head. “I didn’t want to interrupt you and Ted, so I went back to the table; one of the guy’s cousins was in town, and they asked me to dance with her. She was a bit too touchy-feely for me.”

Haven stared at me and went to say something, then quickly shut her mouth.

“Anyway, I saw you were gone and asked them where you went. They said you and Ted came back here. Did you change your mind?”

Now she looked even more confused. “About what?”

“Ummm, well, about, ummm…sleeping with him.”

Haven leaned forward, put her water on the coffee table, then turned to face me. “What are you talking about, Nate?”

“They said you were…well…you were going to sleep with Ted for the first time.”

A look of horror crossed her beautiful face. “They told you that?”

I nodded. “Josephine did. Yes.”

She leaned forward. "Why would they tell you that?"

Shrugging, I replied, "They're *your* friends."

Haven stood and started to pace. She finally stopped and faced me. "I'm sorry, Nate. They lied to you. I'm not even dating Ted any longer. Not that I was officially dating him to begin with. He's a…a…"

"Douche?"

Attempting not to smile, she turned away and cleared her throat. "Something like that."

"At least we agree on something. So, what made you pick that song to sing?" I asked suddenly.

"I didn't. Rosie did."

I nodded, not entirely believing her. "You have a beautiful voice, Haven. I remember hearing it when you were in the choir."

She once again had a look of surprise on her face. "How? When did you ever hear me sing in the choir?"

"The Christmas programs you guys did each year while we were in high school."

Haven slowly sat down on the loveseat once again. "You came to those?"

I gave a one-shoulder shrug. "I did."

Her head slowly shook. "Why?"

Feeling suddenly like a beaming hot light was shining on me, I tried to quickly figure out what to say. In the end, I went with the truth.

"I wanted to see you sing."

Haven swallowed hard as she stared at me with utter shock.

"You came to see me? I thought you couldn't stand me in high school because of what happened with my father."

I felt a look of horror come over my face. Was that what she thought? My stomach churned and for a moment I thought I might be sick. I dropped my gaze to the blue and white rug she had in the living room and took in a few deep breaths. The floors were all wood, and from what I could tell, they continued throughout the apartment. When I finally lifted my gaze, Haven was watching me. Waiting for my answer.

"That's not true, Haven. What happened to you with your father wasn't your fault at all."

She let out a bitter laugh. "You sure have treated me like you couldn't stand me, Nate. Like he somehow tainted me all those years ago. Especially after the barn incident…"

"Haven… It was the opposite."

"The opposite? What do you mean?"

Pushing my hand through my hair, I sighed. "I couldn't be near you, Haven, and it wasn't anything to do with your dad. Well, not in the way you think."

"What do you mean?" she asked, looking at me with eyes that were filled with so many different emotions.

I could feel my heartbeat picking up, and I knew I was about to fuck this all up.

"I just can't explain it."

Her arms folded over her chest. "Try, Nate."

Turning away from her, it was my turn to pace the small area of her apartment.

When I stopped and faced her, I exhaled. "Fuck, I don't know how to say what I need to say to make you understand."

Her head tilted slightly to the side. "Let's start with something easy. Why did you stop that night in the barn if you weren't repulsed by the thought of my father abusing me sexually?"

"Jesus, Haven, I have never once thought that. Never."

"Why did you say what we were doing was a mistake when you screwed some girl from out of town at a wall party?"

"What?"

"Don't play stupid with me, Nate. You'd rather fuck some stranger than even touch me."

I flinched at her words. “Is that what you honestly think?”

Her arms dropped to her sides. “Yes. You’ve never tried to hide the fact that you sleep around, Nate.”

“Did you ever, for once, Haven, think that maybe I was all talk?”

She took a step back and then laughed. “All talk?”

I rubbed at the back of my neck. “Yes, I’ve slept with women. I won’t say I’m innocent. I’ve let plenty of women do…other things to me, but the amount of women I’ve had sex with isn’t all that you think.”

She rolled her eyes. “Other things? As in?”

“Does it matter? None of them meant a damn thing to me.”

“You didn’t sleep with Callie that night at the wall party?”

“I don’t know a Callie, Haven. And what the hell is a wall party?”

“It was the night Michael Mathews was coming onto me, and I guess we argued because you said I was drunk, and Josh drove me home. Josephine said you took Callie back to your truck, and she said you two had sex.”

“You’re talking about something that happened in high school?”

“Yes!” she cried out. “Why could you take a stranger to your truck to have sex, but you couldn’t with me? What is so wrong with me that you can’t even stand to be near me?”

My resolve broke, and I marched over to her. I gently put my hands on her upper arms.

“I didn’t sleep with her, Haven. Nothing happened. I wanted something to happen because I wanted to forget about seeing that asshole put his hands on you. But I couldn’t because it wasn’t you. She. Wasn’t. You.”

She took a step back, her eyes widened in shock. “What do you mean?”

“Do you know how many fucking times I’ve closed my eyes when I’ve been with a woman and dreamed it was you I was with? Every single time a woman has ever touched me, it's always been you."

She sucked in a breath of air as I moved closer to her.

"The number of times I've taken myself in my hands and come to your name falling off my lips? Too many times to even count. And it was always you."

Haven slowly shook her head as she took a few steps back, causing me to let her go. I moved forward, my heart pounding so loudly in my ears I could hardly think.

"It's always been you, Haven. And this feeling I feel." My hand slammed against my chest. "It just grows, and something happens when I see you. That night in the barn, touching you and kissing you made me feel something I had never felt before, and it scared the living shit out of me. *You* scare me, Haven. The only reason I stopped was because I didn't want to hurt you. I don't want to hurt you, ever. That day, seeing what your father did to you—what he was about to do to you—it broke me, and I know it broke you. I am terrified to hurt you because you deserve someone so much better than me, Haven. You deserve the world, and I never want to see you hurt again."

Her mouth opened and then quickly closed.

I started to pace again. "This feeling I get when I'm near you…it fucking scares me because it grows stronger every time, and I don't know how much longer I can hold off. I want you so much, but you have no idea how worried I am that I'll fuck it up and hurt you. You are the last person in this world I would ever want to hurt. I'll burn it all down before I—or anyone else, for that matter—has a chance to hurt you again."

"I scare you?" she softly asked.

Turning to face her, my breath caught in my throat as I looked at those big grayish-blue eyes so wide they nearly made my knees buckle.

"Yes. I'm terrified, Haven."

She slowly turned away from me and sat down on the loveseat. "Is that what you were going to tell me that morning at your house?"

I nodded. "Yes, but Ted the douche showed up."

Haven clasped her hands together and momentarily looked down at her lap before looking back up at me. She stood and walked around the sofa to stand inches away from me. I balled my fists together to keep from reaching out and pulling her to me. What I had with her was magnetic, instinctual. I had no control over it.

"So all these years, you pushed me away because you were worried you would hurt me? I get feeling this way about someone is scary and confusing; trust me, I've sat in my room plenty of nights and cried over you. Wondering why I was so drawn to you. Why you seemed to hate me."

My eyes closed. "God, no, Haven. I was trying to push you away after that night in the barn. I would have made love to you then, but you had been hurt so badly, and I wasn't sure if I was doing the right thing or not."

"You didn't stop because of what he did to me?"

"No! Haven, I swear to you that wasn't the reason at all."

I sighed and dropped my head back. I wasn't sure if I was making things worse or not. "This isn't what I wanted."

She let out a humorless laugh. "My God, Nate. What in the hell do you want? I'm confused."

"I want you, Haven!" I shouted. "It's all I've ever fucking wanted. You."

Her hand came to her mouth as she blinked rapidly at me.

"You're the most amazing woman I have ever met, Haven. You're kind, selfless, and you love your dogs with all your heart, as well as strangers, but mostly the dogs. You are perfect in my eyes, sweetheart."

Haven slowly shook her head as she lightly chuckled at the accuracy of the dog statement.

"I was trying to stay away because…because I love you, Haven. I gave you my heart long ago. You've had it this entire time and never knew it."

"Wh…what did you say?"

Meeting her eyes with mine, I asked, "Which part?"

She closed her eyes and gave her head a quick shake before focusing back on me. "You love me?"

Smiling, I nodded. "I think I've been in love with you since I first saw you."

Her hand came up to her mouth as she stared at me for a few moments before it fell to her side. "Nathan Shaw, I would like to just punch you right now."

My head jerked back. "What?"

"How do you not see what an amazing man you are? Any woman would call herself lucky to be loved by you. And I know in my heart of hearts that you won't hurt me."

"I have before."

"I now know that you weren't doing it on purpose. And I'm sorry I always made cracks about the amount of women you slept with."

I shook my head. "Every woman I've ever been with has been interested in me for one of two reasons. My looks, or my money. None of them ever meant a thing to me, Haven. I need you to know that."

Haven made her way over to me. She placed her hand on my chest, and I felt my heart jump in response. "That's not true, Nate. Not every woman sees that in you."

My eyes searched her face. "What do you see, Haven?"

When her gaze met mine, something in the air crackled between us.

"I see a man who loves his family and would do anything for them. I see a man who is involved in this community. I see a man who pretends nothing bothers him, but I can see the hurt behind his eyes. I see a man who played Santa Claus and bought me new tires for my car—and sent a check to my company to help me follow a dream of mine—and he did it all without anyone knowing he did it."

"How did you know that check was from me?"

Smiling, I rubbed my thumb over his shirt and stared straight at his chest. "It wasn't hard to figure out. The tires and the check all happened the same day."

Confused, I shook my head. "The check wasn't supposed to be mailed out until a few days later."

"Well," Haven said with a soft laugh. "You better have a word with your attorneys because it came the same day. It didn't take me long to figure out it was from you. Once I found out that the law firm the check came from was your family's firm that you use, the puzzle pieces fell into place."

I closed my eyes and shook my head.

"Why did you do that, Nate?"

My hand went to the side of her face, and she gently leaned into my touch. "I want to see you happy, Haven. I want to see your dreams come true, and I want to be a part of all of it—and I don't want to do it anonymously for one more second."

Her eyes filled with tears. "What are you saying?"

Cupping her face within my hands, I leaned down and whispered against her lips, "I'm tired of denying my feelings for you, Haven. I want to take you to your bed and explore every fucking inch of your body with my eyes, my hands, my tongue. I want to make love to you until I don't have the energy to move. I want to make you mine."

Chapter Nine

Haven

The feel of Nate's hot breath against my lips caused my entire body to shiver in anticipation of what would happen next. His words swirled around in my head, and I felt dizzy with happiness. I reached for his arms to steady myself.

He pulled his head back slightly, met my gaze, and asked, "May I kiss you, Haven?"

My eyes closed as a rush of air left my lungs. When I opened them, Nate's intense silver eyes pierced mine, and I said the only thing that I could get out. "Yes. Now. Please."

He smiled, and it was nearly my undoing. The moment his soft lips touched mine, I melted into him. My arms wrapped around his neck, and when his tongue sought entrance into my mouth, I gladly opened to him, letting out a soft moan when our tongues intertwined. The kiss was intense yet gentle. The way Nate wrapped his arms around me, drawing my body up against his, nearly had me exploding with a fierce desire that almost left me breathless.

"Haven," Nate whispered against my lips. "Please tell me if you want this."

My eyes fluttered open, and it took me a hot second to get my wits about me. “I’ve wanted you, Nate, for as long as I can remember. You’re the one who has been pushing away.”

He grinned. “Leave it to you to remind me of that.”

I shrugged but my smile faded. “You aren’t bothered by my…past?”

With a shake of his head, he bent down and kissed me again. “I promise you, sweetheart, I want to help you forget that time of your life and do nothing for the rest of my life but make you happy.”

I couldn’t help the smile that spread over my face. When we both just stood there as if neither of us had any idea what to do, we laughed.

Nate laced his fingers in mine and squeezed lightly. “Haven, I know this is personal, but the last time we talked you were only sixteen and still a virgin.”

I felt my cheeks heat as I said, “I’ve never been with anyone. I mean, I’ve dated, but my experience with men is rather limited. I always found it hard to trust anyone and honestly, I always dreamed you would be my first.”

A pained expression moved over Nate’s face, and he cupped my face within his hands again. “I don’t deserve you, Haven.”

Chewing on my lower lip, I nodded. “I disagree with you.”

Nate placed his forehead to mine and I whispered his name. “Nate.”

Before I knew what was happening, I was in his arms, and he walked us to my bedroom. He stopped when he stepped into the room and then laughed.

“Holy shit, Haven. Do you have enough dog stuff in here?”

Looking around the room, I laughed. I had boxes from Amazon filled with dog treats. Dog toys were stacked in one corner, and a few dog beds were piled up in the other corner.

"I don't have anywhere to keep this stuff. At least not until the dog park is done. I plan on having a storage building onsite as well."

He slowly put me down and walked up to one of the boxes of treats and food. Looking at me, he asked, "What's with all the dog food?"

I made my way over to him and stopped in front of the bags of food that were piled high. "I have a few clients who have run into tough times. They can't pay for the doggy daycare bus anymore, and money is also tight with food. I collected donations from my other clients, and I was able to buy them this food. I just have to take it to them. I was going to just pile it all into my back seat and deliver it tomorrow."

I could feel his gaze on me. "How did this all get up here?"

Turning to look at him, I said, "I carried them up."

His mouth fell open. "Haven, there are ten forty-pound bags. You carried these up by yourself?"

"Well, yes. It took me forever, but I got them all up."

Nate slowly shook his head as he looked back at the bags of food. Turning to face me, he took my hands and lifted one to his mouth, kissing the inside of my wrist tenderly. With the other hand, he kissed my palm.

"I've never met a woman like you before, Haven. Your heart is so pure."

I let out a nervous laugh. "I don't know about that. If you had any idea about what was going through my mind right now, you wouldn't think I was so pure. Not one pure thought is racing through my veins at the moment."

A bark of laughter escaped, and he pulled me to him. "Tell me what is going on in your pretty little head."

I could feel my entire body heat. "I want you to do what you said earlier. Explore my body with your hands and…"

My voice trailed off.

"Mouth?"

I nodded.

Nate took my hand and walked us over to the bed. It was the only thing in the room with nothing sitting on it. My entire body shook when Nate put his hands on my shirt and lifted it over my head. When he knocked on my door earlier tonight, I had just changed into comfortable clothes. Letting off a low moan, he took in my naked upper half.

"You don't have a bra on."

"No," I whispered as he reached up and cupped both breasts, his thumbs moving over the hardened nipples. A rush of raw desire raced through my body.

"You're so fucking perfect, Haven."

Dropping my head back, my fingers slipped into his soft hair, and I tugged when his mouth covered one of my nipples.

"Oh, God!" I cried out, the feeling of pain and ecstasy mixed when he pinched one nipple with his fingers while sucking on the other. "Nate."

Was it even possible that I was beginning to feel my orgasm already start to grow? Just when I couldn't take much more, Nate was gone and the buildup vanished, making me groan in frustration.

With a dazed feeling, I dropped my head to look at Nate as he slid the soft cotton pants I was wearing slowly off of me. He held my hand as I stepped out of them.

He sat back on his heels and stared at me. I had to fight the urge to cover my body under his intense gaze. Instead, I moved uneasily back and forth on my feet.

Nate looked up and said, "Why are you nervous about me looking at your body?"

An anxiety-ridden bubble of laughter slipped through. "I'm not…well, I don't think I'm like the other women you've been with. I've got about ten extra pounds I'm carrying as well as…"

My voice faded away when he pressed his mouth against my lower stomach. He hooked his fingers in my panties and slowly pushed them down.

"Don't say another word if you'll say bad things like that. I can't remember any other woman before you, Haven."

Nate's sweet words caused tears to prick at the back of my eyes.

He gripped my ass while running his tongue around my belly button. "Fucking hell. I've never wanted anyone like I want you. I can smell your desire for me, Haven. I want to taste it."

I swallowed the lump in my throat as I stepped back, butterflies in my stomach making me feel a bit queasy. Nate was still holding onto me.

"I've never, um…my sexual experiences haven't exactly been…um…I don't even know the word. No one has ever done that to me before."

When he looked up at me, I swore his eyes were black. "Good. I'll be the first and your last."

His statement caused me to sway slightly. I reached up and pinched my arm. Nope, I wasn't dreaming. This was really happening.

"Haven, did you just pinch yourself?"

Feeling embarrassed that Nate had seen that, I covered my face in my hands and groaned. When I dropped my hands to my sides, I met his gaze. "You don't know how many times I dreamed of this moment. It doesn't feel real."

Nate stood, cupped my face, and kissed me as he walked me back until I hit the bed. I dropped down to sit, and he never once broke our kiss. When he pulled back from my mouth ever so slightly, he smiled.

"Crawl back onto the bed, sweetheart. When I finish with you, you'll know this isn't a dream."

I hurried back, my chest heaving.

Nate slowly pulled and unbuttoned his shirt and took it off, dropping it to the floor. My mouth instantly watered at the sight of his chiseled chest. His eyes zeroed in on my mouth when I licked my suddenly dry lips.

My gaze fell to his hands, undoing his jeans. Nate kicked off one boot, then the other. With a wicked smile, he pushed his pants and boxers down and I sucked in a breath. He was pure perfection. His thick, long length pulsed against his lower stomach, and I had to squeeze my legs shut to ease the pulsing.

"Need some relief, sweetheart?" Nate purred as I crawled onto the bed like he was on the hunt for something.

The only thing I could do was nod and whisper, "Yes, please."

With a wicked smile, he ran his hands up my thighs, causing my body to shiver. He spread my legs open and stared for what felt like forever.

"What's wrong?" I quietly asked.

He slowly shook his head. "Nothing at all. I'm just taking you in."

I squirmed and Nate put his hands on my hips as he softly kissed the inside of my thigh. Then he was where I needed him. I gasped and grabbed onto the quilt that was on my bed. The way he touched me with his mouth and hands nearly had me exploding with an orgasm. But then he would move, and the delicious build-up would start again. He sucked and licked my core until I was writhing under him.

"Nate. Oh, God, I'm going to come."

He slipped his fingers inside of me and the dam burst. My entire body went tense as ripples of pleasure raced across my body over and over until I could barely take it anymore.

"Nate, I can't. I can't. I can't."

He moved his mouth, and my body trembled as I opened my eyes and tried to focus. The room felt like it was spinning, and I was floating above the bed watching the most erotic moment of my life.

"Oh my God. I think I died and went to heaven. But now it's your turn."

A soft chuckle came from Nate as he placed kisses up my body. "I wasn't planning on this, babe, and unfortunately, I don't have a condom."

I chewed on my lower lip. "Have you ever had sex without one before?"

He shook his head.

"Have you been tested? I mean, for anything…"

My voice trailed off as Nate kissed my cheek.

"I'm clean, Haven, but we can do other things until next time."

"No," I quickly said. "I don't want to wait. I want you. All of you."

He looked unsure, and I was positive he was about to say we should wait.

"I'm on birth control."

"That's not a hundred percent."

Smiling, I ran my finger along the stubble that was starting to grow on his face. "Neither is a condom."

Nate laughed. "Touché."

"I need you, Nate."

He closed his eyes for a moment, then pierced me with an intense look. "Are you sure?"

Lacing my fingers with his, I smiled. "I've never been so sure of anything in my life."

Nate leaned down and captured my mouth with his. The kiss was searing, as if he was trying to pour everything into it. When he slowly drew back, he searched my face. "I'm not going to last long inside you without a condom."

"That's okay," I said, opening my legs as he settled his body over mine. "We've got all night."

Nate chuckled, then grew serious when he pressed against my entrance. He reached down between our bodies and moaned when he slipped a finger inside of me.

"You're so wet."

All I could do was nod.

"I'm going to take it slow since this is your first time."

When he started to rub my clit, I moaned.

"I need you to come again, baby," he whispered as he positioned himself against me. "Does that feel good?"

I nodded. "I need more of you. Nate, please."

"I've got you, Haven."

He pushed in more and I gasped from the pressure of him slowly entering me.

"Tell me if I'm hurting you."

I dug my nails into his back. "Don't stop. Please don't stop."

Rubbing my clit, he pushed in more and I felt the familiar build-up once again. He rocked slightly in and out while playing with my sensitive bud.

"Nate, I'm going to…oh my…Nate!"

My orgasm exploded as Nate pushed all the way in. I gasped at the sharp pain, but it was quickly replaced with pure pleasure.

"Are you okay?"

I practically purred. "You feel so good, please don't stop, Nate."

He leaned down and kissed me with a kiss so searing it nearly left me dizzy. We soon got into a rhythm and moved together as if we were one. Nate never took his eyes off of me as he made love to me. It was unlike anything I ever dreamed it would be…and the best part of all, it…it was Nate.

"It feels so fucking good, Haven. I'm not going to last much longer."

"Don't hold back."

Nate moved faster, and his moves began to be a bit more frantic. He reached under my ass and lifted me, and something changed and another orgasm raced through my body. Nate let out a groan and buried his face into my neck as he repeated my name as if it was a prayer.

When he finally came to a stop, he rested above me with his weight on his elbows. We both were breathing heavy, and when his gaze met mine, we both smiled.

"That was…amazing," I said between breaths.

"More than amazing. It was fucking beautiful."

I ran my finger along his stubbled jaw. "Thank you."

He let out a strangled laugh. "I promise, next time I'll last longer."

With a slow shake of my head, I said, "It was perfect. You were perfect. Everything was perfect."

Nate kissed the tip of my nose. "That's because it was with you."

My heart felt as if it was too big for my chest. I wanted desperately to utter those three words, but wasn't sure. I didn't have to think about it for very long though.

"Haven, I love you."

Tears built in my eyes and I tried to speak but nothing came out. I closed my eyes, drew in a deep breath, and then looked at the love of my life. "I love you more."

He smiled and everything in my chaotic world seemed to simply click into place.

◆ ◆ ◆

My eyes fluttered open, and it took me a moment to realize where and who I was with. Nate was sleeping on his back, his arm over his eyes. I had been snuggled up next to him with my head on his chest. When I lifted my head, I internally sighed with relief that I hadn't been drooling on him.

"Thank you," I whispered as I looked heavenward.

Carefully moving away from Nate, I managed to slip out of bed without waking him. I looked down at the man who slept peacefully and smiled. The memory of him being inside of me would forever be etched into my brain. He had been so gentle and loving, and a part of me wanted to crawl back into the bed and wake him up for round two.

Instead, I reached for his shirt and slipped it over my head. Nate's woodsy smell instantly wrapped around my body, and I took a deep breath.

With one last look over my shoulder, I went to the kitchen to make breakfast. I had plenty of time before picking up this morning's group of dogs. I pulled out the bacon and got it going first before starting the eggs.

As I moved around, I could feel the slight pain between my legs, but it wasn't anything I couldn't handle. A warm bath would fix it, I was sure.

My entire body trembled as warm arms engulfed my body, and Nate kissed me on my neck.

"You snuck away."

Tilting my neck more so he had better access, I smiled. "I wanted to make you breakfast and let you rest."

The feel of his mouth on my skin was making me feel dizzy. I leaned against him and sighed when his hands cupped my breasts and squeezed lightly.

"You wearing my shirt is driving me crazy, Haven."

"It is?" I asked, my knees feeling weak all over again.

When his hands moved under my shirt, I sucked in a breath. He moved lower, and when his hand reached between my legs, they nearly buckled. His other arm wrapped around my body, keeping me against him.

"Breakfast?" I managed to get out before he slipped his fingers inside of me, and my head dropped back against his shoulder. The man was doing wonderful things with those fingers, and I felt myself melting into him.

"I don't mind if I do," Nate replied. Pulling his fingers out, he turned me so I faced him. He put his fingers inside his mouth and sucked on them. My eyes went wide, and I could feel a rush of wetness at my core.

Nate lifted me and set me on the counter, and the cold countertop against my bare skin caused me to let out a slight squeal.

His hands went to my knees, and he slowly pushed them apart. Drawing me closer to the edge of the counter, Nate lowered himself.

"Nate? On the kitchen counter…oh my goodness!" I cried out when his mouth covered my clit. The man could do things with his tongue and fingers that should be illegal.

One hand gripped the counter as my other went to his head. My entire body shook as I closed my eyes and shamelessly rubbed against his mouth, needing more of him.

"Oh, God," I panted as my orgasm built. "I'm so close. Nate, please don't stop what you're doing!"

He growled as he continued to suck and lick. My entire body tingled as the build-up slowly started to take over my body. Then it hit and my goodness, it was one of the strongest orgasms I had ever experienced. I cried out Nate's name over and over as I fell into a sweet euphoria. As I slowly returned to myself, I felt Nate's mouth cover mine. The taste of myself on his tongue shocked me, but the feel of him right at my entrance pushed the shock away and turned it into desire.

"I can't go slow, Haven. I need to fuck you. Are you sore?"

With a shake of my head, I wrapped my legs around him. He pushed inside me, causing me to cry out and him to freeze.

"Shit, are you okay?"

My hands clawed at his shoulders and back. "It burned for just a second. I'm fine! I'm okay!"

This was completely different than last night. Where Nate was slow, gentle, and in complete control, now he was fast, hard, and utterly lost in the moment. I loved it. I wanted more. *Needed* more. This was indeed fucking, and it was raw and intense.

"Fuck, Haven. I can't get enough of you. I want to be deeper inside you," he said as he paused long enough to put my nipple into his mouth. My fingers sliced through his hair, and I held him there momentarily, feeling the tingle begin again. Lord, I was still sensitive from the last orgasm.

He jerked his head back, picked me up, and set me on the floor.

"Turn around and hold onto the counter."

My chest rose and fell in quick bursts of breath. Doing as he said, I looked over my shoulder to see him take his impressive length into his hands and guide it back into me. He pushed in, and we both moaned in pleasure.

"Do you like this?" he asked, kissing my back. I still had his shirt on, but he had pushed it up so that I was completely at his mercy.

All I could do was nod as I pushed back against him. I needed him to move. The feel of him filling me was amazing, but the need for more of him was intense. Would it always be this way?

With another push, I said, "Nate. Please."

His hand caressed my ass as he slowly withdrew, then slammed back inside of me. "Do you like that?"

"Yes!"

"More?"

"Yes. Harder, please."

His fingers dug into my hips as he held me and gave me exactly what I asked for. Each time he pushed in, I felt him go deeper. I was going to come again, and I wasn't sure if I had the strength to keep my legs from giving out with another mind-blowing orgasm.

"Fucking hell, Haven. I need you to come. I can't…wait… much…fuck."

I was so close to coming, but something kept it from happening. When I felt Nate's hands slip down in front of me and play with my clit, I found my release and fell, right along with Nate. It took me a few moments to realize he was kissing my back as he gently laid his body over mine. He was breathing heavily, and every ounce of my being wanted to keep him inside of me. The fullness was simply delicious.

He gently pulled out, grabbed a paper towel, and wet it. "I'm sorry I lost control like that." He gently ran it between my legs before he cleaned himself off.

Turning, I leaned against the counter and tried to get my breathing back under control. "I think I like it when you lose control."

Nate laughed as he shook his head. "You're going to kill me, Haven. Do you know that? I told myself I was going to leave you alone today since you have to be sore, but seeing you in my shirt. I lost all self-control."

Smiling, I replied, "Not if you kill me first. I've never had such intense orgasms like that. Well, at least not from a man."

His brows raised, his interest piqued. "Do you have toys you use on yourself, Haven?"

I could feel my cheeks turn hot. "Sometimes."

Groaning, he closed his eyes.

"Do you want scrambled eggs?" I asked out of the blue.

When Nate peeked one eye open at me, I laughed.

Smiling, he pulled me to him and kissed me like he was afraid I would disappear before his eyes. Once he had thoroughly kissed me, he stepped back. "Go take a hot bath and I'll make us breakfast."

"Are you sure?"

"I'm sure. I've got to make a few phone calls, so I'll make some more bacon and put the eggs on in a bit."

Reaching up, I kissed him on the lips. "I'll be quick!"

I practically skipped back into my bathroom, wearing Nathan's shirt and a smile so wide nothing could wipe it from my face.

Chapter Ten

Nathan

Haven must have decided to take a shower instead of a bath. Once I heard the shower turn on, I quickly returned to Haven's bedroom and grabbed my phone. I pulled up Josh's name and hit call as I returned to the kitchen to pick up where Haven had left off with the bacon.

"Hey, where are you?" Josh asked as I heard what I thought was Blayze and Hunter in the background.

"I'm not going to be coming in today."

He laughed. "Too much to drink last night at The Blue Moose?"

Hearing Hunter make a wisecrack in the background made me roll my eyes. "No, that's not it at all. I'm at Haven's apartment."

The line went silent.

"Josh?"

"I'm still here, just trying to figure out what to ask next. I guess the main one is...why are you at Haven's apartment?"

I quickly paused to hear the shower still going and put more bacon on. "I stayed here last night."

Josh choked on something. "As in, you *stayed*...stayed?"

"I don't know what that means, Josh."

I heard a door softly shut. "It means, did you finally come to your senses?"

Smiling, I replied, "I did."

Josh let out a whistle. "So? Did you guys...you know?"

"Jesus, Josh, we're not eight. Yes, we made love. Twice, and my fucking mind is blown. I'm not sure how I'm feeling right now."

Josh let out a roar of laughter. "You can just take my thousand dollars and donate it to the dog park if you please."

I rolled my eyes once again. "Funny. Josh, I'm being serious. What I experienced with Haven...I've never felt that way before, and I'm not going to lie...I'm freaking out a bit."

"Take a deep breath, Nate. What are you doing now?"

Looking at the open bacon, I pulled some of it out and placed it in the pan. "Making her breakfast."

"Uncle Tanner would be so proud of you."

Sighing, I said, "Josh, stop dicking around. I'm being serious. What do I do now?"

Hearing a chair slide against the floor, I imagined Josh was taking a seat. "What does your heart tell you to do, Nate?"

I pulled the phone out, stared at it, then put it back against my ear. "My heart? What the fuck kind of question is that, Josh? Do I come to work? Do I ask if she wants to have dinner tonight? Should I spend the day with her? I have never done this before."

"First of all, you're overthinking all of this, Nate. Calm the hell down. Ask yourself one question. Do you want to leave, or do you want to spend the day with her?"

"I have to come to work, and she's got to do her dog walking thing today. She doesn't normally do Sunday, but since it's a holiday week, she offered her clients Sunday morning."

He let out a soft chuckle. "You don't have to come to work; it's Sunday. If it were me, I'd spend the day with her. See what she does and why she is so passionate about it."

"Go dog walking with her?"

"That's just a small part of her day. Listen, you have the luxury of taking a day off, so do it. Spend it with her."

I used the tongs to flip the bacon.

"Do you think she'll want me to spend the day with her?"

"Yes, I do, Nate. And I'm glad you stayed this morning and didn't bolt."

"I wasn't going to bolt."

He didn't say anything for a second, but I could silently hear him asking me if I was being truthful.

"I truly wasn't going to leave, Josh. I've never felt like this before, and if I'm being honest, I don't want this day to end."

He chuckled. "Then enjoy the day with her. We don't need you here today. As a matter of fact, I think we're all going to be heading home."

I nodded, even though he couldn't see me. "You're right. Good advice. Thanks, Josh."

"No problem, and, Nate?"

"Yeah?"

"I'm happy you finally admitted your feelings for Haven."

Smiling, I replied, "So am I."

After hanging up with my cousin, I got to work on breakfast. I had no idea what time Haven had to leave, and I was pretty sure after our little fuck fest in the kitchen, she was running behind.

"That smells good," Haven said as she walked into the kitchen dressed in jeans and a blue, long-sleeve shirt.

"I wasn't sure how you liked your eggs, so I fried them. I hope that was okay."

She reached for a piece of bacon and popped it into her mouth. "Yes! I love fried eggs."

Opening a cabinet, she took out two plates and set them on the counter.

"Orange juice?"

"Sure," I replied, taking the toast out and putting two pieces on each plate.

"Here is some butter. Do you want jelly or honey?"

"Honey?" I asked as I took the butter from her offered hand.

Stopping, she stared at me. "You've never put honey on toast?"

"Can't say that I have. I'm not much of a honey fan."

Her eyes went wide. "You don't like honey?"

Shrugging, I replied, "I don't think I've ever had it. At least, not that I can remember."

Her mouth dropped open before she poured the juice into each glass. "Next time, I'm making biscuits, and we will have honey on them."

Next time.

The way that made my damn chest flutter. I watched as Haven piled on the eggs and bacon and slathered jelly all over her toast. I couldn't help but smile. The girl had a healthy appetite.

She was so relaxed and herself, which was odd to me. Most women always put on some kind of show; they are never just themselves. They ate like rabbits and seemed to act the way that they thought I wanted them to act. It drove me insane. It was nice to be with someone who was one-hundred percent herself.

We sat down at her small table and ate in comfortable silence for the first few minutes.

"What time is your first outing?" I asked after setting my orange juice down.

"I pick up the morning crew at ten. Unless it's summer. We try to get out early before it gets too hot."

Nodding, I looked around for a clock.

"It's eight forty."

"So, ummm, I don't have any plans today and I was wondering if you would mind if I went with you today?"

Her fork paused at her mouth. "Really? You'd want to go?"

"Yeah. I'd love to see how you do this. I heard you walk dogs simultaneously, and I always wondered how you did it."

The smile that appeared on her face warmed my entire body. I loved when she smiled big enough that her dimples appeared.

"I would love it if you came. Do you need to go home and change? I assume you don't carry sneakers or hiking boots in your truck."

I winked. "You assume wrong. I always have a change of clothes in my truck. If anything happens and I have to change. Plus, I always carry workout clothes. I have sneakers, but no hiking boots. Will that be a problem?"

She shook her head. "Not a problem at all. You can see what your generous donation helped with."

Smiling, I got back to eating breakfast. We cleaned the kitchen, and I ran to my truck to get my bag. Once changed, I returned to the living room to see Haven frowning at something on her computer.

"What's wrong?"

Glancing up, she let out a breath. "This estimate the contractor sent over. It's much higher than what he originally said in the beginning. The loan we're approved for is at the highest we can get, and he is coming in much higher than he said. I think we have to put a pause on starting until I can find a contractor who isn't going to charge us a fortune."

"Have you signed a contract with him yet?"

She shook her head and suddenly seemed weary. "No, we're still trying to get everything squared away with the business loan. We're approved, but they needed to get all the information from the contractor, and now he's gone and changed everything up on me."

"May I?" I asked as I motioned to her laptop.

Turning it my way, she replied, "It's all yours."

I sat down and started reading it over as Haven stood and paced. I glanced up a few times only to see her wringing her hands as she wore a trail into the wood floor.

"I think you need to go with another contractor," I finally said.

She stopped walking and looked at me. "What did you see?"

"A lot of bullshit talk. This guy is stupid if he doesn't think you'd have someone else read over this."

Exhaling, she dropped to the loveseat. "That's why he was so cheap in the first place. I guess he figures he is a shoe-in, and we'll just take the higher costs."

My hand rubbed at the back of my neck at a sudden ache. Should I stay out of it? No, I was in this for the long haul, which meant helping Haven however I could.

"I know someone. A contractor."

Her head popped up. "You do?"

"Yeah. One of our ranch hands, his name is Solo; his father owns a construction company. He's done several things for us at the ranch, including building my cousin Beck and Avery's house. He remodeled the main barn a few years back and also built my house."

She let out a little bubble of laughter. "You should have led with that. Your house is beautiful."

I felt my cheeks heat. "I can arrange a meeting if you'd like."

Haven jumped up, causing me to quickly stand as well. She threw herself into my arms. "Thank you, Nate! I would love that."

Drawing back, I smiled down at her. I loved that I had made that sparkle in her eyes and those two dimples appear once again. "I'll give him a call now before we leave."

◆ ◆ ◆

We walked up to a blue bus with the words, The Waggin, painted on it in white.

"The Waggin?" I asked as I looked at Haven. She winked, and if I didn't know better, I would have sworn wild horses took off in my chest.

"Okay, so we go to each house, pick up the dogs, then head up to the trail."

She climbed into the driver's seat. "Chad will sometimes help me, especially if I have a full load. This morning is a light load, though."

"What do you need me to do?"

With that big, dimpled smile, she replied, "I'll show you on the first one how to strap them in. After that, each dog will jump into his or her seat and you can buckle them in. Once that is done, just enjoy the dogs."

After getting on the bus, Haven started it. She pulled out a printed-out paper on a clipboard, looked it over, and then we were on our way.

"First up is Monty, a black lab and a total sweetheart."

I looked out the front window as we pulled up to a house. A black lab was sitting on the sidewalk, his owner on the porch. Once Haven came to a stop, she opened the bus doors, and Monty came charging in. He stopped when he saw me, gave me a sniff, headed to a seat, and jumped up into it. Haven clipped on the dog seat belt to Monty's harness, and we were on our way to get the next dog.

"They really know which seat is theirs?" I asked, glancing back at Monty, who I swore was smiling at me.

"Yes! They all know where to sit once they get onto the bus."

We drove to five more houses and picked up Piper, a German shorthair pointer that sat beside me. Lucy was a mixed-breed dog that only had eyes for Monty. Next up was Nelly, a golden retriever who I swore was the happiest dog I had ever met. Lou, a small terrier-type dog, sat beside Nelly and completely ignored me. The last dog we picked up was Ralph. A German shepherd that was a retired bomb dog. According to Haven, Ralph was always on duty, and I shouldn't be surprised if he started trailing something. My job was to get Ralph back into relaxed mode.

"Ralph? That's really his name?" I asked as we pulled up to the parking lot of a trailhead. "Just doesn't seem like a tough bomb dog name."

Ralph barked, and Haven laughed. "I think you better take that back."

Holding up my hands, I stood and faced Ralph. "I think your name is tough, boy. Just like you."

He barked again, and if I hadn't been looking, I would have missed the wink.

"Did he just wink at me?"

Haven laughed once again, and I couldn't deny the way it made my stomach flip as if I were on a ride. I had totally made the right decision by spending the day with her.

"Normally, I take them off the bus in groups, but since you're here and we have a smaller group today, you can help."

"I'm at your service."

Once we got all six dogs off the bus, I watched Haven put on a vest with carabiners attached. She then put each dog's leash on a carabiner, and we started to walk to the trail.

"Um, you know I could hold a couple of them."

She smiled. "I do this every day, sometimes with twelve dogs."

"How do they not drag you along the path?"

Haven chuckled. "They're very well-behaved dogs. Chad has trained a few of them. He's a great trainer. I can't wait for you to meet him."

I wanted to roll my eyes but stopped myself. Clearly, Haven thought of this guy as a co-worker, and I needed to stow away my jealousy.

"I'm going to let them all off. They'll do their business, and then we can head on."

"Do their business?" I asked as I watched her tell each dog to stay while she unleashed them. Once they were all off the leashes, she said the word break, and they all took off. I was impressed by how they stayed close to her.

"Go potty."

She took the vest off, stuffed it into her backpack, and started taking out little blue bags. "It's poop duty time."

I stood there and watched all six dogs go to the bathroom, and Haven got all of it. She put all six bags at the trailhead. "We'll grab these on the way out and throw them away. Ready?"

I nodded, impressed with how organized it all was.

Taking out a long whistle, she called the dogs. "Let's go!"

The five took off down the trail, with Haven and me following them.

"How long is the walk?" I asked.

"Forty-five minutes. We reach a point where they can get in the water and play. They loved it this past summer, but now that the temperatures are cooler, they tend to just get drinks."

"What if someone comes on the trail? What do you do?"

"Recall them all."

"And if that person has a dog?"

"Depends. Some dogs will just come running in, greet each other, and we keep moving. I've learned to read people. If someone appears to be afraid of dogs, I recall them to a spot off the trail, and we let them go by."

"Have you ever had a dog not listen to you?"

Haven laughed. "More than once. You get to learn the dogs as well. I had a young golden once that had to keep on a leash because if she saw a person, she would run and jump all over them. She spent more time on a leash than I would have liked. She didn't do well in this type of setting, so I would usually go and pick her up early in the morning and take her to a park and play with her."

"Why didn't the owners?"

"Oh, they would walk her and such, but she needed a good run around in the mornings, so she got some energy out. Her mom works from home, so it helped her out as well."

We walked silently before she said, "Your donation paid off the bus and the business credit card, by the way. And the rest went into the account for a rainy day. That was what Sophia had suggested we do with it. I want to thank you again, Nate. You have no idea what a stress relief it is to have those paid off."

"I'm glad it helped."

We continued to walk for a bit before I said, "I want to help in whatever way I can, even if it's coming out here and helping you walk dogs."

Haven stopped walking and faced me. "I hope you know that I'm not with you because…"

I put my finger to her lips. "That never crossed my mind, Haven."

Leaning down, I gently kissed her, but was interrupted by a dog squeezing between us. Looking down, I laughed when I saw Ralph.

"Sorry, dude, was I moving in on your girl?"

Ralph barked.

"I swear that dog knows what I'm saying."

After hiking up to the lake and back, gathering up the poop bags, which I would have never seen myself doing before today, and getting everyone back on the bus and to their homes, we headed into town for lunch. And I was pretty damn sure nothing could break the smile that had been on my face all morning.

Chapter Eleven

Haven

Nate and I had decided pizza sounded good. After ordering, he asked me about the Waggin' bus and how I had come up with the vest I used to walk the dogs.

"Well, before I got the bus, I needed to devise an easy way to walk them. Holding all those leashes in my hands wasn't working. So, I came up with the vest idea after seeing someone else on social media doing something similar."

He slowly shook his head. "It's a brilliant idea, Haven."

"Thank you, but it wasn't my original idea. I saw a girl on Instagram who used one, and I took the idea from her. She also gave me the idea for the bus. She was my inspiration for it all. She lives up in Alaska."

"Oh, wow."

I grinned. "I know!"

Our pepperoni pizza came out, and Nate rubbed his hands together. "Man, who would have thought walking those dogs would work up such an appetite!"

We both got our pizza and began eating when Nate's phone buzzed on the table. He picked it up. "It's Doug, Solo's dad. Excuse me."

I watched as he answered the call and walked outside. One glance around the restaurant showed no one was paying us any attention. My own phone buzzed, and when I looked at it, I saw it was Rosie.

Rosie: Did Nate show up at your place last night?

Me: Yes, he did. That was a dirty trick to play on him!

I could see the three dots appear and had to press my lips together tightly to keep from laughing.

Rosie: That's it? Girl...I don't think so. What happened? Did you let him in? Did you talk?

Resisting the urge to giggle, I quickly checked to see if Nate was coming back before replying.

Me: We talked, among other things.

Rosie replied instantly.

Rosie: SHUT UP! Call me.

Me: I can't right now. I'm at lunch with Nate, and he excused himself for a call.

Rosie: He's with you?

Me: He's been with me since last night. He joined me on a walk this morning. We're at lunch now.

Rosie: I can't even right now. My mind is all over the place. Are you...dating?

Chewing on my lip, I wasn't sure how to answer that. We had slept together. Twice. He had spent the morning, and now afternoon, with me, but did that mean something more to him?

Me: Got to go. Talk soon.

I knew Rosie would be upset I had ignored her question, but it was one I wasn't sure how to answer.

Rosie: That is not cool. Not cool at all. I'll be waiting for your call.

"Sorry about that," Nate said, causing me to jump and quickly turn my phone over and set it on the table. "That was Solo's dad, Doug, calling me back. He'd like to meet with you today if that's possible."

"Today?"

He nodded and picked up his pizza. "Maybe drive by the site so he can look at it."

"Yes, yes, that's perfect. Can we swing by my apartment and pick up the plans for the dog park?"

"That's a great idea. That way he has a visual of how your current design is so he can quote it apples to apples with the other quote."

Nate took a bite of his pizza and smiled at me. Did he have any idea how much this meant to me? I wasn't sure if things would work out with Doug, but it was nice to know I had other options. I'd also have to talk to Sophia about it and see if she could meet us.

"I sent a text to Sophia as well to let her know," Nate stated as if reading my mind. "I figured you would want her there as well."

I let out a soft laugh. "I was just thinking I needed to let her know. Thank you for that."

"How's the pizza?" he asked, wiping his mouth and reaching for his Coke.

Glancing down at the barely eaten slice of pizza on my plate, I picked it up. "It's delicious, as always. This is my favorite place to get pizza in Hamilton."

"It is mine too. What are your plans for Thanksgiving? Do you and your mom do anything?"

"Nothing big. It's usually just me and my mom. Um, this year, she'll just come over to my apartment, and I'll make a little Cornish hen or something. She got a promotion at work, so that is good. The extra money is helping her a lot. My father left her with all the bills, and she has slowly been paying off the debt. Plus, the divorce lawyer she hired and had to pay for."

"So, she did divorce him?"

I nodded.

Nate cleared his throat. "Haven, did you ever tell your mother what your father had been doing to you?"

I chewed on my lower lip and looked around.

"We don't have to talk about it here, or at all."

"It's okay. I did tell her. She needed to know the truth. She was sick, literally sick to her stomach and blamed herself of course. I told her about the day you showed up and stopped him from…"

I let my voice trail off.

Nate reached for my hand. "Have you spoken to anyone? A therapist?"

Smiling softly, I replied, "Yes. I have and it's helped me so much."

He closed his eyes and let out a breath. "I wanted to kill him, Haven. And I am so sorry you ever thought I pushed you away because of that. I need you to know that, sweetheart."

"Oh, Nate, I do know that…now. And thank you for never telling anyone."

His eyes went wide. "I would never betray your trust like that, Haven. Never."

I let go of his hand and picked up my pizza. "What about you? What's the plan for Turkey Day?"

"Since my grandfather passed away a few months ago, we try to do everything at my Grams's. Thanksgiving will be there this year with the entire Shaw gang plus the Littlewoods."

"That sounds lovely."

"Why don't you and your mother come to Thanksgiving at the ranch?"

I was pretty sure my eyes went as wide as saucers. "Oh, no, we couldn't intrude like that."

"What do you mean? Your mother and my mother are friends. Besides, with this being the first holiday since Granddad is gone, I know Grams would love to have as many people there as possible."

"It's at her house you said?"

"Yes, she insisted on hosting. Said it would keep her mind busy."

Glancing at the table, I said, "I can't imagine how it is for your grandmother to lose her husband so suddenly. Especially after being married that long."

"She's a tough cookie. Why don't you talk it over with your mom and see if she'd like to come?"

I nodded. "I will. Thank you for the invitation. That was sweet of you."

Nate reached across the table and took my hand in his. "Haven, once today is over, it's not back to usual for us. I hope you know that."

My heart started to race as I asked, "Are you…are you saying you want to date me?"

He grinned. "Oh, I want to do more to you than simply date you, sweetheart."

My cheeks heated, and I pulled my hands free and placed them on my face to cool down my warm body.

Nate shot me a wicked grin. "I think we should go back to your place now."

I raised a brow. "Really? What for?"

"You need to pack a bag."

Confused, I shook my head. "A bag? For what?"

"I want you to come stay with me at my house. I can help you with the dog walks this week as well. Since it's Thanksgiving week I'll have a few days off."

My eyes blinked a few times. "You want to do that again?"

"Hell, yes, I do. It was fun and good exercise, if I do say so. And if I'm being honest, I want to spend as much time with you as possible."

Chewing on my lower lip, I debated whether it was a good idea. I wanted to spend more time with Nate and learn more about him and his family. And I wanted the same for him: to learn more about me, the job I loved, and what my future held. Were we moving too fast, though? I nearly laughed. I had been in love with this man for as long as I could remember, and he was asking me to stay with him at his beautiful home. He also told me that he loved me. I'd be crazy if I said no.

"Okay, I would love to come and stay with you."

A brilliant smile lit up his face. "And you'll talk to your mom about Thanksgiving?"

"Should you ask Stella first?"

Nate laughed. "Grams will say the more the merrier."

I nodded. "I'll talk to her later today about it."

Leaning back in his chair, he looked at the pizza. "Should we take it to go?"

"Cold pizza and a movie sounds like a grand plan."

Nate winked. "I like that plan too."

◆ ◆ ◆

"This is the perfect spot for this dog park," Doug said as he stood in the middle of the field. "You've already got water and electricity here, so that's an expense you won't have to take on."

Sophia and I followed Doug as he looked at the plans and the plot of land donated for the dog park. We wouldn't own it, but the owners gave us a ninety-nine-year lease.

He nodded. "This would be a great project for us and a wonderful way to give back to this community that has been there for me for many years."

We both smiled at Doug.

Sophia cleared her throat. "I can get you a copy of the plans so you can work up a bid. Once we have decided on a contractor, the bank will contact them, and all withdraws will be made to you...or um…them."

Doug looked up from the plans he was studying. "That's fine. For my portion, I'd like to do it pro bono. So, the only costs will come from my subcontractors that I use if I don't have someone in-house to do the work. I have a few on my payroll, like the electrician I'll use for this project. That fee will be pro bono as well as the plumbing."

I shook my head a little and leaned closer to Doug. "I'm sorry, what did you just say?"

About that time, Nate walked up and put his arm around my waist, causing a shiver to run down my spine. This connection we had found within the last twenty-four hours was still new to me, but I wasn't about to complain.

"How's it going?" he asked, looking around at us.

"Well," Sophia started. "Doug just dropped a huge bomb, and I think Haven and I are trying to figure out if we heard him correctly."

Doug laughed. "I try to find a project each year that I call my passion project. A way to give back."

I felt myself lean toward Nate. *Was this really happening?* That would save us thousands upon thousands of dollars that we could put back into the dog park for things we didn't think we would be able to do right away.

My mind raced in a million different directions. "What exactly does it mean when you say you'll do it pro bono? Do we just not pay for your services, but you'll oversee the construction, and we still pay the subcontractors?"

Doug smiled at me. "Yes, that pretty much sums it up. The in-house contractors I use, though, you will not have to pay for."

I slowly shook my head. "That's too much to ask you to do."

Nate and Doug exchanged looks before Doug cleared his throat. "I'm not taking a loss, Haven, if you're worried about that. I have a fund set up where I, as well as other members of our community, donate money, their time, and skills, as well as materials, so that I can do projects like this and return it to the community that helped me to get to the point in my career that I can offer pro bono projects. It's like a giant circle of a wonderful community."

I stifled the urge to jump and scream like a crazy person. "If you do this pro bono, we can make the membership cheaper." Turning to Sophia, I said, "We can also open it to the public, maybe a few days a month for free so everyone can enjoy the park!"

Sophia grinned. "That would be amazing. Everyone could get the chance to enjoy the dog park, not just those willing to pay for a pass."

Tears gathered in my eyes, and I had to quickly excuse myself and walk away from the small group. I could hear Sophia asking Doug questions as I walked toward the area that would be for the large dogs.

I felt Nate before he said a word.

"Are you okay?"

With a jerky head bob, I wiped the tears away. "I can't help but wonder if I'm dreaming. I never in my life imagined all of this would happen. It almost seems…too good to be true."

Nate placed his hands on my shoulders and turned me to face him as I asked, "Did you do this?"

He laughed and shook his head. "No, but I knew Doug did pro bono projects in the community, and I also happened to know he is a huge dog lover. He has six of them."

"Six?" I asked, half laughing, half sobbing. "I'll have to allocate just one day for him to bring his dogs to play by themselves. I'll call it Doug's Doggie Day. Nate…do I deserve this?"

His eyes went wide. "What do you mean? Of course you do, Haven."

Wrapping my arms around my body, I turned away and stared at the mountains in the distance. "When I first thought of doing a dog park, the membership idea was necessary. If I got the loan, I would need a way to repay it, so what better way to help than offer memberships? But that little girl inside of me, the one who used to watch her mother and father count out how much money they had for the grocery store, felt like a traitor to the people struggling to make ends meet. If they couldn't afford the membership for their dogs, they would be left out."

I turned to face him. "Do you know how many times I felt left out growing up? I wanted to go to camp like all my friends, but we couldn't afford it. I wanted to cheer, but my parents couldn't afford the uniforms. I couldn't even play sports because it was hard enough to buy shoes to wear to school, let alone shoes to play soccer in."

A look of pain washed over his face, and I shook my head. "Don't feel sorry for me, Nate. I didn't say that for you to look at me with pity."

He took my hands in his. "Haven, the last thing I do is pity you. You're one of the most amazingly strong and independent women I have ever met. I love that your heart is pure and kind and that you even thought about those less fortunate when planning the dog park."

I chewed on my lip. "It feels like everything has slid into place so easily, which isn't how my life goes. It's crazy and chaotic, and I'm always trying to figure out ways to make ends meet, yet still be able to grow. The whole rob Peter to pay Paul thing. Then Sophia came into my life, then you and I found one another in a way I had only dreamed about. All my dreams are coming true, and I'm…"

My voice trailed off as a frog formed in my throat.

"You're what?" Nate asked.

Lifting my head, our eyes met. "I'm scared the floor will be pulled out from under me, and I'll lose it all. I'll lose you."

Squeezing my hands, he bent down and slowly shook his head. "You're not going to lose me or anything else, Haven. And as far as you not being deserving of any of this, that is plain bullshit. You've worked hard; everything you accomplished is because of that hard work. Just take a deep breath and do what everyone else around you are doing."

Smiling softly, I asked, "What's that?"

He placed his finger on my chin and tilted my head up more. Leaning down, he brushed his lips across mine before he whispered, "Believe in yourself."

Chapter Twelve

Nathan

Haven's eyes started to fill with tears before she blinked them back and softly said, "Pinch me."

Grinning, I looked over to where Sophia and Doug were standing and going over the plans. Meeting her gaze once again, I said, "I think we should save that for later in the bedroom."

Haven laughed. "Thank you for making me see I was having a pity party for one."

"You were not, Haven. You were expressing your feelings, and nothing is wrong with that. I want you to always feel like you can be honest with me."

She bit into her lower lip and shook her head. "Nate Shaw, you may just be the most perfect man in the world."

I scoffed. "Hardly perfect. But I am behind you a hundred percent. I want to see your dreams come true, Haven."

She drew in a deep breath and slowly let it out. "I'm so glad my tire was flat that night."

Drawing her into my arms, I held her tightly as I kissed the top of her head. "So am I. So. Am. I."

Glancing back over to Sophia and Doug, she cleared her throat. "We should get back over there."

"The sooner we get Doug on board, the sooner we can get this project going."

Lacing her fingers in mine, we returned to Doug and Sophia.

"Okay, what's the next step?" Haven asked in a voice that was filled with hope and excitement. Sophia and I exchanged a smile as Doug launched into the steps that needed to be taken next.

My heart felt full with something I had never experienced before as I watched Haven contain the happiness that was clearly about to spill over.

Sophia took my arm and held me back as we all started to walk toward our vehicles.

"Nate, I just wanted to say that I'm so happy the two of you finally found your way to each other. Thank you for believing in her dreams."

I smiled at my future sister-in-law. "I can't explain it, Sophia, but I want to see her happy. I *need* to see her happy."

A wide grin appeared on her face, and she patted me lightly on the chest. "That, Nate, is your heart falling in love."

Sophia started to walk off, and I couldn't help but smile. Six months ago, if someone had told me that, I would have laughed my ass off.

"Looks like Josh is smarter than I thought."

◆ ◆ ◆

"You invited a girl for Thanksgiving?" my sister Lily asked as she held her daughter Maggie while we stood in our parents' kitchen for a family dinner night.

Glancing around the kitchen, I shot my sister a warning look. "Do we have to talk about this now?"

She laughed. "Um, yes. Nate, you've never seriously dated anyone. Who is it?"

I turned to face my sister. "How do you even know?"

Her eyes lit up. "So it's true! Who is it?"

"How did you know?"

Lily rolled her eyes. "Avery."

My mouth fell open. "How did Avery know?"

With a half-shrug, Lily set Maggie down, who then ran over to our mother when she walked into the kitchen.

"How did Avery know what?" Mom asked, looking between me and Lily.

"That Nate is dating someone and asked them to come over for Thanksgiving."

I elbowed Lily in the side.

"Hey, that hurt, you butt munch!"

"Butt munch?" I asked with a laugh. "Seriously, Lily, is that all you've got?"

"The both of you stop it. You sound like toddlers."

At that moment, Maggie cried out, "Butt munch!"

Our mom looked at her granddaughter and then back to us. "See? Are you happy now? You taught your daughter something new, Lily."

Lily giggled, then quickly stopped when our mother shot her the look. The one that all moms have to warn you to stop while you're ahead.

With a sigh, Lily leaned against the kitchen counter. "She'll forget it in an hour."

"We'll see," Mom stated, giving Maggie a piece of banana nut bread and telling her to go find her granddad.

Once Maggie was out of the kitchen, my mother focused all her attention on me. "Who did you invite for Thanksgiving?"

I shot Lily another dirty look to which she simply smiled and folded her arms over her chest as she waited for me to answer.

"She hasn't told me if she is coming yet. It would be her and her mother."

That intrigued both women in the room. I inwardly cursed myself. Less is better with my sister and mother.

"Do I know her?" Lily asked.

"Yes," I replied, taking the garlic bread my mother left me in charge of out of the oven.

"Do I know her?" Mom asked.

Sighing, I replied, "Yes, you're friends with her mother, so I hope you can convince them to come."

"Nate! Who is it?" Lily said as she grabbed my arm and shook it.

I wouldn't win this battle, and everyone would find out sooner or later. I was honestly surprised they didn't know already. My parents had friends everywhere in this town, and somehow my sister was always in the know.

After I took off the oven mitts and set them down, I turned to face them both. "It's Haven."

For a few seconds, neither of them said or did a thing. They simply stared at me. My mother was the first to break the silence.

"Well, it's about damn time!"

Lily jumped and clapped her hands. "Finally! Holy crap, Nate. It took you long enough to open your eyes."

I was pretty sure my mouth was on the ground. "What do you mean, *finally*?"

Lily laughed. "Haven has liked you for as long as I can remember. You finally noticed her."

Frowning, I replied, "I've always noticed her."

Lily folded her arms over her chest. "Have you really? Was that before or during all the times that you treated her like crap?"

"What?" my mother asked horrified.

"I did not treat her like crap."

With another roll of her eyes, Lily said, "Please. You have. You've done everything you could to push her away."

"Nathan Christopher Shaw! Is that true?"

If someone were keeping track of how many looks I shot my sister in the last ten minutes, they would be well over ten by now, surely.

"It's complicated, Mom."

It was her turn to cross her arms. "Explain it to me, I'm an intelligent woman, and I'm sure I can understand it."

"Isn't everything ready for dinner?" I stated, motioning toward the food on the kitchen island.

"Oh, no," my mother said as she slowly shook her head. "You're not getting away that easily."

"Can we at least sit down and eat, and then I'll tell you?"

My mother turned to look at Lily for approval. Lily nodded, followed by my mother. "Fine. Let's take the food out to the table, Nate. Lily, gather up your husband and daughter. Wherever they are, your father will also be."

Lily dashed out of the kitchen, yelling for Maverick and our father. My mother sighed. "Well, I could have done that."

My mother cleared her throat once we had everything on the table and everyone had food on their plates.

"Nate has something he would like to share with the family."

My father looked up. "Really? What about?"

"Haven Larson," Lily blurted out before I could even take a breath.

"Don't you have to feed your child or something?" I said as I looked over to see Maverick cutting up the lasagna for Maggie, who was shoveling it into her mouth with her little fork as fast as she could.

"Mav has it covered," Lily stated with a shit-eating grin.

"Hasn't that young lady had a crush on you since middle school?" Dad asked before taking a bite of his food.

"Yes, she has," Lily stated as if she would remember anything from when I was in middle school.

Before I could utter a word, Lily added, "And Nate has done everything he could to push her away."

"Thank you, Lily, for adding your two cents…again," I stated dryly.

"What did you do to the poor girl?" my mother asked.

"I wasn't trying to be mean to her, but keeping her at a distance was easier."

Maverick looked up at me. "The old '*if I don't have to see her, I won't be reminded of how I feel about her'* trick."

All eyes turned to him. He shrugged. "I felt that way about Lily."

Lily smiled and reached across the table to take his hand. "I love you."

He returned her smile with a wide grin. "I love you more."

"Ugh, seriously?" I said as I shoved a piece of garlic bread into my mouth.

My father laughed. "It's hard sometimes to listen to your heart. Especially when you feel something for someone you've never felt before. It's scary."

Everyone at the table nodded. Maggie joined in when she saw everyone else doing it, and I nearly started to laugh.

"Yes, a part of me was afraid of my feelings for Haven. Happy now, Lily? But there was more to the story."

"Like what?" Lily asked.

I looked around at the four of them; correction, five since Maggie was looking at me as well. "Something in Haven's past hurt her badly and I was afraid that I would hurt her too. Don't ask me why, I just thought it would be better to be friends. But every time I was near her…I felt something more than friendship. So it was always easier to stay away."

This time, it was my father who stated, "Yes, the old '*I'd rather keep them as friends'* logic."

Turning to my father, I asked, "Did you do that to Mom?"

My mother and father exchanged a look before Dad focused on me. "I will admit I was afraid of my feelings for your mother only because I had never felt like that before her. It can be a very powerful emotion. I think it's that fear of rejection or ruining something that keeps them somewhat close to you that you don't want to risk. But you can't have them too close, or then your feelings get muddled."

Maverick nodded in agreement. "Then you think about how you're not good enough for them, and that plays with your head."

I slowly nodded. I had felt all of those things when it came to Haven.

"But the idea of them with someone else nearly drives you mad," I softly said.

My father and Maverick both said, "Yes."

"I will never understand men," my mother stated before drinking her water. "Never."

"Same," Lily agreed with a smile in her daughter's direction.

"What made you decide that it was worth giving a relationship a shot, Nate?"

"I couldn't fight my feelings for her anymore. The bad part of it all is that Haven thought what happened to her in her past was the reason I was pushing her away. That was the worst part."

Lily wore a concerned expression. "What happened to her, Nate?"

All eyes were back on me. I cleared my throat. "It's not my story to tell."

My mother set her fork down. "Does it have something to do with her father?"

"Her father?" my dad asked.

"Mom, I made Haven a promise."

She gave me a soft smile. "I understand."

"The question I want to ask is are you dating her?"

I couldn't help the smile on my face. "Yes."

My mother and Lily both grinned from ear to ear.

"How is it going?" Mom asked.

Glancing down at my plate, I fought to keep my giddiness in check. "It's going amazing so far. It's only been a few days since it was official. Last weekend, to be exact."

Everyone at the table exchanged looks as I went on. "She's an incredible woman with dreams and passions like no one I've ever met. She takes pride in everything she does, from walking dogs to helping less fortunate people; even if she struggles herself, she puts everyone else first."

"Her mother, Grace, is the same way. She always does what she can for the community."

"How long have you known Grace?" I asked.

My mother thought for a moment. "Let's see. Maybe since you kids were in elementary school."

I nodded. "This, of course, stays between us here at the table, but Haven mentioned times were tight for her mom."

Mom cleared her throat. "I know Grace is very private, but times have been tough on and off for years. Especially after that low-life husband of hers up and left her. Grace wanted to stay at home with Haven for as long as she could, which put a strain on the family, but it was important to Grace to be there for as long as she could. Grace works for a dental office and was recently promoted to office manager. I hope the promotion will help ease some of her burdens."

Maverick cleared his throat. "Beck was telling me that Blayze was talking about hiring an assistant for the ranch. Someone to help with all of the bookkeeping, since Stella and Lincoln are both ready to step away from that. Scheduling, doing the payroll, and all of that. I would hazard a guess they would pay more than a dental office."

"Do you think Grace would be interested?" Lily asked my mother.

She shrugged. "I guess it would depend. I'm sure she could handle anything that is thrown at her. The last I knew she didn't have health insurance, but that might have changed with the promotion."

"If she worked for the ranch, she'd have health insurance," I quickly said.

"It would be an opportunity that I think should be presented to Grace."

I nodded. "If they come to Thanksgiving dinner, maybe you can bring it up."

Dad nodded. "I'll talk to Blayze and get all the information for what they're looking for."

Turning to my mother, she smiled. "If Haven and Grace decide to join us, then I will for sure speak to Grace."

My heart felt so full of love for my mother and father that I had to clear my throat. "Thank you both."

Reaching for my hand, my mother squeezed it. "No need to thank us, Nate. We'll do whatever we can to help. I adore Grace and Haven."

The conversation thankfully moved on to a new stallion that was being delivered, and then on to winterizing the ranch. I tried to keep up with it by nodding every now and then and trying to be part of the conversation, but the only thing I could think about was when I would be able to see Haven again.

Chapter Thirteen

Haven

I walked into my mom's kitchen and drew in a deep breath. Something smelled heavenly as I removed my light jacket and placed it on the hook by the door. Late November in Hamilton saw temperatures in the mid to lower fifties. It wouldn't be long before I broke out my full winter gear.

"Mom?"

My mother walked into the room wearing an apron. It took everything I had not to start laughing.

"Hey, sweetheart," she said with a huge smile before kissing me on the cheek. "What brings you by?"

"I was in the area and thought I would stop by. I have some news about the dog park as well."

She turned on the oven light, bent down, and peered inside.

"What are you making?" I asked.

"Spaghetti casserole."

My brows rose. "Wow, look at you being all Betty Crocker."

"She bakes, sweetheart."

Laughing, I reached for a cup and filled it with water. "Did you get off early?"

She frowned. "Yes. I've been working later each day trying to learn everything, and one of the doctors told me I needed to watch my time."

Leaning against the counter, I said, "Did you ask about insurance now that you're the office manager?"

"They said I have a ninety-day probation period before it will kick in."

"Are you serious? But I thought Jane said once you were promoted, they would offer you insurance."

She reached for my hand and gave it a light squeeze. "Don't get worked up, sweetheart. It will all work out. I've gone this long without insurance, and so have you. You really need to look into that."

After letting my hand go, she turned and walked over to get some plates. "Staying for dinner?"

"Of course I'm staying."

"Wonderful. I'm dying to hear about the dog park."

My eyes searched my mother's face, and for the first time I noticed how tired she looked. "Mom, are you okay with bills and everything?"

Her head snapped up sharply. "What?"

I gave a slight shrug. "I just want to make sure you're not struggling. I've got some money–"

Holding up her hand, she said, "Stop. I'm doing fine, and the last thing I would ever do is take money from my daughter who is about to embark on a huge dream of her own. You'll need all the money you saved up, young lady. The last thing I want to see is you get in over your head."

"That's one of the reasons I came to see you tonight. I found a new contractor, and he is doing some of the work pro bono."

She paused and looked at me. "What?"

I smiled and nodded. "Yes! He said he likes to pick a project to give back to the community once a year. He contracts out some of the labor, but some of it he does in-house, and he isn't going to charge us for that! Sophia and I are over the moon. This is going to change everything, and we can even offer less for the memberships now and be able to do open days where people can just come and bring their dogs and not have to pay for a day pass or membership."

My mom looked skeptical and folded her arms over her chest. "What have I always told you, Haven? If something is too good to be true, then it is."

"I know you've said that, but, Mom, there are people out there who do things like this." My mind drifted to Nate and his donation. I couldn't help but smile. "Kind hearts and all of that."

"That is a lot of work and time to give away for free."

I nodded. "It is, I agree, and I struggled with accepting it at first, but then Nate and I talked, and he made me realize I deserve this. I deserve to have someone believe in what I'm doing and want to be a part of it."

My mother's face softened. "Of course you do, Haven. I didn't mean that at all."

I waved off her worry. "I know you didn't."

"Wait, did you say Nate? Nate Shaw?"

Nodding, I felt myself smile. "We recently started dating."

"How recent?"

I shrugged. "Last weekend."

Her brows slowly went up. "Really? Why didn't you tell me?"

"Um, we just started dating, Mom."

She smiled. "You used to have the biggest crush on that boy once upon a time."

I wanted to correct my mother and tell her he wasn't a boy in any way, but I decided to keep that to myself.

"Yes, well, we can thank a flat tire for us getting together."

Mom looked confused. "What do you mean?"

I smiled as the memory of that stormy night came back to me. As I told my mother, my entire body felt warm.

"I was leaving the Shaw Ranch one night and got a flat tire. It was the night of that bad storm. Nate came across me broke down and offered to help. The rest is history."

She huffed. "Never thought I would see that boy settle down with one girl. Are you sure you can trust him, Haven?"

I reached for her arm and gave it a light pat. "Yes, Mom. And don't you also say never judge a book by its cover? Nate is an amazing man, and if I told you what he has done for me… well…let's just say I'm the happiest I've ever been. I have to keep pinching myself because it doesn't feel real. I feel like all my dreams are coming true, and honestly, in the short time we have been seeing each other, Nate has been a part of those dreams being able to come true."

She walked over and pulled me to her, hugging me. "No one deserves that more than you, Haven. I am so proud of you."

Once we sat down at the table to eat, I told her about Doug and Nate and all that had happened in the last few days.

"How wonderful that things are turning out as they are, Haven! I know Doug. He's a patient of ours. He did a playground in town for free one year. It turned out beautiful. I'm not the least surprised he would also take on this project. And how amazing you can open it to those who cannot afford the membership. I know having to charge the membership was a hard decision for you to make."

"Thanks, Mom."

Mom looked back at me and smiled. "So, Nate Shaw, huh?"

I felt my cheeks heat. "Yes, Nate Shaw."

"I know you said you just started dating, but how serious is it?" she asked.

I shrugged. "I think it's progressing along nicely."

"I'm so happy for you, sweetheart. I know how much you liked Nate and what he did for you with your father."

A feeling of sadness swept through the air, and I decided it was time to change the direction this conversation was going.

Taking my napkin, I wiped my mouth and set it on the table. "Nate has invited us to Thanksgiving at his grandmother's house tomorrow."

My mother stared at me for a few moments before saying, "He did?"

"Why are you frowning?" I asked.

Mom cleared her throat. "I'm sorry, sweetheart; I didn't mean to frown. I guess I'm just surprised. What made him invite us if you've just started dating?"

"Well, he invited me, and I told him I would most likely be having you over to my apartment. He asked me if you would like to come as well. After all, you are good friends with his mother, Mom."

My mother nodded. "Yes, Timberlynn and I go back many years. Since you kids were in elementary school."

"Mom, there isn't anything behind the invitation. I think Nate simply wants to be with me and he knows family is important."

My mother smiled and said, "I think it's a lovely idea. I'll ask Timberlynn if she wants us to bring anything. Come to think of it, I haven't spoken to her in a couple of months. We need to catch up."

I nearly exploded with happiness while at the same time sighing in relief. "I'm so glad you agreed to go. This means the world to me. I care deeply for Nate, and I know things are new between us, but…well…it means a lot to me that we can all be together on Thanksgiving. I'm sure it will help Stella as well."

"I haven't seen Stella in years. I did send her a card after Ty passed away. I can't imagine what she is going through. My heart hurts for her. For the whole family."

"I still can't believe he's gone. He was such a nice guy."

"That he was. So, are you up for dessert?" Mom asked.

"Wait, you made dessert as well?" I asked with a giggle. "Now I can call you Better Crocker."

Mom stood. "I did, indeed. Lemon bars. You stay here and I'll get them cut up and bring them out."

After setting down a plate of lemon bars and handing me a small plate, Mom smiled and asked, "How is the sex?"

"Mom!"

"What?" she asked, all innocent. "It's a valid question."

"Maybe from my best friend, but not my mother!"

She gave a one-shoulder shrug. "I've seen those Shaw men. I'm going to assume it's good. Otherwise, your face wouldn't be so red."

"My face is red because my mother just…" I lowered my voice. "…asked me how the sex was with my boyfriend."

She winked. "Gotcha."

"No, I don't think you do!"

"I was a girl your age once, I get it. I hope he pleasures you first. It's important that you have a lover who doesn't just think of himself."

Dropping back in my chair, I stared at my mother. "Please tell me you're not going to tell me about your past lovers."

She laughed. "I wouldn't do that to you, darling. But, when I was your age–"

I quickly stood. "No. Just no! I'm going to do the dishes."

The rest of the time was spent with my mother helping her clean up while she told me about her new job promotion, and how she was slowly learning everything. I watched as she spoke and wondered if she ever got lonely. She'd gone out a few times since the divorce, but nothing serious. I suddenly had the urge to see Nate. I took my phone out and sent him a text.

Me: I'm having dinner at my mom's house. She said yes to Thanksgiving. I'm going to be heading home soon.

It didn't take Nate long to reply.

Nate: I'm so glad she said yes! I'll let Grams and my mother know. Leaving the ranch now and heading home. Why don't you come here instead?

Smiling, I peeked up to see my mother reading something on her phone.

Me: I'll swing by and pack a bag. I'll text you once I'm on the way to your house.

Nate: Perfect. Be careful driving. See you soon.

I set my phone on the table and gathered the dessert plates. Mom stopped me. "No, leave those, Haven."

"Mom, you cooked. Let me clean up all the way for you."

She sat as I finished up the last few dishes.

"Timberlynn texted and asked if I was planning on coming for Thanksgiving."

I glanced at her over my shoulder. "And did you tell her yes?"

She smiled. "I did. I asked if we could bring something, and she said no. Then texted back and said to bring sneakers and dress comfortable."

I looked at her and frowned. "What?"

With a nod, she looked back at her phone. "What in the world do they do on Thanksgiving?"

Shrugging, I folded the dish towel and set it on the counter. "I guess we'll find out tomorrow!"

◆ ◆ ◆

Before I got out of my car, Nate appeared on the front porch of his house. The smile on his face made my stomach flip with anticipation. I quickly grabbed my purse and bag and got out of the car.

"Want to park in the garage?"

I glanced at my old car. "I think it will be okay."

Nate met me halfway and took my bag before leaning down and kissing me.

"I missed you."

"It's only been a day since I saw you."

He smiled again, and my stomach felt like butterflies were in there. "I know, it's crazy. I never in my life imagined I'd be feeling this way."

Pulling me into his arms, he kissed me again.

"Well, if this is how you act when we're apart for a day, what would it be like longer?"

Nate laughed, took my hand, and led me to the front door. "Let's not find out."

Once inside, Nate helped me with my jacket and hung it up. "Did you bring a heavier coat? It's supposed to snow tonight."

"No, I need to unpack all of my winter clothes."

After taking my bag and bringing it to his room, Nate met me in the kitchen where I was peeking at the soup he had on the stove.

"What are you making?"

"Beef stew, my mom's recipe."

I drew in a deep breath and moaned. "That smells heavenly."

Nate winked at me, and my heart jumped in my chest. "I was about to put the rolls in the oven."

"Is there anything I can do?" I asked as I looked around the kitchen.

"You can go get into something comfortable. I know you already ate, but after I eat, I thought maybe we could watch a movie."

"You're sure you don't need help?"

Nate shook his head. "I'll let you pick out the movie."

"Are you sure about that?"

He shut the oven door and turned to face me. "You're going to pick out a romance movie, right?"

I felt my cheeks heat. "I was thinking Hallmark. All the Christmas movies are playing."

Nate closed his eyes and let out a sigh. When he opened them, I was trying not to laugh. "Fine. But if you tell anyone, especially Josh, that I watched Hallmark, I will deny it until my dying day."

Jumping in excitement, I kissed him and said, "Deal!"

I spun around and quickly made my way to Nate's bedroom. He had placed my bag on his bed. Unzipping it, I took out the clothes I had brought and the pajamas. I wasn't sure why I brought those since I was hoping to be naked and snuggled up next to Nate all night. I also wasn't sure what to wear for Thanksgiving, so I didn't pack anything, figuring I would be leaving to pick up my mother anyway.

The small bathroom bag was at the bottom of the bag. I took it out and headed to the bathroom. I set it on the counter. Putting it on Nate's counter felt weird. I didn't want him to think I was trying to move my things in. With this relationship still so new and my worry that it was too good to be true, I wasn't even sure I could take anything out and leave it here.

I looked in the mirror and frowned. The dark circles under my eyes showed where I hadn't slept the night before. I felt happier than ever, yet something was nagging at the back of my mind, and I wasn't sure what it was. I left the bag sitting toward the back of the counter, but didn't take anything out.

Making my way back into the bedroom, I pulled out a pair of sweats and a long-sleeve T-shirt from Glacier Park. I pulled my hair up into a ponytail, and last but not least, took off my shoes and put on my favorite warm and fuzzy socks.

After making my way back to the kitchen, I found it empty. "Nate?"

The rolls were in the oven, the beef stew simmering, and no Nate.

I decided to get everything out for the stew. Bowl, spoon, and butter for the rolls. It smelled so good I decided to have a small bowl myself, even though I had already eaten at my mother's. The sound of the front door shutting caused me to look over my shoulder.

"Were you outside?" I asked.

Nate looked at me. "Yeah, I wanted to check on something outside."

I nodded. "Is the temperature dropping?"

He walked up and let his eyes roam over me. "Yes, it's for sure colder outside. You look adorable."

Glancing down at what I was wearing, I screwed up my face. "I do?"

Nate nodded, took my hand, and pulled me to him. Dropping my hand, he cupped my face and stared into my eyes.

"I'm sorry I pushed you away for so long. I was a stupid idiot."

My heart started to beat faster. "It doesn't matter. All that matters is now."

He dropped his forehead to mine and let out a soft breath.

"Nate? Is everything okay?"

When he said nothing, I drew back and looked up at him. "Nate?"

He smiled. "Yeah, everything is fine." He saw the two bowls. "Are you still hungry?"

Smiling, I replied, "It smelled so good I decided to try it!"

"I'll get the rolls and drinks, and you dish out the stew."

We worked silently as I ladled some stew while Nate buttered some of the rolls and put them on a small plate. As I brought our bowls to the kitchen island, Nate placed two glasses of water down.

"Do you want another drink besides water?"

I shook my head as I slid onto a stool. "Water is perfect, thank you."

Nate followed my lead and sat down.

"This smells so good, Nate."

"Let's just hope it tastes good. I've made it a dozen or so times, but it never seems to be as good as my mother's. I follow the recipe, but something seems missing."

I laughed as I blew on my stew and then tasted it. Closing my eyes, I let out a moan. "This is heavenly!"

Nate tasted it and shook his head. "It's missing something."

"A mother's touch?" I asked with a smile.

He chuckled. "Maybe that's what it is."

"It's like when someone else makes a sandwich like a BLT or something. It is the best sandwich you've ever had, even if it is just a BLT."

Pointing to me, he said, "Yes! That is exactly like that."

"I think it is amazing. Warms me up as well."

He took another bite. "It is pretty damn good."

We ate in silence for a few minutes before Nate broke it.

"How are things coming along with the dog park? I know Doug just came on board, but do you have a start date?"

I leaned back in my chair, full of the stew and the roll I ate. "I think everything is finally set. The bank has all of Doug's information now, and I think we'll be ready to go in a couple of weeks. I'm just not sure how much we can get done with winter coming."

"You'd be surprised by what they can do, even in the winter."

"I hope everything goes okay. I have to admit, I'm nervous."

Nate reached for my hand. "It's okay to be nervous. I'd be worried if you weren't."

"Thank you, for everything you have done. You'll never know what it means to me."

Looking down at our clasped hands, Nate softly said, "The feelings that I feel for you, Haven, is nothing I've ever experienced before. When you're not with me, I can't stop thinking about you. I never again want to ever bring you pain or sadness. Ever."

"You won't."

Nate closed his eyes as he spoke. "When you're with me, I feel like I can…breathe. I don't know if that makes sense."

I could feel tears burning at the back of my eyes.

"Life just seems to make sense now, and the only thing I can think about when we're apart is you. What are you doing? Are you safe walking the dogs all alone? What can I do to make your dreams come true?"

A sob slipped free as I slid off the stool, bringing Nate with me. "You have no idea what you've done for me, Nate."

"You would have done the dog park without me."

I shrugged. "Well, I don't ever want to find out."

"My biggest regret is the time we lost out on because of me."

Placing my hand on his face, I drew in a slow, deep breath and exhaled. There were so many things I wanted to say to him, but I wasn't sure where to even start. I'd loved this man for so long, and a part of me had given up ever being with him. Now he stood before me, baring his heart and soul, and the only thing I wanted to do was tell him I felt the same exact way.

Placing my hands on his chest, I stared at one of the buttons on his shirt. "I read a quote a few years back from Zora Neale Hurston. 'Love makes your soul crawl out from its hiding place.' I never really knew what that quote meant. To me, if you loved someone, you screamed it from the top of your lungs. But, that's not how love works, and the push and pull of us over the years left me even more confused."

He went to say something, and I pressed my finger to his lips. "I love you, Nate Shaw. I've loved you for as long as I can remember, and I only want to focus on our future. You and me and where this takes us. Because I honestly cannot imagine ever returning to a life without you in it."

Before I could say anything else, Nate lifted me into his arms and took me straight to his bed, leaving everything a mess in the kitchen.

Chapter Fourteen

Nathan

"Nate, stop pacing in my kitchen. You're making me nervous."

I stopped and looked at my grandmother. "Is there anything you need me to do?"

She paused from mashing the potatoes and stared at me. "Like I would give you a job to do. Your hands are shaking like a leaf on a windy fall day."

Holding up my hands, I quickly balled them into fists. They were shaking.

"Nate, why are you so nervous?" Aunt Lincoln asked from across the kitchen, where she was stirring something on the stove.

"Well, let's see. I'm dating a woman for the first time. Not just any woman, but someone I can't stop thinking about whenever she isn't with me. I've invited her and her mother to my family's Thanksgiving, which the entire family will be in attendance. Uncle Brock and Ty are arguing about one of the games for a special holiday edition game night, which I might add no one informed me we had a game night tonight."

"It didn't scare Sophia away, and from what I know of Haven, she doesn't seem to spook very easily," Aunt Lincoln stated.

"She doesn't, and I don't think she will be fazed by it, but her mother will be."

Grams turned off the mixer, put the lid on the potatoes, and put them in the oven warmer. She wiped her hands on her apron and tilted her head as she regarded me. "Are you embarrassed by your family, Nate?"

I was pretty sure there was a look of horror on my face. "Of course not, Grams. It's just…you know how things get on game night."

She nodded. "I do. But game night is a part of this family, and we don't get to have it nearly enough anymore."

I could see the sadness in my grandmother's eyes, and I wanted to walk over and hug her. It had only been a few months since my grandfather had passed away, and I knew this wasn't easy for her. My problems seemed pretty damn stupid compared to my grandmother going on with her life without Granddad here by her side.

"You're right. I don't know why I'm so worried."

"It's because you care for Haven. That's why you're worried," Grams said softly. "Don't be worried, Nate. I've met Grace, and she is a wonderful person. Nothing we do here will make her grab her daughter and run for the mountains."

Right at that moment, Rhett and Ryder, my cousin Blayze's six-year-old twins, came running through the kitchen. Rhett held a baseball bat, while Ryder held a cell phone and yelled, "I'm live! I'm live and have witnesses!"

The three of us watched them run back out of the room.

"That's something you don't see or hear every day," Grams said.

"What did he mean, he was live? I don't think he is even allowed to have a phone yet," Aunt Lincoln said, making her way out of the kitchen to track down her two grandsons.

When I looked at Grams, she was fighting to keep back a smile. "What was that about them not running for the mountains?"

"I don't suppose we can lock those two up in a bedroom, right?"

I laughed. "I don't think Blayze and Georgiana would like that much."

"The table is all set," Mom said as she entered the kitchen. "We're just waiting on Rose, Bryson, Greg, and Haven and her mother."

My nerves started up again. When Haven had left my house earlier this morning, I had offered to go with her to pick up her mother, but she insisted it would be better to arrive on their own. "Maybe I should have invited them to a small family dinner."

"What are you talking about?" Mom asked, her eyes darting from me to Grams.

"He's worried we're going to overwhelm them. Or scare them."

Mom waved her hand, saying, "Don't be silly. Grace is from a large family back east. She'll be used to it. And Haven, well, from how I have seen that girl look at you over the years, nothing could scare her away. Plus, she deals with a lot of dogs at one time every day, she can handle our chaos."

Rhett and Ryder came running back through the kitchen. "Take that back, or I'm going to use your head as a baseball!"

"Ryder Shaw!" Georgiana yelled as she chased after them. "Put that bat down this instant!"

"That's Rhett!" Blayze added as he pulled up the rear.

Once they were all back out of the kitchen, I turned to my mother and raised a brow.

Clearing her throat, Mom said, "I'll just see if I can help them get that bat."

Before I had a chance to say anything, the doorbell rang. Rose wouldn't ring the doorbell, meaning it was Haven and her mother. Like a madman, I rushed out of the kitchen, crying, "I'll get the door!"

Right as I was almost there, Josh appeared. He had a wide, shit-eating grin on his face.

"Well, what do we have here?"

"Get out of the way, Josh."

He folded his arms over his chest. "I do believe you owe me some money."

Rolling my eyes, I grabbed him by the arm and yanked him out of the way. "I believe you told me to donate it…remember?"

Josh stood there and waited for me to open the door. "Did I?"

"You can leave now."

"Are you kidding me? This is the first time you're bringing a woman home. I'm not missing any of this."

I turned away from him and opened the door to find Haven and her mother. A light snow was falling and dusting the ground.

Haven smiled up at me, and my heart tripped over itself. Without even thinking, I took her hand and led her in, kissing her in the process.

"Bold move with the parents right here," Josh whispered from the other side of the door.

"I'm glad you could make it," I said as I reached for Grace's hand while she walked through the door.

"Thank you for having us. It's been a long time since I was on your family's ranch," Grace said. "I think the last time was picking Haven up from your mother and father's place."

"A lot has changed," I said as I took Grace's coat and Josh took Haven's.

"I'll put this in the office right down the hall here," Josh said, motioning down the hall.

Haven smiled. "Thank you, Josh."

I smiled and said, "Come on in, and I'll introduce you to everyone. I'm sure you know almost everyone, though."

Taking Haven's hand in mine, I guided the three of us to the family room. When we walked in, I expected chaos; it was, after all, my family. My very large family. Instead, we found everyone sitting down somewhere in the room, all eyes on us.

Josh walked in and started to laugh. "History has been made, and all it took was Nate bringing a girl home!"

My mother was the first to break the strange silence. "Haven, it's so wonderful to see you!"

She hugged Haven and then turned to Grace. "Grace, we can't go so long between seeing one another."

"I agree," Grace replied, hugging my mother.

When my mother looked at me with wide eyes and a nod to the rest of the family, I cleared my throat.

"Right, um, introductions. Family, this is Haven and her mother, Grace Larson. And this is my family."

Everyone stared at me as Haven giggled from next to me.

"Nathan Christopher Shaw," my mother slowly said as Josh laughed beside me.

Lily laughed. "Not the full name being brought out."

I turned and shot her a look before focusing back on my mother.

"You can't possibly expect me to go down the entire family tree and introduce them, do you?" I asked.

Her hands went to her hips, and I knew my ass was grass. "That is exactly what I expect."

"But dinner will get cold!" I argued.

"Rose isn't even here yet," Grams stated as she sat down on the arm of one of the sofas. "We've got plenty of time."

I drew in a deep breath and slowly let it out. "Okay, Grace, Haven, you might want to take a seat."

Haven and Josh both laughed.

"You already know my mother and father," I said, motioning to my parents. Grace smiled.

"Next to them is my sister, Lily and her husband, Maverick. And sitting on Maverick's lap is Maggie, who is four."

Maggie waved.

Haven waved back to Maggie.

"You probably know my uncles, Brock and Ty."

"How are, Brock, Ty?" Grace asked with a warm smile.

I went around the room and introduced everyone to Haven, at least those who she didn't know already. I hadn't really realized how damn big my family was until I finally got to the last person. Haven seemed to think so as well because she looked at me and crinkled her nose in the most adorable way.

"I hope I'm not quizzed on everyone!"

Smiling, I replied, "It's multiply choice."

Grams stood and clapped her hands. "Now that introductions are done, and everyone is here, let's eat! Should we get the kids fed first?"

"That's a great idea," Aunt Kaylee said as she gathered the little ones. Once everyone was seated, small conversations broke out.

"Why is your leg bouncing up and down?" Haven asked in a lower voice.

"We're having game night tonight as well."

Haven's brows drew down in confusion. "Game night? That sounds like fun."

"Fun? Fun?" I huffed. "It can start out as fun, but quickly becomes a competition between everyone."

"There isn't anything wrong with a bit of competition between people."

I stared at her. "You have no idea. The last thing I want to do is scare you or your mom."

She smiled as she looked at her mother. "Don't worry about us; we can handle some competition. We're made of sterner stuff and all that."

Exhaling, I looked down at the large table we were sitting at and saw my mother and Grace were seated at another table in a deep conversation with Grams.

"Your mother seems to be fitting in just fine."

Haven nodded. "I think so as well. Helps she knows some of your family and Stella."

Her eyes moved to my grandmother. "How is Stella doing?"

"I think she's okay. I'm sure she has good days and bad days. Being surrounded by family helps. I heard her and my aunt Kaylee discussing a trip with Grams. She's always wanted to go to Banff but has never been."

"That sounds like fun. I've never been out of the state."

I finished chewing my bite. "Where is someplace you'd like to go?"

"Like, in the US or anywhere?"

"Anywhere. Sky is the limit."

Haven thought about her answer for a few moments. "If it was here in the US, I think I would like to see the coast. Maybe Oregon or even the East Coast."

"Oregon is beautiful. The whole Pacific coastline is."

"Have you been back east?" Haven asked.

With a shake of my head, I replied, "If you count Europe. When Avery got married, we all went to France."

She smiled softly. "I remember that. I bet it was a beautiful wedding."

"It was, but I've seen some beautiful weddings right here on the ranch." She nodded and looked down the table toward her mother. "What about outside the US?"

Haven's eyes met my gaze. "Let's see, I think it would be maybe Ireland or Scotland. London would be pretty cool to visit. A lot of the historical romance books I read are based in London."

With a smile, I said, "Maybe we can go there someday."

Haven laughed. "Right now I just want to get through this winter and what it's going to be like building the dog park."

I took her hand in mine and gave it a squeeze. "Everything is going to be great. Don't stress."

She nodded. "Easier said than done."

Once everyone was finished up eating, and the food and kitchen cleaned up, it was time for game night. My gaze swept over the living room until I found Haven sitting next to Lily. Their heads were bent low in what had to be a private conversation. I couldn't help but smile. Two women in my life who meant the world to me. When I turned to my right, I caught my mother watching me. We both smiled at one another, and I tried to ignore the way my face felt heated.

A bell rang and everyone turned to see Uncle Brock standing next to Grams.

"The time has come, family. It's family game night… Thanksgiving edition."

I closed my eyes and groaned. When I opened them, Haven stood in front of me.

"What was that all about?"

Taking her hands in mine, I said, "Do you remember last night, in my kitchen? That thing I did with my tongue?"

Her face instantly went red as she quickly looked around, then focused back on me. "Nate!"

"Do you remember?"

She rolled her eyes as she sighed. "Of course I remember."

"Good," I said, nodding my head. "Remember that once we get into the throes of family game night."

With a small frown, Haven went to say something, but snapped her mouth shut. A look of worry crossed over her face when she looked past me. "Is…is Rose stretching?"

With a quick glance over my shoulder, I said, "She knows something we don't! Quick! Do some stretches!"

Haven looked shocked when I grabbed her hand and pulled her to the side of the living room and started doing some jumping jacks.

"Nate?" she softly asked. "What is happening?"

Turning to her, I said, "It's too late to do any reconnaissance work, if someone knows the games, they won't tell us now."

Looking even more confused, Haven asked, "Reconnaissance work?"

Josh made his way over to us. "Rose knows something."

"I know. I saw her stretching."

Josh leaned in closer. "I saw Lincoln earlier today blowing up orange balloons."

"Orange balloons?" Haven and I both asked in unison.

"And my father made a podium. He's been trying to hide it from me, but I saw it."

"Wow, you guys really take game night seriously, don't you?" Haven asked with a lighthearted laugh.

When Josh and I both turned to her, her smile faded. "If we break up into teams, you need to be ready, Haven."

She swallowed. "Ready?"

Josh and I both nodded.

Her hand came to her chest as she searched the room. "I wonder if my mom needs to leave?"

"I need everyone out back. Grab something warm to wear, but dress in layers!" Uncle Brock called out as he motioned for everyone to follow Uncle Ty.

Grabbing Haven's hand, I gave her a slight tug. "The chance to save yourself is over! Let the games begin!"

Chapter Fifteen

Haven

I wasn't sure what in the world had happened to Nate. It was like a switch went off when Brock had announced it was time to start game night.

My mother walked up next to me and leaned in to whisper, "They take game night seriously here, don't they? Did you see how everyone instantly started putting their…game faces on?"

"I noticed," I replied. "I think it's too late to say we'll sit this out."

"What are they carrying!" my mother said, jerking her head to where Josh and Brock were walking.

"What does he have in his arms?"

"Sacks, Haven. Burlap sacks. I think this is going to get physical."

I laughed. "I've never heard of any horror stories on the local news about the game nights, so I think we're fine."

Brock stopped, dropped the sacks, and then turned to face everyone. On one side of the large backyard, there were ropes set up to make lanes. Thank goodness the snow had stopped falling; otherwise, it could get a bit slippery. The other side was where all of the orange balloons were. There was also a smaller course next to the big one, and a smaller patch of balloons next to the larger patch. I was guessing those were for the little ones.

Brock clapped his hands and got everyone's attention.

"First game up is the pumpkin patch stomp."

All the little kids jumped and cheered.

"Mom and Lincoln will be in charge of the kiddos' games. They are the only two who have an exemption from participating in our event. Everyone else is playing."

"Oh, dear," my mother whispered.

"How are the teams going to be divided?" Rose called out.

"Girls against guys!" Lily shouted.

Before I knew it, the women were on one side of the yard, and the men were on the other. The kids were already playing their game and not paying attention to the grownups at all.

"First up, the sack races," Brock stated with what I could only describe as an evil smile.

"Gather around, ladies!" Rose called out.

Once in the circle, I noticed Sophia was on my left, Kipton was on my right, and Rose was in the middle.

"Okay, I'm pregnant and not so sure the race is something I should participate in. Anyone else preggers?"

Everyone glanced around the circle, and all eyes landed on me.

"Me?" I squeaked out. "Why are you all looking at me?"

A few of them shrugged as my mother's eyes went as wide as saucers.

"Well, I can tell you, I'm not pregnant."

"Anyone else?" Rose asked, slowly scanning the group. Once she was sure no one else was pregnant, she smiled. "Okay. I discovered they are drawing names on who is going up against whom. I want you to give it your all, ladies. We have a streak of winning anytime it is girls against guys." Her eyes found me again. "Are you prepared to give it your all?"

Sophia cried out, "She is! She's a fighter!"

Everyone clapped, including my mother.

"Mom? You're doing the sack races?" I asked.

Giving me a look that said I had just asked a stupid question, my mother laughed. "Of course, I am."

"But...you just said?"

Waving me off, my mother clapped her hands and cried out, "Let's beat the guys!"

Rose pointed to my mother. "See, that's what I'm talking about, people. Get your game faces on!"

They all put their hands in the middle, and I quickly joined.

"On the count of three, women rule. Got it?" Rose asked. "One. Two. Three!"

"Women rule!"

Everyone drew their hands back and clapped, then broke apart. It was then I noticed my mother running in place. My mouth fell open as I watched her start stretching.

"What is happening?" I felt like I was in the Twilight Zone.

Sophia leaned in. "I know. It's like this weird power that comes over you when it's game night. I had to play it cool my first time."

I slowly turned and looked at her. "You had to play it cool?"

With a nod, Sophia said. "Well, yeah, you can't let them know you've got it in you. I advise you to play it like you're worried, then unleash the dogs when it's your turn!"

"The dogs?"

"Don't mind me. I just said the first thing that came to mind. Blame it on the adrenaline."

"Did you eat or drink something I didn't?" I asked, looking back at my mother, who was now doing bendovers and touching her toes. "I think my mother had the same thing as you."

Then I saw Nate. He had his ankle in his hand and was stretching his quads. "Oh my God. They've all gone crazy."

When Rose blew a whistle, I jumped. Since Rose was sitting out the race, she had declared herself the person to announce the teams.

"First up is Lily and Tanner."

Lily fist-pumped, pointed to her father, and yelled, "You're going down, old man!"

My hand came up to my mouth as I tried not to laugh.

Tanner rolled his shoulders. "Bring it on, little lady. Bring. It. On. I brought you into this world and, well, you know the rest…"

I watched as they climbed into the sacks and got to the line.

Rose had clearly taken over as she called out, "Each team will go to the end, ring the bell, then come back. The next team will be ready to go."

"Do we each get a sack to climb into and get ready, or do they have to take off their sack and let the next person get in it?" I asked.

All heads turned to look in my direction as Hunter pointed to me. "Yes! I like that idea better. Makes it harder and should be some good laughs."

Everyone nodded and started to agree. Brock hit Nate on the back. "I like her. I like her a lot."

Nate winked at me, and I felt my cheeks heat.

"Okay, listen up for your number and pay attention to who is up before you so you know when to get up to the line!" Rose stated.

Lucky for me, I was last and paired with Nate.

"Last spot," Sophia said as she looked at me with a concerned expression. "Yikes."

I instantly panicked. "Why yikes? Why do you say that?"

She shrugged. "I just don't think I would want to be bringing up the rear. What if the girls are winning and you mess up?"

"Why…why would I mess up?"

Another shrug. "I'm just saying, I wouldn't want to go last."

Before I had time to ponder her words, the sack races started. And I had never laughed so hard in my entire life. Lily had started strong, with Tanner running slightly behind. But when it came time to get out of the sack and get Kipton in, who was second and jumping against Blayze, everything that could go wrong did. Lily's bracelet got stuck in the sack, and in a rapid decision, Rose declared nothing from the previous jumper could be left in or attached to the sack. Sweet Kipton, who on all accounts appeared to be the loveliest of them all, screamed out, "Rip the mother f'er off! Hurry!"

It went on each time. Someone's leg got stuck, or their hair got stuck. Ty's watch somehow got stuck in Maverick's hair, and since it wasn't stuck to the bag, Rose declared it was okay. I laughed until I almost peed as Maverick jumped down the lane with the watch hitting his eyes with every jump.

My mother and Brock were next. I stood there stunned, hearing my mother screaming for Timberlynn to jump faster as Beck somehow stumbled and fell.

"What are you doing, man?" Brock cried out. "Get your butt up, son, and move!"

"What happened to my mother?" I asked as I stared at my mother. When my mother accidentally bumped into Brock, I heard some of the men screaming for a penalty. Rose waved her hands.

"She stumbled, yet no one said anything when Bryson ran into Avery!"

I soon found myself yelling for my mother to go faster.

"Haven!" Rose cried out. "You're up next, so get into place."

I quickly made my way to the starting line. Nate stood next to me.

"Good luck!" I said with a smile.

"Do not wish him luck!" Lily cried out. "He's the enemy."

Blinking a few times, I looked from Lily to Nate. He was focused on his uncle Brock hopping toward him. The look on his face nearly had me laughing.

"It's just a game, Nate."

He snapped his head to me. Then he smiled. A smile that said he was confident he was going to win this one for the boys.

I stood up straight. "You don't think I can beat you, do you?"

With a half smile, he turned back and started yelling for Brock to go faster. My mother was barely in front of Brock.

"Jump faster, Mom! Kick his ass!"

"Little ears!" someone shouted from behind me.

"Not now, Mom!" Rose cried out. "She's getting into the spirit finally!"

"Mom, jump faster!"

My mother must have dug deep because she started jumping longer distances and speeding up.

"Yes! Go! Go! Go!" I cried out. I quickly removed my shoes, which no one else had done until then. I pulled off my necklace and tossed it up into the air.

"Hey, that hit me!" Nate cried out.

"Stop whining!" I shouted as I started to run in place. My mother was almost there, but Brock was close behind.

"Sir, I don't mean to yell at you, but hurry the hell up, old man!" Nate cried out.

My mother fell to the ground and quickly slipped out of the sack as I picked it up, climbed into it, and took off. Brock slipped right before the finish line, and I could hear Nate yelling for him to get out.

"Move, man, move!" Nate cried out.

I knew the moment Nate was jumping in the sack when the men started shouting. I didn't dare look behind me. I needed to focus. The girls were counting on me, and it was my first game night at the Shaws', so I wasn't about to let them down.

"Go, Haven, go!" I heard my mother yell out.

Running along the side of the course, Rose was shouting out encouragements.

"Should you be running?" I called out once I got to the end and turned. Nate was close behind. Our eyes met, and he smirked—he actually smirked.

Rose motioned with her arms for me to keep going. "Focus, man! Focus! Stop flirting with the enemy!"

I could see the finish line. It was right there. I could also feel Nate gaining on me.

Think, Haven! Think!

Nate came up alongside me, and I quickly looked at him. I couldn't let him win. A memory of us playing dodgeball came to mind from when we were younger. Nate had thrown the ball so hard, hitting me in the face. He instantly ran over to me and asked if I was okay. That's when it hit me. I knew what I had to do.

"My ankle!" I cried out, acting as if I was about to fall to the ground. Nate turned to look at me, obviously out of concern, stumbled, and lost his balance. I took advantage of the moment and jumped as fast as possible.

"You little cheater!" Nate cried out as he pushed himself up and started coming for me faster. I gave one last jump and crossed the finish line. I was quickly surrounded by women taking turns hugging me while I was still in the sack. When they stepped back, I saw Nate standing there. He wore a smile, but there was something dark in his eyes that made my body shiver, and it wasn't from the cold. He walked up to me, cupped my face, and kissed me. The crowd erupted into cheers, and I was pretty sure I heard my mother clear her throat.

When he drew back, I gasped for air. "What…what was that for?"

He winked at me. "For playing like a Shaw. Well done with the fake injury."

I felt my cheeks heat. "I'm sorry, it was the only thing I could think of doing except for pushing you over."

He laughed. "I don't know what it is about game night, but it brings out another side of people. Definitely the darker side."

I was still trying to regain my breath as I nodded. "I don't think I've ever wanted to win so badly before in my life."

Timberlynn, Nate's mother, walked up to me and hugged me. "Don't worry, darling, we've all been there. Let's head on over to the next game, shall we?"

Nate took my hand as I slipped out of the sack. After I put my shoes back on, he laced his fingers with mine as we walked to the second event that was to be played.

"This time, it's couples. The couple who pops the most balloons wins," Stella stated as she pointed to bags filled with orange balloons. "Each bag has the same amount of balloons. So when it is each couple's turn, they get a new bag."

"Who thought up this game?" Beck asked as he stood behind Avery, his arms wrapped around her.

Stella's smile slipped some as her voice caught in her throat. "It was one of the games Ty Senior had written down to play on Thanksgiving."

A somber mood quickly washed over the large crowd before Nate clapped his hands. "Then let's play this game so he has a good laugh upstairs."

Stella beamed at her grandson. "Shall we start with the older couples and work our way down?"

"Kaylee and I will go first," Ty said as he took his wife's hand. They entered the area that had been made into a small pen with panels set up in a large circle. I was assuming it was so the balloons would stay in that area.

"Okay, there are fifty balloons. You have one minute to try and pop as many as possible!" Stella said as she held up a stopwatch. "On your marks, get set, go!"

Ty and Kaylee started stomping on the balloon, but each one kept slipping from under their feet. They ended up laughing more than anything. In the end, they had only popped seventeen balloons, but they both wore huge smiles on their faces.

Stella used a blower to blow the balloons out of the make-shift corral. Then the kids all started playing with the balloons.

Ty brought another bag in and dumped the balloons out.

"Goodness, who blew up all of these balloons?" I asked Nate.

"If I know my grandmother, she has a machine she used to do it."

"You guys take game nights seriously, don't you?"

Nate looked at me and laughed. "We do."

The next couple was Brock and Lincoln. They had popped twenty-five. Tanner and Timberlynn were next. Timberlynn was laughing so hard that she started to do the pee-pee dance and declared she was about to pee her pants, to which her granddaughter Maggie said, "Do you need a big girl diaper, Grammy?"

Blayze and Georgiana were next. They argued for the first twenty seconds about how to pop the balloons and only got ten.

Morgan and Ryan got thirty-one, the highest yet. Rose and Bryson sat out the game, as did Avery and Beck.

Kipton and Hunter tried to beat Morgan and Ryan but only tied them.

When it was Lily and Maverick's turn, they smiled and declared they would be the winners. They were nowhere close to being winners, with only nine balloons popped since they were both laughing too hard to even try.

All eyes turned to Bradley and Mackenzie. When her face turned bright red, and she shook her head, Merit, Bradley's mother, gasped. That caused Lincoln and Timberlynn to do the same.

"What's happening?" I asked Lily.

"Mackenzie is pregnant."

"What?" I asked. "How do you know?"

"How far along are you?" Merit asked.

Bradley took Mackenzie's hand in his. "Fifteen weeks," Mackenzie softly said. "I'm due March 19th."

Cheers erupted as everyone waited patiently to congratulate the happy couple. I'd met Mackenzie often over the last few years. She helped run the you-pick-it farm that Merit and her brother Michael owned. Once the congratulations were over, Josh and Sophia stepped into the corral. They ended up getting thirty-six."

My mother and Stella went next. They spent more time on the ground laughing than anything, which in turn had everyone else laughing.

"Last but certainly not least, Nate and Haven."

Nate took my hand and pulled me into the corral. He bent his head so only I could hear him. "Okay, we need to play this differently."

"How so?" I asked.

"We need to sit on them."

My head lifted, and I looked at Nate and grinned. "You're brilliant."

He nodded. "I know."

With a roll of my eyes, I pushed him away. "You take that side, and I'll get this side."

"No amount of planning is going to help you!" Josh cried out. "You can't beat thirty-six."

Nate scoffed and said, "I'll bet you a thousand dollars we can!"

"You kids ready?" Stella asked.

"Let's do this!" I said, jumping in place and cracking my neck. Nate looked at me and laughed.

Once Stella said go, I dropped to my ass and started sitting on as many of the orange balloons as I could. Pop! Pop! Pop! It was one balloon after another. I could hear cheers coming from all around me. I didn't dare look at Nate, but from what I could hear, he was popping as many balloons as I was.

"Ten seconds!" Stella called out over the balloons popping. When the whistle blew, I fell back and stared at the sky. I had long since shed my jacket because all the running, jumping, and cheering had overheated me. I rolled to my side and moaned.

"There are only five balloons left!" Tanner called out. "That is forty-five balloons! Nate and Haven are the winners!"

Nate stood over me, a wide grin across his handsome face. "We won."

I nodded. "I think I broke my tailbone. All that dog walking didn't prepare me for this battle."

Nate chuckled and reached down to help me up. When I stood, I winced. "Okay, maybe it's just a bruise."

Moving his mouth to my ear, he whispered, "I'll massage your battered body tonight."

My lower stomach instantly tightened with the images that popped into my mind. "I would like that."

He moved his mouth and kissed my forehead. "You're a trooper. Thank you for doing all of this."

As Stella said to leave all the popped balloons, everyone started heading back into the house. Hot chocolate, dessert, and a movie were waiting for everyone.

As I started following my mother, Nate stopped me and took my hand. He was holding my jacket.

"Oh, I forgot about that."

He drew me closer to his warm body, and only then did I feel how cold it was outside. "Thank you."

Smiling, I asked, "For what?"

His gaze searched my face. "For being you. For fitting in with this crazy family of mine. For cheating at the sack race."

"I did not cheat!"

Nate raised his brows.

"Fine, I may have cheated a little. I had to win it, Nate."

His finger came up and traced down my cheek lightly. "I never knew I could be this happy."

My heart hammered in my chest. "I'm glad you're happy. I am as well."

He shook his head. "You know it's all because of you, right?"

Biting my lip, I looked down at the ground. Nate tipped my chin up so our eyes met. "I…I would love if..."

Josh poked his head out before I could ask Nate what he was trying to say. "Grams said to get inside, it's getting colder, and the movie is about to start."

Taking my hand in his, Nate guided us to the house. I inwardly cursed Josh for his timing. Once we stepped back into the house, everyone claimed seats in a room with a large screen that had dropped from the ceiling. Stella had a theater room in her home, with theater seating in the back, and tons of bean bags on the floor toward the screen. Most of the little ones had taken up the bean bag chairs, but Nate secured one big enough for us both to sit in.

"How did you manage to snag this one?" I asked as I sat down, a bag of popcorn in one hand and a box of Junior Mints in the other. Stella had a table filled with movie snacks, not to mention the desserts from Thanksgiving dinner, which included apple, pumpkin, and cherry pie.

"I had to bribe Rhett and Ryder to give me this one."

I laughed and looked around the room. Everyone was so happy, and that made my heart feel full. I knew this had to be a hard Thanksgiving with Ty Senior not here.

Nate set two bottles of water down and then sat next to me. The lights dimmed, and *A Charlie Brown Thanksgiving* started to play. I snuggled deeper against Nate and couldn't help but smile. I wanted every Thanksgiving to be exactly like this one.

Chapter Sixteen

Nathan

Haven sat beside me in the bean bag chair and intently watched *A Charlie Brown Thanksgiving*. At some point, Maggie made her way over and sat with us. Haven had started playing with Mag's hair and braided it. I wasn't the least bit surprised that Haven was good with kids. She had a heart like no one else I had ever met.

I glanced at her once more and smiled. I had been about to ask Haven if she would move in with me but then Josh had interrupted us. I'm glad I hadn't, though. It was too soon to be suggesting that, even if I wanted to spend every moment of the day with Haven as I could.

Haven leaned closer to me and whispered, "Do you need anything? I'm going to run to the restroom."

I shook my head. It was then that I noticed Maggie had fallen asleep. Haven carefully lifted the little girl from her lap, gently laid her on the bean bag, then ducked down and high-tailed it out of the room.

Maggie wiggled and sat up. "Where did Miss Haven go?"

"She had to go potty. She'll be back."

Maggie nodded, then made her way onto my lap, where she promptly snuggled against my sweater. "I'm cold, Uncle Nate."

I wrapped my arms around her, causing her to giggle. "Oh, no! Let me get you warmed up, little one."

"I'm not warm yet!" she stated with a twinkle in her eyes.

"Not yet?" I asked in a whispered voice. Suddenly, a small blanket made its way in front of me, and I glanced up to see my sister smiling down at me and her daughter.

"This might help."

I took it and covered up Maggie. "Thanks, Lily."

"Want me to take her?"

With a shake of my head, I held onto my niece tighter. "No, she's fine here. I hardly ever get to spend time with her."

Lily was bent down, attempting not to block the screen from those in the back. "She's going to fall asleep."

Kissing the top of her brown curly head, I breathed. What was it about little ones that made them smell so good?

"She's fine. Go spend some time with your husband."

My sister reached over and kissed my cheek. "You know, Nate, someday you're going to make a wonderful father."

I nearly choked. "A father? Let's not put the cart before the horse, Lily."

She shrugged. "I'm simply pointing out a fact. By the way, I really like Haven."

Smiling, I nodded. "I do too."

"Me twee," Maggie mumbled as Lily and I both chuckled.

"If you get tired, just send her my way."

"I won't get tired, so please go spend some time with your husband."

Lily looked over her shoulder. "He's asleep. I lost him about ten minutes in."

Turning around, I tried to let my eyes adjust to the room's darkness. Sure enough, Maverick was sitting in one of the recliners sleeping.

"Mommy, I don't feel good," Maggie suddenly said, pushing off of my chest. "I think I'm going to twow up."

I had never stood and handed my niece to my sister so fast. Lily laughed and cradled her daughter to her chest. "Come on, sweetness. Let's go see what we can do for that upset stomach."

"Nate, sit down!" Josh whisper-shouted.

Instead of sitting back in the bean bag, I decided to see what was keeping Haven. I quickly made my way out of the theater room and started toward the kitchen. Faint voices could be heard, and I slowed when I heard Haven.

"Are you excited about the dog park?"

The question came from my mother.

"I am. I'm also a bit scared. Meeting Sophia was a huge blessing, and lifted a large weight off of my shoulders, but it's still daunting. Nate has helped me so much as well."

"He has?" my mother asked.

"He tried to be sneaky and made an anonymous donation, which allowed me to pay off the van and the business credit card."

"That sounds like Nathan," my mother replied. I could hear the smile in her voice. "He has one of the kindest hearts I've ever known, and I'm not saying that just because he is my son."

Haven let out a soft chuckle. "There might be some bias there."

Before they could keep talking about me, I cleared my throat. "What are you two doing in here?"

Haven looked up and smiled so big it made my heart jump in my chest.

"Girl talk," my mother answered.

"I heard my name," I stated as I walked up, kissed my mother on the cheek, and then kissed Haven.

Haven and my mother exchanged a look. "I was telling your mother about your donation."

"Oh, that."

With a roll of her eyes, Haven replied, "Yes, that. It was one of the kindest things anyone has ever done for me."

I drew in a breath and exhaled. "I just want you to be happy, Haven."

Her breath drew in sharply as my mother touched her heart. "Oh, so very much like your father."

"I'll take that as a compliment."

My mother winked at me.

"Oh, Haven, there you are," Grace said as she walked into the kitchen. "I hate to do this, but I am exhausted and ready to head home. I've already said goodbye to Stella and thanked her for having us."

My mother walked up to Grace and drew her in for a hug. "Let's plan to get the girls together for lunch soon. It's been so long."

Uncle Brock made his way into the kitchen. "Grace, I wanted to catch you before you left. Do you have ten minutes to give to me?"

Grace looked to Haven who said, "Yes, please go ahead, Mom. I'm not in a rush."

"Great! I won't keep her long," Uncle Brock stated as he motioned for Grace to follow him to Granddad's office.

Haven wore a worried expression on her face.

"It's nothing to worry about," I said as I leaned against the kitchen counter.

Haven's head snapped to look at me. "Do you know what it's about?"

I looked at my mother who gave a slight nod of her head.

"Um, yes. We're looking to hire someone on the ranch to be an administrative assistant. Someone to help Blayze with the day-to-day office work, as well as payroll, appointments, etc. The position pays well and would include health insurance."

Haven's eyes went expansive and hopeful. "Oh my goodness, what made you think of my mother for the position?"

My mother reached for Haven's hand. "We all thought it would be something Grace might be interested in."

Haven's gaze met mine, and she smiled. A sense of relief washed over me. I had been worried Haven might have looked at it as a job offer made out of pity. I knew how proud she and her mother were, and none of us wanted them to think that was the case.

Haven walked over to me. "Did you have something to do with this?"

I shrugged. "Maverick said he had overheard Blayze and Hunter talking about the need to hire a full-time person to help them in the office, and my mother and I thought of Grace."

She took my hand in hers. "Thank you. That was sweet of you to think of her."

"Are you leaving with your mom, or did you drive separately?"

She grinned. "I left my car at her house."

"Do you want me to drive you there to get it? You can stay the night with me if you want. I have the rest of this weekend off."

Her eyes lit up. "I don't have any dog walks planned this weekend. Most of my clients are either out of town or spending it with their family."

I placed my hand on her hip and drew her a bit closer to me so I could lower my voice. "So, what you're saying is, we have the whole weekend together?"

"That's exactly what I'm saying."

The urge to lean down and kiss her was almost too much, so I stepped back and dropped my hold on her. My chest squeezed when her eyes darkened.

"Can we leave now?"

Haven giggled. "I need to go say goodbye and thank you to Stella. I'll be right back."

Reaching up, she kissed me quickly, then made her way out of the kitchen.

I leaned against the counter and brought my hand up to my chest to rub at the familiar feeling I got whenever Haven was near me. Was that something I would get used to, or would I always feel this way? If I was being honest, it wasn't anything new. The last few years I got this feeling whenever she was near me, but not as strong as over the last week.

"I've seen that look before."

My mother's words brought me out of my thoughts. "What look?"

She smiled. "The look of someone head over heels for another person."

I couldn't help it. I felt the corners of my mouth tip up. "I am head over heels for her. I've never felt this way before, Mom. Every day, it seems to grow stronger and stronger. She's all I think about. When I'm at the ranch, I want to be where she is. When I'm with her, I'm thinking about how to keep her with me longer. It's pure insanity."

She laughed. "That, my dear, is called being in love. And it's pretty clear she feels the same way about you with how she watches you when she doesn't think anyone notices."

I glanced to the floor and kicked at nothing. "I don't know why I didn't take the risk of loving her before now, but I'm glad I finally opened my eyes."

I felt her hand on my arm as she gave it a tight squeeze. "You opened your heart along with those beautiful eyes of yours. The big thing now is not to mess it up."

"Do you think I will?" I asked, my stomach instantly feeling sick.

A lighthearted laugh came from her. "No, I don't think you will."

Haven walked back into the kitchen only to have Grace and Uncle Brock arrive only seconds later.

Grace looked at Haven and smiled. "Looks like I found a new job."

Haven let out a small squeal of delight and hugged her mother. "That's wonderful, Mom. Congratulations."

Uncle Brock looked my way and grinned. "I'm going to head on back to the movie. You take care, and we'll see you next week."

Grace shook his hand and replied, "Thank you, Brock. You've given me the most amazing opportunity. I cannot thank you enough."

Uncle Brock nodded his head, said his goodbyes to Grace and Haven, and made his way out of the kitchen. My mother walked everyone to the door while I grabbed their jackets. The temperature had continued to drop, and when I opened the front door, a burst of cold wind went past me.

Turning to my mother, I hugged her. "Tell Grams I said thank you for everything. I'll call you tomorrow."

She kissed me on the cheek and said, "Be careful driving. If you want, dinner Sunday at our place."

"I'll be there."

"Bring Haven as well."

I smiled. "Happy Thanksgiving, Mom."

"Happy Thanksgiving, sweetheart."

◆ ◆ ◆

After picking up Haven's car from her mother's house, we drove straight to my house. We weren't in the door two seconds before I pulled her into my arms and kissed her. Haven melted into me, and we were soon lost in the kiss.

We broke apart, and I leaned my forehead to hers. "Thank you for coming today."

Smiling, she replied, "I had so much fun, Nate. So did my mother. Your family is amazing."

"I think they are as well."

"And the job offer for my mother, you should have heard her on the way home. She couldn't stop talking about it. And the best part is health insurance! She's never had that before, so this is huge."

"It was perfect timing."

Haven nodded. "It really was."

I took her bag and started toward my bedroom. "You know, you should bring some stuff to keep here."

"Stuff?" Haven asked, sitting on my bed.

"Yeah, you know, like, a toothbrush, shampoo, extra clothes, things like that."

Her brows pulled down slightly. "You want me to keep stuff here?"

I smiled. "Yes. It would make it easier for you on the nights you stay here. You don't have to pack all your stuff up."

The corners of her mouth twitched. "You don't think it's too soon for me to bring my…stuff…to your house?"

I sat down on the bed next to her. "If I'm being honest, I almost asked you to move in with me earlier before Josh interrupted us."

"That's what you were going to say! I was wondering."

We both turned to face one another. "I know I'm moving at warp speed, Haven, with telling you I love you and now asking you to move some of your things in with me, it's just…"

"It's just what?" she asked.

"Now that I have you in my life, I want to spend every second I can with you. I don't want to miss out on anything. I want to ask you how your day was as we cook dinner together. I want to kiss you goodnight and make love to you each morning."

Haven took my hands in hers. "I love that you want all those things because I want them as well. And as much as I want to scream yes, I will move in with you, we honestly don't know much about each other, Nate. Do you leave your towel on the floor or, worse yet…on the bed when it's wet? Do you put the dishes in the dishwasher, or do you let them stack up in the sink until you have to load them in the dishwasher?"

I laughed. "I hang my towel up after I dry off. I cannot stand dishes in the sink, and one of my favorite things to do to de-stress is clean."

Haven stared at me for a few seconds. "Okay, could you be any more perfect?"

I winked. "I could try."

She giggled. "How about we do this. I'll bring a few things over to make staying the night easier. Then we take it day by day and see how things go."

"I'm not letting you go now that I have you. I hope you know that."

"That's good because I feel the same way. I've been in love with you for far too long to let you just push me away ever again."

I stood and reached for her. "Trust me, Haven, I will never push you away again. Not ever."

Haven wrapped her arms around my neck and lifted to kiss me. "Now that we have that settled, what should we do now?"

"How about we make some popcorn, change into something comfortable, and settle in for a movie?"

"That sounds wonderful to me. Do you have any movie candy like Stella did?"

I frowned as I thought about what I had in the pantry. "I have some Milk Duds and Mike and Ikes."

"I love Milk Duds! That is perfect," she said as she grabbed my hand and pulled me out of the bedroom and into the kitchen. "You pop the popcorn, and I'll get the Milk Duds. Once the popcorn is done, we can put the Milk Duds in it."

"Whoa…what?"

She turned and looked at me as she opened the pantry door. With her nose crinkled in the most adorable way, she asked, "You've never mixed candy in with your popcorn before?"

"No! That is gross, Haven."

Her mouth fell open. "How is that gross?"

I shrugged as I stepped around her and walked into the pantry to get the popcorn. "Here are the Milk Duds."

I took two bags of popcorn and headed back into the kitchen to put them in the microwave.

"I cannot believe you've never mixed anything in with your popcorn. The hot popcorn melts the chocolate some on the Milk Duds and it is so yummy."

Leaning against the counter, I watched as Haven took a few boxes of the Milk Duds and poured them into a large bowl. "I'll give it a try, but I'm not sure I'll like it. I like my popcorn full of butter. Hence the Butter Lovers popcorn."

She giggled. "Just trust me. Once you have this, you will never eat popcorn alone again."

"I find that hard to believe."

"Just wait. Which movie did you have in mind to watch?" she asked.

"Your pick tonight."

Her eyes lit up. "Really?"

"Really, really."

Tapping her finger on her mouth, she looked up as she thought about it. "How about we watch *Love Actually*?"

"Who is in it?"

Haven's mouth fell open. "You've never watched *Love Actually*?"

I shrugged. "Can't say I have."

She jumped and clapped her hands. "Oh, this is going to be amazing!"

"I take it it's a chick flick."

With a quick shake of her head, she said, "You are in for a treat!"

I laughed. "What do you want to drink?"

"How about we open a bottle of wine?"

"You want to eat popcorn with Milk Duds in it and drink wine?"

She nodded, and those dimples appeared. I knew right then and there there was nothing I would deny Haven Larson. Nothing.

Chapter Seventeen

Haven

Two weeks had passed since Thanksgiving, and I had slowly started to bring more and more of my things to Nate's house. Winter had officially set in also with a good snowstorm that had blown in—unfortunately, the day before we were set to break ground on the dog park. All part of living in Montana and building something in winter. Doug was amazing and assured me that all would be fine. He had stopped by my mother's house last night since I was there having dinner with her to tell me what the plans for today were as far as what would be happening. The excitement of it all had fully hit me this morning when I woke up.

"How did you sleep?" Nate asked, his arms wrapping around me from behind as he kissed my neck.

"Like a baby. How about you?"

"Same. When you're here, I sleep so good."

I laughed. "Does all the sex have anything to do with that?"

He grinned at me in the bathroom mirror. "That might have something to do with it."

Turning in his arms, I reached up and gently kissed him on the mouth. "Today is the day."

"Today is the day. I was planning on going with you, if you didn't mind."

"You don't have to work today?"

He shook his head. "I took the day off. I wanted to be there with you today. Josh also took the day off to go with Sophia."

Wrapping my arms around his neck, I smiled up at him. "Thank you. That means a lot to me."

"Wouldn't miss it for the world. We did get a bit more snow last night, but I don't think it will impact much today."

"I hope not."

Nate pushed a piece of hair behind my ear. "You get ready, and I'll go make us some breakfast."

I shook my head. "I honestly don't think I can eat. My stomach is a mess with nerves."

He drew back some and looked down at me. "Why are you nervous?"

With a one-shoulder shrug, I replied, "Today makes it all real. I just really hope I'm not biting off more than I can chew."

"You're not. The dog park is going to be a huge success, Haven. You and Sophia have everything planned out down to the very last detail. You're in good hands with Doug, and you have support from all of us."

"All of us?"

"Yeah," he said, kissing the tip of my nose. "Your mother, me, and my entire family."

Smiling, I said, "Your dad asked me when he can buy a membership. I asked him when he got a dog, and he just smiled at me."

Nate tossed his head back and laughed. "That totally sounds like something my father would do."

"Stella also asked about one. She said she was thinking of getting a dog."

His brows rose. "She did? I think that's great. It would be nice to have something to keep her company."

"I agree. She asked me about some breeds she should look at. She even asked if she could come on a walk with me so she could be around the dogs. I offered to do a smaller walk around the park, and she said she would like that a lot."

"I love that. What kind of pup do you think she would like?"

"She said she didn't want a little dog, so I suggested a golden retriever. They're loyal and as sweet as can be. I told her she should look into maybe finding one out of the puppy stage, but she insisted she wants to raise it."

"A puppy? Grams wants to get a puppy?"

I laughed. "That's what she said."

"Wow. Well, when she's ready, I hope she asks you for your help."

"I offered it to her, and she told me she would let me know when she was ready."

Nate stepped back. "Will you at least try to eat some toast?"

I chuckled. "I just need to get dressed. You take a shower and do what you need to do, and I'll go and make us something. You're right; something on my stomach would help a lot."

"You're sure?" Nate asked.

"Positive. Doug said he will be at the site after nine."

"Sounds good. Are we meeting Sophia there?"

I nodded. "My mother also wanted to meet us."

Nate had turned on the shower. Looking back at me, he asked, "Your mom?"

Smiling, I leaned against the counter. "Doug stopped by her house when I was there for dinner. I think my mom has a crush on him. Do you know if he is married or single?"

A huge grin appeared on Nate's face. "He is single. He got divorced about five years ago."

"Really?" I replied as I chewed on my lower lip.

"Don't tell me you're going to play matchmaker with your mom, Haven."

"No, not really. But how they kept looking at one another makes me want to play matchmaker."

Nate had stepped into the shower. "I would stay out of it."

Chewing on my thumbnail, I replied, "I will."

"Why do I not believe you?"

I pushed off the counter and said, "Because you know me. I'm off to make us breakfast."

Once Nate and I finished breakfast, I texted Sophia to let her know we were on our way to the building site. We pulled up in Nate's truck and parked next to Josh's truck. Sophia and Josh were already standing with Doug, and I was surprised to see my mother there as well.

"My mother is already here," I said as Nate opened my door and held out his hand to help me out.

He chuckled. "I can't help but wonder if she came to watch, or simply to see Doug."

I smiled. "You know, I wouldn't mind if she dated him. He is such a nice man, and my mother deserves someone who will cherish her."

Nate took my hand in his. "So do you, Haven."

Stopping, I faced him. "I found him in you."

Leaning down, he gently brushed a kiss across my lips. "I love you."

I placed my hand on the side of his face. "I love you more."

Tapping the tip of my nose, he replied, "Impossible."

Taking my hand once again, we started to make our way toward the small group. Heavy equipment was pulled up and parked, and about twenty guys were marking out things with survey sticks.

"Sorry we're late," I stated as I walked up and hugged my mother and then Sophia. "I hope you weren't waiting for us."

"We just got here as well," Sophia said as she rubbed her hands together. "It's so cold out."

Doug laughed. "It is, but the sooner we get going, the better. We haven't gotten much snow, so it's perfect to get things marked out. The next step will be to use the heavy equipment to prep the area."

"How exciting!" I said as I looked out. "What are they marking now?"

"That is the building. I met with Rose the other day over Zoom. She has some great ideas, and I really like the idea of doing a small area out here for the fire pit."

"Yes," I said as I looked at the plans. "We just need to figure out a way to keep it safe so the dogs don't get near the fire."

"That should be easy enough. Also, I want to make sure we are a go for the splash park."

Turning to look at Nate, I smiled before focusing back on Doug. "Yes, that is a go."

"Great. I don't think I have any other questions as of now. Let's take a walk, and I can show you a rough layout of the park."

I nearly jumped and clapped my hands. I was so excited. I could not believe my dream of the dog park was finally coming true.

As we walked around the area, I was surprised to see how big the park actually was.

"I had a few people reach out to me about making a donation in the form of memorial benches for people to sit on, as well as some covered areas for the benches. You could even offer something like plaques in memory of a pet that people lost."

"Really?" Sophia and I said at the same time.

"Yep," Doug replied as he kept walking ahead of us.

Sophia held me back. "Who do you think donated the benches and covers?"

I shrugged. "I'm not sure. Maybe someone who is excited about the dog park?"

"Let's ask Doug if he knows who it was."

We quickly caught up to everyone else.

"This will be the small dog park. Over here will be the covered seating, the poop station, and the dog washing station."

"How exciting!" my mother said as she did a three-sixty turn. "I can't wait to see it."

"Me too," Josh said with a wide smile.

"Doug, do you know who made the donations?" I asked.

"Yes. They reached out yesterday and wanted to donate in memory of their grandmother, a dog lover."

Sophia's hands went to her chest. "That is so sweet. What a wonderful idea."

My mother turned and looked at Sophia and me. "What if you built a brick entrance into each dog park and gave people the option of buying a brick in a loved one's name? It could even be in the name of a fur baby if they wanted?"

Looking at Doug, I asked, "Is that possible? The brick sidewalk?"

He nodded. "That's a great idea. Do you have a website yet for the dog park?"

Josh answered, "We do. It's live, but there isn't much on it, just a few drawings of what the dog park will potentially look like."

"I would make a section on the website for people who would like to buy a brick. While you're at it, you can never have enough benches, so you could have people make donations for memorial benches as well."

"You could even name the splash park in someone's memory if they wanted to make a larger donation," Mom added.

"That's a great idea, Grace," Nate stated. "You don't have a name for the dog park yet, right?"

I shook my head. "Not yet."

"What if you do a community event where they get to submit their name ideas, and you can pick a winner?" Nate said.

"That is a great idea!" I said as I felt another wave of excitement building. "We could do it at the community center and make it a family fun event where people can bring their pets."

Doug pointed to me. "That's a great idea. By getting the community involved, you're giving yourself free marketing. Plus, if they feel like they were a part of the process, they will most likely be more connected to it, which means they'll buy a membership."

"Aunt Kaylee can help plan it. She used to do party planning," Josh said as he and Nate exchanged looks. "And I bet Grams would love to be a part of it."

"It would help her stay busy, which would be good," Nate added.

Sophia took out her phone and started to type. "Okay, I'm thinking we do this sooner rather than later. The faster we have a name for the dog park, the faster we can get marketing done."

"I agree, we should plan it soon. How long do you think it will take to plan something?"

Nate cleared his throat. "I can talk to Uncle Brock and see when the community center is available."

I chewed on my lower lip as I thought about what we could do. "If we could get it before Christmas, maybe we can do a holiday-themed party. People can bring their dogs dressed up in holiday clothes."

"That would be so fun!" Mom said as Sophia nodded.

"I'll call him as soon as we're done," Nate said.

Doug cleared his throat. "I think all of this sounds great. Keep me updated on the plans. I can also get the word out. Let's finish up with the short tour; then, we need to get started while we have the weather on our side."

◆ ◆ ◆

The last week had been a whirlwind. Chad had covered a few walks for me since I was busy helping Sophia and Kaylee with plans for the holiday party we were planning for the community to help name the dog park.

"I can't believe Christmas is next week!" Sophia said as she set a box of decorations down in the middle of the large gym where we were holding the party.

"Have you and Josh put up a tree yet?" I asked as I worked on decorating the large tree we had bought for the party.

"We're going tomorrow to pick one out. What about you and Nate?"

"I have a small artificial tree for my apartment, but I'm hardly there anymore, so I haven't even decorated. We've put up some of Nate's decorations, but haven't gotten a tree yet."

"You should come with me and Josh tomorrow," Sophia said as she turned and looked at me with a wide smile. "We could make it a tradition of getting our trees at the same time!"

I let out a soft laugh. "That would be fun. I don't think Nate has anything going on, so I'll ask him. What time are you going to be heading out?"

She shrugged. "No real set time. Probably later in the morning, I would think."

"I'll ask Nate, but I think it would be fun to do that together."

"How is everything going?" Kaylee asked as she walked up to us with another box of decorations.

"Good," I replied. "I'm almost finished with the tree and was going to work on the table decorations next."

Kaylee nodded. "It looks like we've had nearly a hundred-and-fifty people RSVP."

Sophia gasped and I was pretty sure my mouth fell open. "Are you serious?"

She smiled. "Yes! I'm so glad I told the caterer to plan for one seventy-five. We should have plenty of food."

I slowly shook my head. "I never dreamed we would have that many people say they would come."

Sophia clapped and did a little jump. "This is amazing!"

I hung the last ornament on the tree. The only thing left was the tree topper, which we would need one of the guys to put up.

"You know, we should make this an annual thing," I suggested as I glanced around the large room. Round tables were set up with chairs. "If this one is successful. Maybe we can even pick a charity to support each year and donate the proceeds from the dinner."

Kaylee looked up from a box she was looking through. "Haven, that is a wonderful idea! There are so many businesses here in Hamilton willing to donate their time and goods that I think we could make that happen."

I smiled. For throwing this party together so quickly, we had lucked out with the caterer who had donated her time and the food. The decorations were from the city of Hamilton that they had donated to the community center a few years ago. The tables and chairs were owned by the community center, and since Brock Shaw owned the community center, we got to use it for free.

"Did Jo get back with you about the menu she was doing?" I asked Kaylee.

She stood and wiped her hands on her jeans. "She did! She is going to do antipasto skewers, savory s'mores, cranberry and feta pinwheels, and pear and pomegranate salad. Each table will also have a hummus wreath, baked brie puffs, seven layer-dip cups, and last but not least, roasted butternut squash french bread bites."

My stomach growled and Sophia and Kaylee both laughed.

"She is doing all of that and doing it for free?" I asked, still surprised that she had offered to do it all on her dime.

Kaylee winked but didn't answer me.

"Kaylee, is she doing this all for free?"

She looked everywhere but at me.

"I'm going to take that as a no."

Finally looking at me, she sighed. "Okay, she is being paid, but the person paying her is doing it as their part of helping out."

"Who is it?" Sophia asked.

Kaylee chewed on her thumbnail. "I promised I wouldn't say."

"Josh?"

"Nate?"

Sophia and I had asked at the same time.

Kaylee laughed. "No, but you're not far off."

"Is it a member of the Shaw family?"

"Oh, yes. A founding member."

I laughed. "Stella?"

Kaylee reached for my hand. "Please don't tell her I told you. When she heard we were going to keep the food simple, she insisted we had to do something more. She has worked with Jo numerous times, and they came up with the menu together, and Stella is covering the costs."

"I've never met a family who does so much for their community like the Shaws," I said as I sat down in one of the chairs.

Kaylee smiled. "They are an amazing group of people, and I'm so proud to be a part of it."

"I can't wait to be a part of it," Sophia stated as she sat down in another chair.

Taking Sophia's hand in mine, Kaylee took a deep breath and slowly let it out. "I can't wait either."

I felt tears prick at the back of my eyes. What would it be like to be a part of such a loving family? My mother, of course, loved me and did her best to make my life as good as possible, but I knew she still struggled with what had happened with my father. She blamed herself, while I blamed myself for not having the courage to tell her what was happening.

"Haven? Sweetheart, what is wrong?" Kaylee asked, reaching up and wiping a tear from my face. I hadn't even realized I had been crying.

Reaching up, I felt the wetness on my face and buried my face in my hands.

"Haven," Sophia whispered as I felt her kneel before me. "What in the world is wrong?"

I dropped my hands and tried to speak, but nothing but a sob came out. Kaylee sat in the seat next to me and took my hand. "What is it, dear?"

With a deep breath, I slowly exhaled and attempted to get myself under control. What in the world had just happened to me?

"Haven?"

The sound of Nate's voice caused me to look to my right and see him. He wore a pained expression on his face.

"What's wrong?" he asked as he quickly made his way over to me.

I stood and was about to tell him everything was fine, but a sob slipped free. Nate quickly wrapped me in his arms and held me as I cried into his chest. I wasn't sure what had happened and why the dam had decided to break at that moment, but being in his arms instantly made me feel better.

"What happened?" Nate asked.

"I'm…I'm not sure. She just got upset," Sophia stated.

"Most likely the stress of everything got to her," Kaylee softly said as she rubbed my back.

Once I got my crying under control, I stepped back. Nate cupped my face in his hands and looked into my eyes.

"Are you okay, princess?"

Oh…my heart tumbled in my chest as I stared back at the man I had been in love with for as long as I could remember. With a nod, I whispered, "I'm fine. I'm okay."

Turning to Kaylee, I tried to smile. "I'm so sorry for breaking down like that."

"Oh, you don't have to apologize at all, sweetheart. We all have moments like that, which is nothing to be ashamed of."

Nate pulled me back into his arms. "Do you want to go home?"

"No, honestly, I'm okay. I just had a moment."

When I stepped back, Nate searched my face once again. "I'm here now and can help with whatever you need."

I smiled as I drew in a breath. "I could use help doing the table decorations."

Nate stood up straight and clapped. "My specialty."

I laughed along with Kaylee and Sophia.

Taking my hand in his, Nate gave it a slight squeeze. "Tell me what you need me to do."

Chapter Eighteen

Nathan

"I am exhausted," Haven said as she dropped onto the sofa in the family room.

Handing her a beer, I sat next to her. "So am I."

"I think the community party was a success. Don't you?"

With a nod, I replied, "I do. And some of the suggestions for the name are hilarious."

Haven giggled. "My favorites are The Puppy Playhouse, The Cozy Pup Playground, and Wag More, Bark Less."

I smiled. "It was a good idea to let the community vote."

"Yes, that was a brilliant idea. And the way your uncle Brock got the Hamilton newspaper there to cover the party and do the voting was brilliant."

"I think so as well. This will be the dog park to end all dog parks."

"From your lips to God's ears."

"I think people liked getting to meet you and Sophia. The faces behind the dog park and the bus."

She nodded. "I had a lot of fun. Thank you so much for everything you have done to make this all happen."

"You're the one making it happen, princess. I'm just along for the ride."

She set her beer down with a wicked grin and crawled into my lap. "Speaking of rides."

"I like where your thoughts are at."

Haven pulled her shirt over her head and tossed it to the floor before helping me with mine.

"I need you, Nate. Now."

Our hands were everywhere on each other's bodies as we practically ripped our clothing off. Haven positioned herself over me, and when she finally slid down my length, we both let out a moan.

"You feel so good," she whispered as she slowly rocked her body, taking me all the way in.

My hands went to her hips while I dropped my head back against the sofa. Being with Haven was one of my favorite pastimes. Every time we made love, it felt better and better. If I could live inside of her, I would.

"That's it, baby, take what you want."

She moved up and down as her hands cupped her breasts. I was about to explode as I watched her pinch her nipples. Leaning forward, I took one in my mouth. Haven let out a moan of pleasure.

"I'm so close, Nate. I just need…I need…more."

I placed my hand between our bodies and found her clit. It only took me a few strokes, and Haven was crying out in pleasure.

Once I knew she was done with her orgasm, I placed my hands on her hips and started to pump up into her.

"Oh, yes," she gasped. "Harder, Nate. More!"

I moved faster and harder, and when I felt Haven's body squeeze around me, I knew she was about to come.

"Nate!" she cried out as we both came together. It felt like my orgasm went on forever as I spilled into her. Haven collapsed against my chest, and we both dragged in breaths.

"That…was…amazing."

I chuckled. "Yeah, it was."

Lifting her head, her dimpled smile made my heart tumble. I loved this woman more than I could have ever imagined. "Now I'm really exhausted."

I brushed a strand of her hair behind her ear. "How about we shower, change, and watch a movie?"

"I honestly don't know if I'll be able to keep my eyes open long enough to watch a movie."

"Fair enough. Shower then bed?"

"That sounds like heaven."

I stood, took her hand in mine, and led her back upstairs and to my room. After starting the shower, we stepped in, and I kissed her slowly. Haven seemed to melt into my body as the kiss deepened. She opened her eyes and laughed when her hand moved down my body.

"Ready already?"

"I have always wanted to make love in the shower."

She bit down on her lip before saying, "Who am I to deny you that."

Picking her up, I pushed her back against the shower wall and got lost in her once again. I would never get tired of making love to Haven Larson.

◆ ◆ ◆

The smell of coffee, bacon, and something else caused me to open my eyes and sit up. I glanced at the clock to see it was seven a.m. I pushed the covers off me, swung my legs over the bed, and stood.

I headed to the bathroom and splashed my face with cold water to wake up. Last night, Josh and Sophia had come over, and we exchanged gifts and had dinner. I had never dreamed how wonderful my life could be until Haven had entered it completely. I had planned on asking her to move in permanently after the new year since her lease was up in January. She spent all of her time now at my place and had even brought over some of her supplies for her business and stored them in the garage.

After brushing my teeth and slipping on some sweats and a long-sleeve T-shirt, I made my way out to the kitchen. The sound of Nat King Cole's Christmas album filled the space, and I couldn't help but smile as I saw the Christmas tree lights on, as well as some of the other lights Haven and Sophia had hung up. It smelled like apple cinnamon in the house mixed with bacon. My stomach growled the closer I got to the kitchen.

I stopped and watched as Haven stood before the stove singing softly to "The Christmas Song" along with Nat. An overwhelming sense of love filled my chest. How had it only been barely a month since we had finally found ourselves as a couple?

My mind drifted to last week when I walked into the community center to see Haven crying. She had admitted to me that night that it was because of the conversation about my family, and she had thought of her father. I had wanted to track him down and beat the shit out of him. I hated that he could still make her feel defeated and sad. I made a vow to do whatever I had to do to help her, and that included suggesting to her that we go together to a therapist. When she had broken down again, I held her until she cried herself to sleep.

The song ended, "Deck the Halls" came on, and Haven started dancing as she flipped the bacon. I pushed off the wall and made my way to her. Once I was behind her, I wrapped my arms around her waist. She stopped dancing and leaned against me.

Turning her head slightly, she looked back at me. “Good morning, and Merry Christmas Eve.”

“Merry Christmas Eve. Don’t let me stop you from singing and dancing.”

She laughed. “I’ve never been this excited for Christmas. I can’t wait to spend it with your family.”

“I can’t wait to share them with you as well.”

Turning around, she wrapped her arms around my neck. “I feel like I’m in a dream, Nate. Everything is perfect, and I’m just waiting for the rug to get pulled out from under my feet.”

I ran the back of my hand down the side of her beautiful face. “Stop worrying, Haven. For once in your life, I wish you would believe you deserve this happiness.”

She chewed nervously on her lower lip. “I’m trying, it’s just…”

Her voice trailed off, and her gaze dropped to my chest. Placing my finger on her chin, I lifted her gaze to mine.

“Our life is only just beginning, Haven. There are so many wonderful moments that we’re going to experience together. So many places I want to whisk you off to and show you.”

Her dimples appeared as she asked, “Really? Like where?”

“Anywhere you want to go.”

“Anywhere?”

I laughed. “Anywhere.”

“Like I said before, I’ve always wanted to see London.”

“Then we’ll go to London.”

Rolling her eyes, she said, “Maybe we should start here in the US. Maybe Oregon?”

I nodded. “We can do that.”

She sighed. “Maybe after the dog park is up and running.”

“I don’t think we should wait. We’ve waited long enough.”

Her finger ran along my jawline. “I love you for wanting to make me happy.”

"I don't only want to make you happy, princess; I want to see all of your dreams come true."

Tears filled her eyes. "They are coming true because of you."

I shook my head. "It's not because of me, Haven. You would have done all of this without me. You're more than capable of bringing your dreams and goals to life; I'm just along for the ride."

"How do you do that?"

"Do what?" I asked.

"Make me feel as if I can do anything I want."

"Because you can."

Haven let out a sigh. "Pinch me."

I waggled my brows. "That game again, huh?"

Laughing, Haven turned back to the bacon. "I was going to make us some French toast."

"That sounds good. I don't think I've had that since I lived at home with my parents."

"I have a secret ingredient that makes mine amazingly good."

"Really? What is it?"

She raised a brow. "It wouldn't be a secret if I told you."

"I'll get it out of you; just wait."

She shrugged, removed the bacon from the pan, and put it on paper towels on a plate.

I sat at the kitchen island and watched Haven move about my kitchen as if she had been doing so since day one.

"Move in with me."

She paused and glanced over her shoulder. "What?"

"Move in with me."

With a soft laugh, she said, "Nate, are you being serious?"

"It feels like the right step in the right direction."

I watched as she beat the eggs and then went into the pantry. She set a bunch of things down and looked at me. "Are you being serious?"

"Yes!" I said with a laugh. "Your lease is up next month. Do you really want to renew it? You're here all the time anyway. Let's make it official."

She stared at me momentarily before a huge smile broke out on her face. God, how I loved those dimples of hers.

"Okay, I'll move in with you."

I got up and made my way to her. Lifting her, I spun her around and kissed her. "I love you."

"I love you too."

Once I put her down, she patted my chest. "Now go away so I can add my secret ingredient."

"When can we go and get your stuff?"

"Nate! It's Christmas Eve!"

"So what? We don't have anything going on today."

Her mouth fell open. "You want to do it today?"

"Yes. What all do you want to bring with you?"

She bit down on her lower lip. "Well, I don't have much furniture, and it's not really worth anything. Besides, your house is full of furniture. I could probably give it all away. I really just have a few kitchen items and my clothes. The dog stuff, of course, but other than that, it's all I have."

Frowning, she added, "That's kind of sad."

"No, it's not. You've put all your time and money into your career; nothing is wrong with that."

With a grin, she asked, "Do you have boxes?"

I let out a whoop of laughter, picked her up, and spun her around again before setting her back on the floor and kissing her soundly. "If you've got this, I'll head to the garage and look for some boxes. If I don't have any, we can pick them up."

"On Christmas Eve?"

As I approached the garage, I called out, "Home Depot is open!"

Chapter Nineteen

Haven

I was moving in with Nate.

I still couldn't believe it. I had been planning on going month to month on my lease, figuring that eventually, I would move in with him, but I hadn't thought it would be this soon. Nate was right, though; it felt right. I hardly ever stayed at my apartment anymore. As a matter of fact, I hadn't even been there since before the community party for the dog park.

"Excited?" Nate asked as he held my hand while we pulled into the apartment complex's parking lot.

"I am excited. There has been so much change the last few months, and it's all good, but life feels like it's just flying by, and I need to take a break and enjoy it some."

"I can see that. Do you ever take a vacation?"

"A vacation? No, I've never taken any time off. My dog owners rely on me to walk their pups."

Nate chuckled. "You don't think they would understand if you decided to take a week off and do something for yourself?"

I shrugged. "I'm sure they would; I just could never financially afford to take time off. And now, with the dog park and the loan, I can't see myself taking any time off because I need all the money now."

"What if you didn't have to pay for any of it?"

"No, that's not how we're going to do this, Nate. As a matter of fact, we should talk about the living arrangement before we pack up my apartment. I want to pay my share of the bills."

He stared at me like I had lost my mind. "Haven, you just said money was tight, and you needed all you could get, and you want to pay half of my house bills?"

"Yes, what's wrong with that?"

"How much was your electric bill in your apartment?"

"It depends on the time of year, but on average, around a hundred and twenty-five, give or take."

"Okay, mine is higher since I have a full house compared to your smaller apartment. I'm not going to ask you to pay half of that when I can easily afford it."

I twisted my hands in my lap. "I'm not living for free, Nate."

"That's fair. How about you pay me what you paid here at the apartment?"

"Even my rent?"

"Can we negotiate that one?"

I thought for a moment. "Okay, if you won't let me pay toward your mortgage, then we have to figure something else out."

He drew in a breath and slowly let it out. "Princess, I don't have a mortgage."

My eyes went wide. "Oh, well, okay. Then how about I buy the food for us, and you let me pay you toward the electricity and gas?"

"Not half of it, but what you paid here at the apartment."

I reached my hand out, and he took it. Instead of shaking it, he brought it to his mouth and kissed it softly.

"Has anyone told you you're romantic?"

Nate laughed. "I have never been told that in my life."

Smiling, I replied, "Then I guess you've saved it for me."

He winked. "I guess so."

We stared at one another for a moment before Nate broke the trance. "I'll grab the boxes and meet you in your apartment."

I leaned over and kissed him. "Sounds good."

Nate went to the back of his truck to get the boxes we had bought at Home Depot as I made my way up the steps to my apartment. I unlocked it and felt a rush of cold air when I stepped in.

"Shit," I mumbled as I quickly went to the thermostat. It was set at 68 and chilly in the apartment. I turned it up to 71, then went to the kitchen. Setting down my purse, I surveyed my small place. Where should I start? I opened a few cabinets and let out a soft laugh. I honestly didn't have very many things to pack up. Taking out the bowls, I set them on the counter. A sound coming from my bedroom caused me to stop and glance over my shoulder. Had Nate come in, and I had not heard him?

"Nate?" I called out as I made my way toward my bedroom. When I stepped in, no one was in there. I headed to my bathroom and froze when I felt a strange sensation wash over me. Slowly turning, I let out a small scream.

"Merry almost Christmas. Surprised to see me, Haven?"

Fear clogged my throat as I tried to find words to speak.

"So surprised you can't speak?"

My father sat on the floor, his back against the wall with a gun pointed directly at me.

"What are you doing here, and how did you get in?"

He let out a laugh that made my skin crawl.

"I picked the lock. What? Aren't you happy to see your old man?"

"I can't say that I am."

His smile faded. "Where is your mother?"

I slowly shook my head. "My mother?"

"Yes, Haven, your fucking mother. She hasn't been home in two days."

A feeling of dread washed over me. "What did you do to her?" I cried out.

He looked surprised. "I haven't done shit to her. Like I said, she hasn't been home, so where is she?"

My mind raced as I wondered if my mother had told me she was leaving town. I had just spoken to her last night and she was fine, but hadn't told me she wasn't home. Maybe she was with Doug. "I…I don't know where she is."

"You mean to tell me you haven't spoken to her in two days?"

"What are you doing here?"

He slowly stood. "I saw you in the paper. Looks like you're doing good for yourself. Building some stupid dog park, throwing parties for the community. Is your boyfriend paying for it all?"

I turned to look at the bedroom door. Nate would be walking into the apartment any moment and would be caught off guard by my father—my father who was holding a gun.

"What do you want?"

"Isn't it obvious?"

"Not to me it isn't."

"I want my family back."

A humorless laugh slipped out as I stared at him in disbelief. "Your family? You don't have a family anymore."

He snarled. "That's your fault," he said as he walked across the room. I stood perfectly still, afraid that if I made one wrong move, he would shoot me.

I saw Nate walk into the bedroom from over my father's shoulder. I didn't dare draw attention to him at all. I could feel my breathing increase, and I felt for my phone in my pocket. It wasn't there, and I wanted to let out a frustrated cry.

"If you so much as lay a finger on me, I swear I will kill you."

He stopped walking. "You'll kill me? If you haven't noticed, I'm the one holding the gun, Haven."

I could see Nate slowly making his way toward my father. He had something in his hand, but I couldn't see what it was.

Focusing in on my father, I took a step to the side. "If you're looking for money, you've come to the wrong place. Everything I have is tied up in the dog park."

"I'm sure you can get some from your rich boyfriend."

I shook my head. "He wouldn't give you the shirt off his back."

My father laughed. "You think he's with you because he loves you? You're a piece of ass for him, Haven, that's all."

Smiling, I replied, "How wrong you are. It's really rather sad that you had to come crawling back to your ex-wife and daughter asking for money. What's wrong, Dad? Couldn't find a new family to take advantage of?"

My father stood there and stared at me. He lifted the gun and pointed it directly at my chest. "I'm going to enjoy watching you die, Haven."

Before I could say a word, Nate lifted what was in his hands and hit my father over the head, causing him to instantly fall to the floor.

"Get out of here, Haven!" Nate called as he kicked the gun away and pulled my father's hands behind his back.

"No! I'm not leaving. You need something to tie up his hands."

Turning to run out of the room, I nearly ran into the police officer who was rushing into the room. I stumbled back, and he reached out to steady me. Two other officers were behind him.

"We've got him, sir," the one said to Nate as he pulled out handcuffs and put them on my father.

Nate looked like he didn't want to let go, but he eventually stood and took a few steps back. He turned, and when our eyes met, he quickly made his way over to me. Drawing me in, he held me close to him.

"Are you okay?"

I held onto him tighter. "Yes, I'm okay. I'm fine."

He gently pushed me back some and studied me from head to toe.

"I'm okay, Nate. Just a little rattled."

"Thank God you didn't come here alone. When I heard you scream, I nearly killed myself getting up here. Then I heard your father talking."

"Did you call 911?"

He nodded. "I did. The second I heard him, I called."

Closing my eyes, I let out a shaky breath. "That could have gone a completely different way."

Nate framed my face with his hands. "But it didn't. You're safe, and I swear to God, he will never hurt you or get near you again. I'll make sure of that."

"I need to call my mother and make sure she's okay. It sounds like he was looking for one of us between our places."

Frowning, Nate asked, "You don't know where she is?"

I shrugged. "I don't. I assumed she was home, but I panicked when he said she hadn't been home for two days."

"You give her a call and check on her, and I'll talk to the police."

"Okay."

The police had pulled my father up into a standing position and were walking him out of the apartment. Nate followed as I headed to the kitchen to get my phone. Pulling up my mother's name, I hit call.

"Merry Christmas Eve!" she singsonged.

"Mom, where are you?"

"What do you mean, where am I?"

"Have you not been home for two days?"

The line went silent. "How did you know that?"

"Just answer me this: are you okay? Safe?"

She let out a nervous laugh. "Of course I am, Haven. What is wrong?"

With a breath, I walked over to my sofa and sat down. "Something happened."

"Are you okay? Is Nate okay?"

"Everyone is okay, for the most part. Nate asked me earlier this morning to move in with him."

She let out a little squeak of happiness. "Haven! That is wonderful. Did you say yes?"

"I did say yes. We stopped at Home Depot before they closed for the holiday, picked up some boxes, and then headed to my apartment to pack some things. Nate wanted to do it as soon as possible."

Mom laughed.

I closed my eyes. I had no idea how to say what I needed to say, so I just decided to be blunt.

"I came up to the apartment first while Nate was getting the boxes out of his truck. Dad was in my apartment waiting for me."

I was met with silence on the other end of the line. "Mom?"

"What did you say?"

"Dad was in my apartment waiting for me. I'm okay, he didn't do anything, but he did have a gun."

She gasped, and I heard what sounded like a chair slide across the floor. "Oh my God," she said.

"When I saw him, I screamed, and Nate heard me. He ran into the apartment and heard Dad talking, so he called 911. He was able to approach Dad without him knowing, and he hit him over the head. The police arrived within seconds of Nate knocking him out."

"Oh, Haven, I'm so sorry, sweetheart. I'm so glad you're okay."

"I am. He mentioned you hadn't been home for two days, and I got worried because you didn't mention you would be out of town. Thank God you were, Mom. I'm not sure what he would have done if he had found you home alone."

She let out an exhale. "I'm at Doug's."

I drew back in surprise. "Doug's? Like…as in staying with Doug?"

"Yes, I'm sorry I didn't tell you. It's just so new for me, and Doug and I are enjoying our company together, and well…"

Her voice trailed off. "Mom, you're a grown woman and can spend your time however you would like. I'm thrilled you and Doug have hit it off as well as you had. I knew you had gone out a few times, but I had no idea it was that serious."

"I should have told you I was staying with him. I planned on telling you tomorrow."

"Mom, you don't owe me any explanations."

"What is going to happen with your father now?"

I looked at the front door. "I'm not sure. Nate is down there talking to the police now. I'm sure they'll need me to make a statement."

"Haven, you need to tell them what he did to you. He needs to be held accountable for his actions and be kept away from you."

"From both of us, Mom."

The door opened, and Nate walked in. "They need to talk to you, Haven."

"I need to go, Mom. I'll call you later and give you an update. I'm glad you're safe and happy, Mom."

"You as well, sweetheart. Call me when you can."

I stood. "I will. Bye."

Hitting End, I slipped my phone into my back pocket and grabbed my coat as I headed down to the police with Nate holding my hand. Seeing my father sitting in the back seat of a police car should have been a relief, but it wasn't. What if he got away with this and was let go? Then what would we do?

"Ms. Larson?" the female officer asked as she approached me and Nate.

"Yes, Haven Larson," I replied, holding my hand out to shake hers.

"Officer Miller. If you're up to it, I need to ask you a few questions."

I nodded. "Yes, of course."

"Can we go to the police station and speak?" Nate asked. "It's getting colder."

Officer Miller nodded. "Of course. We can meet you there."

Nate nodded. "Thank you. We'll go lock up her apartment and then head straight over."

She smiled at Nate and then looked at me. Her smile softened, and she nodded. "See you in a bit, Ms. Larson."

Nate faced me. "I'll go get your purse and lock up the apartment. Go to the truck and start it up; I'll be right back."

I felt numb, and it had nothing to do with how cold it was. It was knowing that my father was only a few feet away from me. Yes, he was sitting in the back of a police car, but knowing how close I had come to him hurting me again, my entire body shivered in fear.

"Haven?"

Nate's voice pulled my gaze away from my father. "Yes, I'm sorry. I'll go wait in the truck."

He leaned down and kissed me on the cheek. "I'll be two seconds."

I took the keys from him and quickly made my way to his truck. Climbing into the driver's side, I started it and turned up the heat before crawling into the passenger side and sitting down. I stared through the window and watched the three police cars slowly pull out of the apartment parking lot.

Chapter Twenty

Nathan

Haven walked out of the police station with her shoulders back, and her head held high, but I could see it in her eyes. She was exhausted, both mentally and physically. During her interview with the police, she told them of the history of abuse from her father. I also told them about the time I had walked in and stopped him before he raped her.

It turned out that her father had multiple arrest warrants, one of them being sexual assault where his DNA was matched through a database. After filing for a restraining order and agreeing to speak to the district attorney after the holidays, they assured Haven that her father wouldn't get out of jail anytime soon.

"Hey, are you okay?" I asked as I held the truck door open for her to climb in.

She nodded. "I am. It's just been an exhausting few hours."

I held her hand as she climbed in. When I got in and started the truck, Haven dropped her head back against the headrest and covered her mouth.

"Hey, it's okay, Haven. He's not going to get near you ever again."

She wiped her tears away and looked at me. "It's not that. I'm not worried about him hurting me. What I'm upset about is if I had just gone to the police like you wanted to, maybe that other girl wouldn't have gotten raped."

Reaching for her hand, I brought it up to my lips and kissed it. "Haven, please don't blame yourself for your father's actions. You were young and scared and wanted to put it all behind you. You couldn't have known he would do what he did."

She sniffled and nodded.

"Hey, look at me, okay."

Doing as I asked, I tried to give her a reassuring smile. "None of what your father did was your fault. I didn't go to the police either. Your good-for-nothing father is going to rot in jail and never hurt another person again. I promise I will do whatever I need to do to ensure it."

She gave me a half smile. "Thank you for that."

"Haven, there isn't anything I wouldn't do for you. For your happiness, your safety, your love. You are my entire life, and now that you're mine, I swear I will never let you hurt like that again."

Wiping her cheeks once more, she nodded. "I know, and I love you so much."

Drawing a breath, I asked, "What do you want to do? Head back to the house or your apartment?"

She exhaled. "I'd like to go to my apartment and get what I want to bring to your house. It's not going to be much. I'm ready to start fresh and leave it all behind."

"We can get as much or as little as you want. We'll figure out what to do with everything after Christmas."

"That sounds good."

Pulling out of the police station parking lot, we returned to Haven's apartment. She packed up a few things from her kitchen, the rest of her clothes, and everything for the dogs. The rest she was going to donate.

Once we returned to my house, we carried the boxes into the house and left the dog boxes in the truck for later.

"How about you go take a hot shower, and I'll make us up something to eat?"

She let out a small gasp. "We were supposed to have dinner at your parents' tonight."

"Don't worry about that. I texted them and told them we'd be late."

Her eyes went wide with shock. "I didn't mention what happened."

When her body visibly relaxed, she almost looked like she was about to collapse.

"I think you should take a bath instead of a shower."

"That sounds lovely. You don't need help with making something to eat?"

With a shake of my head, I took her hand and led her to our bathroom.

Our bathroom. I couldn't help but smile, knowing this was no longer *my house but ours*.

As I helped her undress, I placed soft kisses on her bare skin. I started the bath water, put a towel on the counter, and helped her into the tub. She sank in the bubbles and let out a long exhale.

"You okay for a bit?"

She nodded. "This feels like heaven, thank you."

Reaching over, I turned on the radio I had in the bathroom and tuned it to a station that played calming music. Haven closed her eyes and let out a long exhale. Shutting the door, I headed to the kitchen to make dinner. The doorbell rang as I was walking by. When I opened it, I saw my mother bundled up in a winter jacket, hat, and gloves. "It's starting to come down! Looks like we'll have a white Christmas! I was worried."

"Mom, what are you doing here?"

She stepped in and stomped her feet to get the snow off. I glanced past her and said, "We just got home a bit ago, and it was barely coming down."

Smiling, she took off her coat and hung it up, then stuffed her hat and gloves in the pocket.

"I'm here because we've been trying to call you since we hadn't heard from you or Haven about dinner since you texted you would be late. I got worried, so I told your father I was coming over here to make sure you both were okay."

I closed my eyes and cursed. "I'm so sorry, Mom. Things got a bit crazy, and I completely forgot to let you know we weren't going to be able to make it."

Her smile faded, and she studied me. "What's going on, Nate?"

"Why do you think something is going on?"

"You look…tired."

I laughed. "I am tired, Mom. Follow me while I make some dinner for me and Haven."

"Do you not want to come over? We have plenty of left-overs."

Pulling out a stock pot, I turned to her. "Haven's had a pretty rough day. I don't think she would be up for visiting," I said.

"What happened?"

"Well, the day started amazing when I asked her to move in with me, and she agreed."

Another smile broke out across her face. "That's a wonderful thing!"

"It is," I agreed with a grin. "We decided to head over today to pack up some things since her lease renews in January. We stopped at Home Depot to pick up some boxes before they closed and then headed to her apartment."

She sat down on the stool.

"Wine?"

"No, thank you, but I will take some water."

"Haven made lemonade if you'd like that. It's homemade."

"Yes! I'll take that."

I poured her a glass, and she waited patiently for me to go on.

"While I was getting the boxes, Haven went on up. Turns out her good-for-nothing father had been waiting for her in her apartment…with a gun."

My mother gasped and covered her mouth with her hand. "What? Is Grace okay?"

I nodded. "She's fine. He had also been waiting for her, but she had been staying with Doug for the last couple of days. I think he was going between Grace's house and Haven's apartment."

My mother's eyes went wide. "She is!"

I chuckled. "Yeah, Haven was surprised as well. Happy, but surprised."

"I am as well. She deserves someone good like Doug. But anyway, what happened?"

"When I was heading up the steps to Haven's apartment, I heard her scream. When I stepped into her apartment, I heard her father talking. I quietly stepped back out and called 911. Then, I made my way back in and waited for the right time to overtake him. He was pointing the gun at Haven, and I can't even begin to tell you how scared I was."

She slowly shook her head. "I'm sure you were. I'm so glad neither of you were hurt. Haven is okay, right?"

"Yeah, yeah, she's fine. Just shook up."

"How did you overtake him?"

"Hit him over the head and knocked him out. The police arrived seconds after it happened. Haven had to go to the police station and file a report. She also filed for a restraining order against the bastard."

"What in the world made him come back to Hamilton now of all times?" she asked.

"I guess he saw a news article about Haven and the dog park. He was looking for money."

She sipped her drink and watched as I opened a can of corn and diced tomatoes and added it to the water heating up in the stock pot. I pulled out some chicken and added it, then a packet of spices for chicken tortilla soup.

"That poor girl. Like her father hasn't done enough in that girl's life, now he has to show up and try to take money from her and threaten her with a gun. Did anyone tell Grace?"

"Haven did. What do you mean about what her father did to her?" I asked.

My mother shrugged and glanced behind her.

"She's taking a hot bath."

Focusing back on me, my mother lowered her voice. "I don't have any proof, and to be honest, I never thought it was my business to ask Grace, but I always suspected that David was abusive to both Haven and her mother."

I felt the blood drain from my face. My mother tilted her head and narrowed her eyes. "Was he?"

Swallowing the lump in my throat, I said, "It's not really my story to tell."

She gave a single head nod. "I never liked that man. I hope he rots in jail."

"So do I. I do know that he will never get near Haven again."

Smiling, she asked, "Does she need to speak to anyone?"

"She has a therapist."

"That's good. Do you need any help making the soup?"

"Nah, I've got it."

She stood. "I should get back home."

I followed her to the front hall and took her coat off the hook. "Be careful driving home."

Leaning up to kiss me, she replied, "I will. Tell Haven I'm sorry I missed her."

"I will. She'll be sorry she missed you."

Slipping on her gloves, she said, "Don't forget—we're having a Christmas brunch at your grandmother's this year."

"We won't. Haven is making something to bring."

She smiled and placed her hand on the side of my face. "I love seeing you so happy, Nathan. I've always adored Haven."

"I've never been so happy, Mom. I feel like my life is complete with her in it. I'm just mad it took me so long to open my eyes."

With a soft laugh, she replied, "I think it is in the Shaw blood."

I laughed and kissed her on the cheek. "I love you, Mom. Merry Christmas Eve."

"Merry Christmas Eve, sweetheart. I'll text you when I get home."

Walking her out, I shivered as the cold wind blew. The snow had slowed down, but there was a white dusting everywhere. "There is your white Christmas."

She looked back at me and winked. "Enjoy your evening."

"You too. Tell Dad I'm sorry we missed dinner."

With a wave, she climbed up into my father's truck. I watched until she made her way down the driveway before I turned back and headed into the house.

Once I returned to the kitchen and the soup, I heard Haven.

"Was that your mom I heard?"

"Yeah, she had been trying to reach me since we didn't show up for dinner, and she was worried."

Haven was dressed in baggy sweats and one of my long-sleeve shirts. Her hair was pulled into a loose bun on the top of her head. She looked so fucking adorable. All I wanted to do was pull her into my arms and kiss her.

"Something smells good."

"Tortilla soup. Shouldn't take too long."

"Anything you need me to do?"

"It would be great if you could grab the rolls out of the freezer and heat them up."

"On it."

We worked silently for a few minutes before I asked, "How are you feeling now?"

She smiled at me. "I'm so much better. Thank you for suggesting the bath. I'm sorry I missed your mom, though."

"That's okay, she understood. I gave her a short rundown of what happened. Told her your dad showed up and was waiting in your apartment with a gun demanding money."

Haven nodded and put the rolls into the oven.

"She said something to me, though."

Leaning against the counter, she asked, "What did she say?"

"She said she always had a feeling that your father abused you and your mother."

Her brows shot up. "What?"

I nodded. "I told her that was your story to tell, not mine. She, of course, didn't press on the issue; just said she hoped your father rotted in jail."

"So do I." Lifting onto her toes, she brushed a soft kiss across my lips. "Thank you for being there for me today."

I slipped a loose strand of her hair behind her ear. "I'll always be there for you, Haven. Always."

Wrapping her arms around my neck, she smiled at me. "I'm suddenly hungry for dessert."

"Dessert, huh?"

She nodded. "I think I can manage that."

"I need it fast and hard, Nate."

"That I know I can manage."

Dropping to my knees, I slipped the sweats and her panties down. Haven stepped out of them, and I tossed them to the side.

"Fast and hard, you said?"

She nodded.

"Turn around and hold onto the counter."

Her tongue dashed out, and she licked her lips. "Okay."

I undid my pants and took myself in my hand while I whispered, "Spread your legs, princess."

She did, and I could hear her breathing pick up.

Slipping my hand between her legs, I pushed my fingers inside her and moaned when I felt how wet she was.

"Nate, please."

"I've got you."

"No, if you had me, you would be inside me already."

I laughed. "Impatient little thing."

She pushed her ass toward me, and I lined myself up with her hot entrance. One push, and I was seated completely.

"Oh, God! Move, Nate! Move!"

I gripped her hips and did precisely what she asked for. Hard and fast.

"Yes! Oh, God, yes, that feels so good," Haven cried out as she pushed back against me. It wasn't going to take me long to come, and I could feel Haven's body squeezing around me.

"Baby, I'm not going to last long."

"Harder, Nate."

Bringing my hand back around to her front, I found her clit, and it only took a few swipes of my fingers and Haven was crying out my name as I came with her. I dropped my head to her back as I tried to catch my breath.

"That was so good," Haven said between deep breaths.

"Beyond good."

Kissing her on the back, I pulled out of her and grabbed a hand towel to clean us both up.

“Did that help?” I asked as I helped her put her sweats back on.

“I think I found a favorite new dessert.”

Laughing, I zipped my pants and took the towel into the laundry room. When I returned, Haven was moving about the kitchen with a smile and a glow on her cheeks. I paused for a moment to take in the sight before me. I never in my wildest dreams ever thought I could love someone as much as I loved Haven Larson. She was more precious to me than the air I breathed.

“Rolls are done!” she said as I walked up to the stove and stirred the soup.

“Soup is done as well. You get the bowls, and I’ll cut up an avocado.”

After eating, we went to the family room, where I poured two beers while Haven looked for a movie.

“How about *The Polar Express*?” Haven asked as she snuggled under a blanket.

“I haven’t seen that in years.”

She grinned. “So yes?”

“Sounds good to me. Do you want popcorn?”

“Do we have any Milk Duds?”

Laughing, I shook my head. “I’m afraid you’ve eaten them all.”

She frowned. “I’ll pass then.”

I handed her the beer, and she took a drink and set it on the table beside her.

Once we settled in and the movie started, I noticed Haven struggling to stay awake. She had to be exhausted after the shit day she had. I turned off the movie, picked her up, and carried her upstairs to our bedroom.

Our bedroom.

“Nate,” she whispered as I gently set her on the bed and covered her up.

"Shh, go to sleep, princess."

She sank into the pillow and mumbled, "The movie."

"Can wait until tomorrow night. Get some sleep."

It didn't take long for her to fall back asleep. I pulled the chair in the corner of the room closer to the bed and sat down. I was mesmerized by watching her sleep. She looked so peaceful and content. I wanted her to feel that way for the rest of her life. I wasn't sure how much time passed before I got up and walked into my closet. Bending down, I pulled the small safe out and opened it. The first thing I saw was the blue jewelry box.

Reaching for it, I sat down on the floor and opened it. Twelve mine-cut diamonds surrounded the oval sapphire set in a platinum band. It was one of the most beautiful rings I had ever seen. I took it out of the box and held it up. My mother had given me the ring a year ago and told me to hang onto it for when I finally met the one woman I wanted to spend the rest of my life with. Truth be told, the first person I thought of when she showed it to me was Haven. Her favorite color was blue, and I couldn't help but think how stunning the ring would look on her finger. I had taken the ring without arguing with my mother. It had been her grandmother's ring. Her father had given it to her, and she held onto it for me to give to the woman I wanted to marry.

I stood, the ring in my hand, and walked back into the bedroom. Sitting back in the chair, I watched as Haven slept. This woman had wrecked me in the most beautiful way. She was the one I wanted to spend the rest of my life with, and I knew that down to the depths of my soul.

Closing my hand around the ring, I stood and walked over to the side of the bed. Leaning down, I gently kissed her on the forehead.

"I'm going to marry you someday, Haven Larson. And I promise to love you with my entire heart, forever. Merry Christmas."

Chapter Twenty-One

Haven

"Haven, we're going to be late!" Nate called.

I stared at myself in the bathroom mirror and exhaled. "This is it. This is the moment."

"Haven? We're going to be late," Nate said as he walked into the bathroom. "What's wrong?"

My eyes met his in the mirror. "What if no one shows up?"

He laughed. "What are you talking about? You've already sold how many memberships?"

"A lot."

"Yes, a lot. People are going to be there. Besides, it's open for all the public today, so that means even more people will be there to see what it's all about."

Turning, I nodded my head. "You're right. You're absolutely right. I'm just nervous."

He took my hands in his. "I would be worried if you weren't nervous."

I forced myself to smile. "It feels like it's taken forever to get here, and at the same time, it feels like the last seven months have flown by."

Nate returned my smile. “A lot has happened, hasn’t it? Rose had Milly. Mackenzie had Tyson, and Lily is pregnant again and due in a few weeks.”

“Josh and Sophia are getting married in a few months. My mother and Doug got engaged,” I said with a slight laugh. “Lots of things have happened. I’m so happy Doug could get this done as quickly as he did with the winter we had.”

“Told you he was the best.”

I placed my hand on his chest. “Yes, you did.”

“We really should get going if we want to be there before everyone starts showing up. Josh texted and said they were there.”

Nodding, I drew in a deep breath and exhaled. “You’re right, let’s go.”

Nate took my hand as we walked through the house and to the garage. My nerves settled a bit once I was in the truck, but I was still worried. The drive into town was quiet except for the radio that played softly in the background.

When Nate turned the corner and I saw the dog park come into view, I couldn’t help but smile. There were a number of cars in the parking lot, but I could tell who most of them belonged to.

“Your parents are here?” I asked.

“Of course they are. Everyone is here for the big day.”

Over the last seven months, Nate’s family had quickly become my family. With each dinner and game night, I felt more and more like I was part of something beautiful. Never once did I feel anything other than love coming from everyone. Being part of a family that truly loved and cared for each other was such a beautiful feeling. And now, my mother was experiencing that with Doug.

Nate parked next to Josh’s truck, and I turned to look at him. “Ready?”

"So ready!"

"Then let's do this!"

As I walked toward the main building, I felt my heart racing. It wasn't the first time I'd seen it, of course, but now that it was finished, it was more than I could have ever expected. The sidewalk led you up to a gate that all visitors walked through. The main building, which housed the main office, the bar, and the snack bar for dogs was the first thing you encountered when you walked in. There was also a self-serve machine to buy a day pass or a membership. Once you purchased it, you got a code that unlocked the gates for both the small and large dog parks.

Sophia was behind the counter, along with Lenny, the bartender we had hired. To purchase drinks, you had to show your ID and get a bracelet that allowed you to do so. There was also a strict limit on how many drinks you could purchase. Outside the park in the parking lot was a food trailer that would be here Thursday through Sunday, and a groomer who would be at the park every Friday and Saturday. They were both here for opening weekend.

"How is it going so far?" I asked as I stepped up to the counter.

Sophia grinned and said, "Lenny is teaching me how to make some of the drinks."

"I'm making the pupsicles!" Avery said as she held up one and smiled proudly.

Laughing, I said, "We may just hire you!"

"Did you guys need anything?" Nate asked.

Lenny shook his head. "We're all good here. Some people stopped by earlier asking when the park would open. We told them today, and they promised to come back with their pups."

"That's wonderful!" I said, clapping my hands. "Are the gates unlocked?"

"They are," Sophia replied. "I also checked the machine, and everything is working perfectly."

"Wonderful. I'm sorry I'm late. I was…nervous."

Sophia reached through the window for my hand. "No need to be, Haven. Everything is beyond amazing."

Glancing around, I nodded. "I'm going to walk around and check everything before we officially open."

Sophia smiled.

Turning to Nate, I exhaled. "Let's go check it all out."

Nate and I headed toward the large dog park. You had to walk through the first gate, where you entered your code. Then, down a sidewalk with donated bricks to another latched entrance. Once inside that area, there were two dog washing stations. I unlatched the third gate, and we entered the large dog park. Straight in front of us was the splash pad. Two dogs were already playing there. Lily and Maverick's golden retriever, Winnie, and Doug and my mother's boxer, Mr. Maple.

Turning to the right, you followed another sidewalk directly into the large dog park. The grass we had picked was hardy, and I hoped it would hold up with all the pups. Picnic tables were at the end of the park near the bar. Directly across from us were the cabanas that you could rent. They were covered with bench seating and a TV in each cabana. They were available for people to rent for parties and such. Opposite the picnic tables and at the other end of the park was a covered stage for live music on the weekends. A giant screen TV was at the back of the stage, and Nate and Josh had already purchased the NFL ticket so that they could play the football games come fall. *Paw Patrol* was currently on the TV.

Four large troughs were filled with water for dogs to cool down in. An ice pool would also be filled with ice during the summer months.

"We need to remember to fill the ice pool before we open," I said to no one in particular. The staff we hired to monitor the park were all wearing bright yellow shirts with The Cozy Pup

Playground on them. It was the name that the community had voted to win.

Several Adirondack chairs were scattered throughout both parks for dog owners to sit and relax as their pups played. They were all made with poly lumber and would last much longer than wooden chairs. Nate suggested the chairs, and they were one of my favorite additions to the dog park, besides the cabanas that Doug suggested.

"Wow, everything looks amazing, Haven," Nate said as he walked up to me holding a drink. "Want a taste of my puparita?"

Laughing, I nodded and took a sip. "That's good."

"I know. I also tried the bark and sip."

"The one with the vodka and ginger beer?" I asked.

"Yes. It was good. Lenny informed me I had already met my two-drink limit."

I laughed once again.

Spinning around, I took everything in. "Have we missed anything?"

Nate took another drink and looked around. "I don't think so. The only thing you need to do is fill up the ice pool with ice, and I asked Bryson to help Josh get the ice."

"Why didn't you help him?" I asked with a grin.

Nate held up his drink. "I'm sampling the drinks."

With a roll of my eyes, I walked over to the cabanas. "I'm not sure about the pillows. I have a feeling they won't last long."

Nate picked one up that had a paw print on it. "They're cute. And when the cabanas aren't rented out, these will be closed up, right?"

"Yes."

"I wouldn't worry about it. If you see they're torn up, we just don't replace them."

I nodded.

"Why are you wringing your hands?"

A nervous bubble of laughter slipped free. "I just want everything to work out. I want people to love the park."

"Hey," Nate said, setting his drink down on the table in the cabana. "Everyone is going to love it, Haven. Your vision and Doug's wonderful work have brought to life something special. I've never seen a dog park like this before. It's going to be a hit."

"It did turn out to be even more than I ever dreamed."

"I don't think I've told you how proud I am of you, princess."

Tears pricked at the back of my eyes. "I couldn't have done this without you."

He smiled. "Yes, you could have, and you would have."

I shook my head. "Not like this. You've helped in so many ways, Nate."

"Well, if you think you can handle one more surprise, I'd like to give it to you before we open."

"A surprise?" I said with a wicked smile.

Nate laughed. "That surprise will be later when we're alone."

Taking my hand, we started to walk toward the picnic tables where everyone was gathered. Nate's entire family was here, and I loved seeing the kids running around with the dogs. It was exactly what I pictured when I thought of this park.

Nate stopped and got everyone's attention. "I want to thank all of you for your help, time, money, and prayers that you put out to make this adventure happen. I know I speak on behalf of Sophia and Haven when I say this couldn't have happened without all of you."

"Yes," I added. "If it wasn't for all of you, I'm not sure we could have made this dog park what it is."

"I second that!" Sophia said as she put her arm around Josh's waist.

"It was our pleasure, girls. Nothing is better than watching someone's dreams come true," Stella said as she walked up with Tanner walking alongside her holding a box. "And now, we get to witness yet another beautiful moment."

Confused, I looked around before seeing Tanner hand Nate the box. Sophia walked up and took my hands, turning me away from Nate.

"Close your eyes, Haven."

"What?" I asked with a laugh.

"Close your eyes!"

"But why?"

"For the love of all that's holy, Haven Marie Larson, close your eyes!" my mother called out.

Closing my eyes, I asked, "What's going on?"

"It's your surprise," Sophia softly said as she placed her hands on my shoulders. "Keep your eyes closed until Nate tells you to open them."

Feeling giddy, I nodded and let her turn me around. Everyone was quiet, and it struck me that this was the first time I had heard the Shaw family this silent.

"Ready?" Nate asked.

"Yes! I'm ready!" I said, excitement filling my voice.

"Open your eyes, princess."

When I opened them, I saw Nate on one knee holding a chocolate lab puppy. My hands came to my mouth as I drew in a breath.

"Haven, these last seven months with you have been the greatest months of my life. Watching your dreams come true has been a gift I will forever cherish."

I wiped the tears from my cheeks as Nate cleared his throat and went on.

"When I'm with you, the rhythm of your heart echoes within my soul. I never dreamed I would find a love like this, and every morning when I wake up and see your beautiful face, the fire of my love for you grows stronger and stronger."

"Nate," I whispered as I lowered down to the ground. It was then I noticed the puppy had a bow tied around its neck.

"You once said you wanted a dog but couldn't have one in your apartment. I thought now was the perfect time to gift you with your very own pup. I also needed his help to ask you a very important question."

My hands started to shake as Nate handed me the puppy. That sweet puppy breath filled my senses, and I laughed when the little guy started licking my face.

"Hello there, little baby," I said as I hugged him to me. "What's his name?"

Nate smiled. "I figured you would want to name him."

Holding him up, I chuckled when I saw his paws. They were huge. "I think we should name him Bear, 'cause he looks like he's going to be as big as a bear."

Nate laughed. "Bear, it is. If you'll look on his bow, Bear has something for you."

I found the little note and untied the bow. My hands shook as I opened it and read the note.

I'm so happy to finally meet you, Mommy. Daddy picked me out because he said I would be the perfect addition to the family, and he needed me to help with the second part of your surprise.

I glanced up and nearly dropped the poor puppy when I saw Nate holding open a jewelry box that contained a beautiful sapphire ring surrounded by diamonds. I instantly started to cry when Nate took the ring out and took my left hand in his.

"Haven, would you do me the honor of becoming my partner for life?"

Setting the puppy down, I launched myself at Nate, nearly knocking him over.

I heard everyone start cheering while Nate laughed. "I'll take that as a yes."

Drawing back, I looked into those beautiful silver eyes that had captivated me years ago and said, "I would love nothing more than to marry you, Nate Shaw."

With a wide smile, Nate slipped the ring onto my finger as everyone around us erupted into more cheers.

Nate stood and helped me do the same. Once I was on my feet, I wrapped my arms around his neck and kissed him. Everything else faded away, and it was the two of us for a few short moments. When Nate drew back, he rested his forehead to mine.

"I love you, Haven."

"Oh, Nate, I love you too."

The puppy barked and we both looked down at him sitting next to us, staring up. I reached down and picked him up. "You cannot be here once this place opens up, little man."

"I've already got someone coming to get him and take him home for us. She'll pet sit until we're finished up here today."

I slowly shook my head. "You have it all covered, don't you?"

He winked. "I tried."

Sophia walked up and pulled me into a hug. "We should have a double wedding!"

Laughing, I said, "Let me get used to the idea that I'm engaged first!"

My mother stepped up and took my hand. "That is stunning, Nate. Just beautiful."

"Thank you, Grace. It was my grandmother's ring."

That little bit of knowledge made me start crying again. How special was it that Nate gave me a family heirloom.

"It's breathtaking," I softly said as I stared down at the ring.

Once my mother stepped back, the line formed for everyone to congratulate us.

"Haven, this is Karen. She applied for a job here and reminds me of a younger you," Nate stated as a young girl about seventeen walked up.

"I dog walk too! I started doing it after you picked up our dog Monty."

With a tilt of my head, I stared at the young girl. "Oh my gosh, Karen? When did you grow up?"

She laughed. "According to my mother, it happened overnight."

"I'd say!"

"Don't worry, I'll take good care of Bear today for you, so you don't have to worry."

I reached down and picked up Bear, giving him a hug and kiss. "I hate letting you go when I just got you!"

Nate reached down and kissed Bear on the head and I fell in love with him a bit more. "He'll have fun. I bought out PetSmart and gave Karen three bags of toys to take to the house."

I chuckled. "Spoiled already, I see."

"Nothing but the best for my son."

My head snapped up to look at Nate. "Your…son?"

He grinned. "Yeah. He's the perfect addition to start our family."

If we were alone, I would drag Nate off to a corner and have my way with him.

I handed Bear to Karen and kissed him goodbye. After everyone had given us their best wishes, they broke out into smaller groups. Stella was sitting with Lincoln and Timberlynn, each with a drink in their hands while they smiled and talked about something. I had a feeling they were talking about weddings.

Nate held onto my hand as we walked Karen out of the park and to her car.

"Take care of him," I said as I gave him yet one more kiss. I hated letting him go after just getting him.

"Don't worry. We're going to work on some commands and hopefully get him started on potty training."

"Do I see a little trainer in our future?" I asked.

Karen nodded. "Yes! That is my plan."

"Maybe those plans might include working here as a trainer," I stated.

Karen's eyes lit up. "That would be amazing, Ms. Larson."

"Call me Haven."

She smiled. "Haven, it is!"

Karen put Bear in the front seat and clipped a dog seat belt to his little harness. She waved as she got into her car.

"I'm sorry to give him to you, then take him away," Nate said as we both watched Karen drive off.

"He's beautiful, Nate."

"I was hoping you wouldn't be upset that you didn't get to pick him out."

Facing him, I shook my head. "I loved that you picked him out. He's perfect."

With a quick look at my engagement ring, I added, "And this ring is just…it's stunning, Nate."

"Did I surprise you, then?"

"I'll say!" I laughed. "But you're not the only one with a surprise."

He waggled his brows, put his hands on my hips, and drew me to him. "Oh, yeah? What's your surprise?"

I chewed on my lower lip as I placed my hands on his chest. "It's a big one."

"Really? How big?"

"Big."

He laughed. "Please tell me you didn't adopt a great dane or something. I'm not sure we can handle two dogs."

I ran my finger along his shirt. "No, it's not a great dane."

The sound of a car pulling into the parking lot had us both looking in that direction.

"People are starting to show up," Nate said, excitement filling his voice. He focused back on me and said, "So, are you going to tell me what my surprise is? Maybe a new piece of lingerie?"

"That's not it."

"Okay, well, are you going to make me wait or tell me?"

Reaching into my back pocket, I pulled out a small envelope and handed it to him.

He took it and grinned. "You wrote me a note too?"

I shook my head. "It's not a note."

He opened the envelope, took out the paper, and stared at it. My heart pounded in my chest as I studied his face. He blinked a few times and finally pulled his eyes from the paper to look at me.

"Holy shit."

I nodded. "Holy shit is right."

Nate's eyes went wide. "We're going to have a puppy and a baby…at the same time?"

Laughing, I nodded. "Looks like we'll be growing that family sooner than you thought."

Nate looked at the sonogram again, then at me. "Did you know?"

I shook my head. "I had my yearly appointment and mentioned I was a few weeks late. She decided to take some blood work and test my urine. When it came back positive for pregnancy, she did the sonogram."

"How far along are you?"

"Seven weeks."

Nate picked me up and spun me around before setting me down and kissing me like he had never kissed me before. When we broke the kiss, he looked at me and laughed.

"A baby."

"You're happy, then?"

"Happy? Haven, I'm fucking over the moon!"

Looking past him, I saw Sophia speaking to the group of people who had walked up to the window. She was explaining about the park and the membership system to them.

"I was thinking we could keep this to ourselves for a bit. I'm so early on in the pregnancy, and with the park opening, there is going to be so much going on."

Nate laced his fingers in mine. "I agree. I'd like to keep this between us for now."

"Me too."

"I cannot wait to get you home and make love to you."

I giggled. "I was already wishing there was a place we could sneak off to, but I guess it wouldn't look good for us to not be here when the place opens!"

Nate tossed his head back and laughed.

More people started to pull in and park.

"Come on, my future wife and mother of our child. Let's get our party hats on and open up this dog park."

As we walked back through the gates and I saw our families laughing and having such a wonderful time with the dogs that were slowly filling the park, I reached over and pinched myself.

"Nope, not dreaming."

Epilogue

Nathan

Eleven Years Later

"I cannot believe Rhett and Ryder have graduated," Haven said as we walked up to Uncle Brock and Aunt Lincoln's house, our ten-year-old daughter, Emma, and six-year-old son, Walker, walking between us.

"Is it true that Uncle Blayze and Aunt Georgiana mixed them up after they were born?" Emma asked.

I laughed. "I think they have been mixing them up since their birth."

"How do we know Rhett is Rhett and Ryder is Ryder, then?" Walker asked.

Haven took that question. "One of them has a birthmark, and that is how they can tell. But Rhett and Ryder like to play tricks on their mom and dad and pretend to be the other one."

"I wish I had a twin," Emma said. "Then we could trick you and Daddy!"

"I don't want a twin," Walker interjected. "I do wish we had a goat, though."

Haven and I stopped walking and looked at our son.

"A goat?" we both asked at the same time.

Walker nodded. "Like Aunt Lily has. She has goats."

Haven looked at me, confused. "She does?"

I shrugged. "If she does, I didn't know about it."

"Bear would chase the goats, Walker," Emma said, her little hands on her hips. She reminded me of her mother so much that it was unreal.

"He's too old to chase anything," I replied to Emma.

Haven took Walker's hand once again and started up the steps. "He still has spunk left."

"Daddy?" Emma asked, pulling me to a stop.

Dropping down to look my daughter in her eyes, I asked, "Yes, darling?"

"Are you and Mommy going to have more babies?"

Walker cried out, "I hope not!"

I peeked up to see Haven smiling down at us. I winked and focused on my daughter. "As a matter of fact, we are going to have one more baby."

Her eyes lit up. "You are? When?"

Haven and I hadn't talked about when we were going to tell the kids about our happy little accident, but she was out of the first trimester now, and we would be telling our family sooner rather than later.

"Well, can you keep a secret?"

She nodded as Walker said, "I can! I can keep a secret, Daddy!"

I ruffled his hair. "I'm glad to hear that. Since you're both the best secret keepers ever, we can tell you that Mommy has a baby growing in her tummy now."

Walker's mouth dropped open as Emma jumped for joy.

"Shhh," I said as I put my finger to my lips. "It's a secret!"

"Does this mean I won't be the baby anymore?" Walker asked, tears filling his eyes.

Dropping down, Haven pulled him against her. "You'll always be my baby, and so will Emma. We'll just have a younger baby now."

"Do I still get to do Sunday snuggle day?" Walker asked.

Haven smiled at him, and he smiled back. Walker had inherited his dimples from Haven. "Of course we will. Nothing will ever stop Sunday snuggle day."

Walker looked relieved. "Oh, good. Then I'm glad about the baby. I think Bear will be too."

Haven stood along with me. "I think he will be as well."

"Are we ready to go in? We're probably the last ones to arrive," I said as I rang the doorbell.

Two seconds later, the door opened, and Grams stood there with a broad smile. "The last of my great grandkids has finally arrived." She held her arms open as Emma and Walker ran to her and hugged her.

"Easy, Emma and Walker," I said, motioning for Haven to walk in first.

"Oh, hush. I'm not that old, Nathan Shaw."

"You're not young either, Grams," Walker stated with a solemn expression on his face.

Grams laughed. "Out of the mouth of babes."

"Come on, Walker," Emma said, grabbing her brother's hand. "We need to tell everyone that Mommy is growing a baby!"

My mouth fell open as Haven started to laugh, and Grams let out a little yelp of excitement.

"You're pregnant?" Grams asked as she took Haven's hand.

"I am."

"It was a bit of a surprise since, you know, I'm not supposed to be able to shoot bullets anymore."

Grams laughed. "Well, sometimes the snip-snip doesn't work."

"Sometimes," I said with a roll of my eyes before smiling at Haven.

We had barely walked into the family room before people started coming up and congratulating us.

"Well, so much for counting on the kids to keep any secrets," Haven said as she hugged my mother.

"Another grandbaby!" Mom said as she went from Haven to me. "How did this happen?"

"Your son never went back in to see if he was shooting blanks," my father replied as he shook my hand, then pulled me to him for a hug and a slap on the back. "You and Lily will be having one together."

"What?" Haven asked. "Lily is pregnant?"

Dad leaned in closer. "Don't say anything, it's a secret."

Haven turned to me. "Must be the Shaw blood."

"Must be," I said, kissing her on the cheek.

As we walked into the crowded living room, I surveyed everyone. Grams was in the thick of it all, smiling as all her grandkids and great grandkids surrounded her. There was a bit of sadness in her eyes as she looked at some of her great grandchildren. Rose and Bryson's daughter, Milly, who was the same age as Emma. Tyson, born a month before Milly, was holding a kitten in his arms as Grams asked him what her name was. Josh and Sophia's daughter, Katelynn, sat on the floor with another kitten in her lap and giggled every time it tried to grab and bite her hand. Grams never did get a dog of her own, saying she simply needed to focus all her time on the kids.

Katelynn, Milly, Tyson, Emma, and Walker had never had the honor of meeting my grandfather, nor would our new baby, but I knew he was looking down on everyone with a smile. He was still so missed all these years later, and there was a constant hole that never seemed to fill. No matter how many new babies were born.

"Are you okay?" Haven asked, squeezing my hand lightly.

I nodded. "Yeah, I was just wishing Granddad was here to see everyone. He would have loved all of these grandkids."

"He would have," Haven agreed. "But he's looking down on all of us."

I smiled. "You said out loud what I was thinking only moments ago."

Exhaling, I let my eyes take in the room. We may not get together as often as we used to, and family game night had slowly dwindled to monthly, then quarterly, until it was only done on Christmas, but when we all got together, it was a wonderful reminder of the love we shared for each other. These moments were devoted to family, and only family, and were some of my most treasured memories.

Aunt Lincoln stepped into the family room and got everyone's attention. "If everyone would like to head on out back, we've got Rhett and Ryder's cake and we're ready to cut into it! Remember, there is a book for each of them to take if you want to write in it. It can be anything, congratulations, or maybe if you'd like to share some words of advice for them both as they head off to college this fall. I know they will treasure it."

"Where did our kids go?" Haven asked as we held back and waited for everyone to leave the room and head outside.

"I saw them walking out with Katelynn and Sophia."

Haven turned and looked at me, her beautiful smile on full display. "Do you know, almost eleven years ago you asked me to marry you, and I told you I was pregnant with Emma?"

I nodded. "Seems like it was just yesterday."

"It does."

"Are you happy, Haven?"

Taking my hand in hers, she replied, "I've never been so happy in my entire life."

I pulled her to me, cupped her face in my hands, and kissed her. When I drew back, I met her gaze. "I have a surprise for you."

She laughed. "Do you now?"

With a smile of my own, I nodded. "It was going to be an anniversary present."

"Oh!" she said with wide eyes. "Diamonds?"

"No."

"Pearls?"

"Nope."

"A new swing set for the kids?"

I chuckled. "Hardly. I ordered it…for lack of a better word…a couple of months ago, not knowing we'd have another baby."

Haven's smile slowly faded. "Oh, no."

"Oh, yes."

"Nate, you didn't."

"I did."

She slowly shook her head. "Why?"

"Because I thought it would be nice for the entire family."

Haven dropped onto the sofa. "I was a lot younger then and could handle it."

"Please, you're only thirty-four."

She sighed. "And always tired. It's one thing chasing around a baby, but a baby and a lab puppy."

I rubbed at the back of my neck. "Yeah…about that. It's not a lab."

Haven slowly lifted her head and narrowed her eyes. "What do you mean, it's not a lab? What kind of dog is it?"

Clearing my throat, I mumbled the answer.

She leaned forward. "I'm sorry, what was that?"

"Does it really matter what kind of puppy it is? Just think how happy the kids will be. And remember how wonderful it was having Bear grow up with Emma. They love each other so much."

"He loves Walker just as much."

"True, but it seems like a full circle moment."

Haven stood. "Nathan Shaw, what kind of puppy is it?"

"Have I told you how beautiful you look today? Pregnancy looks good on you, princess."

"Nate."

"It's a Dalmatian."

Haven's eyes went wide as saucers. "I'm sorry. Did you say you bought a Dalmatian puppy?"

"Yes."

A small scream startled us both. We turned to see Emma standing there. "You got a puppy? We're going to have a puppy and a baby? I have to go tell everyone!"

Laughing, I said, "Looks like there are no returns now."

Haven turned, folded her arms over her chest, and glared at me.

"Would you prefer diamonds or pearls?"

"I think a babymoon trip."

"You've got it. Anywhere you want."

Her brows lifted. "Anywhere?"

Taking her hand and kissing it, I whispered, "Anywhere."

When her dimples came out, I knew all was forgiven.

THE END

If you liked this series, you will love my
Cowboys and Angels series. You can find
out more about the series by visiting
https://kellyelliottauthor.com/library/#cowboys

Wait…here is a sneak peek at my next series,
Moose Village, coming March 2025.
Visit https://kellyelliottauthor.com/library/in-the-works/
for more information!

Welcome to Moose Village! A tiny slice of heaven tucked into the beautiful Adirondack Mountains. In Moose Village, you will discover a whole new world to fall in love with.

In *This Moment*, our heroine is on the run from a past she would rather leave buried. But when her boss's nephew moves back home and starts showing her around, she finds that the only thing she wants to do is tell him the truth. Before she gets the chance, though, her past catches up with her.

In *This Feeling*, we find our heroine in a fake relationship and falling for none other than her fake boyfriend's, brother! Talk about feelings!

In *This Memory*, we find two childhood crushes in a situation neither would have expected to be in. Will they figure out a way to make it work, or will they kill each other first?

In *This Heart*, our heroine finds herself helping her best friend's brother as he tries to navigate being a single dad. When sparks fly between them, they must decide if they are willing to risk their newfound friendship for a chance at love.

Sit back, grab your favorite drink, and snuggle in for a series that will have you swooning, laughing, and wishing you could move to Moose Village!

ABOUT THE AUTHOR

Kelly Elliott is a *New York Times* and *USA Today* bestselling contemporary romance author. Since finishing her bestelling Wanted series, Kelly has continued to spread her wings while remaining true to her roots with stories of hot men, strong women, and beautiful surroundings. Her bestselling works included *Wanted, Broken, Without You,* and *Lost Love*. Elliott has been passionate about writing since she was fifteen. After years of filling journals with stories, she finally followed her dream and published her first novel, Wanted, in November 2012.

Elliott lives in Central Texas with her husband, daughter, and two pups. When she's not writing, she enjoys reading and spending time with her family. She is down to earth and very in touch with her readers, both on social media and at signings. To learn more about Kelly and her books, you can find her through her website, www.kellyelliottauthor.com.

CONNECT WITH KELLY ELLIOTT

Kelly's Facebook Page
www.facebook.com/kellyelliottauthor

Kelly's Amazon Author Page
https://goo.gl/RGVXqv

Follow Kelly on Instagram
www.instagram.com/authorkellyelliott

Follow Kelly on BookBub
www.bookbub.com/profile/kelly-elliott

Kelly's Pinterest Page
www.pinterest.com/authorkellyelliott

Kelly's Author Website
www.kellyelliottauthor.com

Made in the USA
Columbia, SC
27 June 2025

59939582R00171